WM

D0672311

DOUBLE-CROSS
A Western Story

DOUBLE-CROSS

A Western Story

STEPHEN OVERHOLSER

Five Star
Unity, Maine

W
Ove
c. 1

Five Star First Edition Western Series.
Published in 2001 in conjunction with
Golden West Literary Agency

Set in 11 pt. Plantin by Minnie B. Raven.

Printed in the United States on permanent paper.

Library of Congress Cataloging-in-Publication Data

Overholser, Stephen.
    Double-cross : a Western story / by Stephen Overholser.
— 1st ed.
      p. cm.
    ISBN 0-7862-2387-1 (hc : alk. paper)
    I. Title.
PS3565.V43 D68 2001
813′.54—dc21   00-057798

DOUBLE-CROSS

A Western Story

Chapter One

The prisoner could not sleep. He paced the ten feet of empty darkness in his cell, and then stepped up on the cot to look out the barred window, open on a summer night. A rich odor of fresh-cut pine came to him. Outside, starlight cut shadows on sawn timbers, the heavy lumber forming the base of a gallows.

He stood there a long time, watching moonrise cast an orange glow on the horizon. A full moon came up like a huge pumpkin. Slowly climbing into the sky, it turned bone white. The white light illuminated the prisoner's clean-shaven face, showing the angular line of his jaw, a cleft in his chin, and high, sharp cheek bones. His eyes were of the palest blue, gray in this light, and his hair, cropped short, was black.

Stepping down, he sat on the cot. Then he swung his feet up and stretched out, lacing his fingers behind his head. He studied the shadows of the barred window, lines slowly lengthening on the wall like ropes drawn tight. Sounds carried from Denver's saloon district—the squawk of a fiddle and tinny piano music along with the rough laughter of men and the squeal of a woman—all the raucous noises of midnight, all familiar to him.

After daybreak other noises came through that window, and he realized he had slept at last. He opened his eyes to the rasp of cross-cut saws, the clink of loose nails in carpenters' aprons, and the rhythmic pounding of claw hammers. Late in the morning the prisoner overheard the conversation of workmen who had sought shade under the jail cell window.

"Waste of good lumber, you ask me."

"Sheriff says we gotta do this thing legal and proper.

Hangman's coming to test the trap door with a hunnert-pound bag of sand. Then he'll tie the noose. Once all that's done, the execution won't take a minute."

"To hell with that. The bastard shotgunned a woman, didn't he? Take him out to the nearest cottonwood tree and hang him. That's what folks are saying."

"It's politics."

"Huh?"

"Ain't you heard? Colorado Territory's up for statehood next year . . . Fourth of July, Eighteen Seventy-Six, the centennial. The eyes of the nation are on us, and everything's gotta be done legal and proper."

"To hell with all that."

"Don't matter what folks are saying. The killer had his day in court, and the judge handed down the verdict, lawful like. Now we'll hang him, lawful like."

"Waste of good lumber, you ask me."

Matt MacLeod crouched in a stand of lodgepole pines, peering ahead. The slender trees grew close together, too thick to allow passage for a man on horseback. He'd left his mount behind and followed boot prints to this place, advancing slowly, wary of an ambush. He figured the prospectors were using every trick they knew to dodge pursuers.

Matt had started tracking this pair yesterday after a couple of cowhands had discovered a slaughtered calf on Two-Bar range. Theft was one thing, but the carcass had been crudely butchered with most of the meat and all the innards left to rot. It was the type of crime that raised a rancher's ire. The owner of the Two-Bar, Old John Souter, had offered Matt a twenty-five-dollar bonus for each thief he brought in, vertical or otherwise.

The other men riding for the Two-Bar were top hands,

paid to work cattle and tend the horse herd, not to ride hell-for-leather after rustlers and risk their lives in a gun battle. Matt MacLeod was a different story. An Army tracker for a good part of his youth, he had lived by his gun, and his skills were honed to a fine edge. Old John, being a man who firmly believed every problem outside of the weather and possibly women could be solved by money, had offered Matt enough cash to balance off the dangers of the job.

The earth was darkened by blood at the site of the butchering. Matt had ridden in a widening circle, separating out tracks left by cowhands from two sets of blunt-toed clodhoppers—one large, the other smaller. Two yahoos afoot. Matt had swung up into the saddle, and made a hard ride to close the distance.

It was not a difficult task, this chase. The pair had made a beeline for the mountains, and by the time Matt reached the forest of lodgepole pines on the slope of a ridge, he could darned near smell them. On foot, they had made their way through the trees without a donkey to carry their goods, or any other beast of burden. A drawback, maybe, limiting the weight of their tools and supplies to what they could carry in rucksacks, but it was a sure way to lose mounted pursuers.

These prospectors were not the first to cross Two-Bar range on horseback or afoot. Far from it. Ever since the *Rocky Mountain News* in Denver had published stories claiming "color" had been panned in Spruce Creek, the rancher known throughout the territory as Old John had found sign—the leavings of prospectors trespassing on their way to easy fortunes in the mountain gulches. Their numbers were increasing, and a goodly number of them took nourishment on the hoof.

Matt knew the mining skills of prospectors ranged from inexperienced to flat ignorant, overeager men caught up in

9

the common knowledge that placer gold in a sandy creekbed had flaked off a vein somewhere upstream. The lode was just waiting to be discovered, and the finder would be "sudden rich," as the journalists wrote.

Matt edged forward on a carpet of pine needles and scattered pinecones. Clear-cut tracks were not visible, but his trail-wise eye did not miss dried pine needles disturbed here, a broken twig there—sign that led straight ahead.

He drew his revolver. He had left his Winchester behind in the saddle scabbard. At close quarters, a revolver was the better weapon. For once, though, he wished he owned a cut-down shotgun. A double-barreled .12 gauge Greener would get the job done in this forest where slender pines grew as thick as the hair on a dog's back.

A tangle of fallen trees gave him a start. He came up on it and halted, knowing he was too close. If the prospectors were in there, awake and watchful, he was a dead man. Standing perfectly still, he stared, trying to see through the matrix of shadows. Movement under a jagged limb made him take quick aim, trigger finger drawing tight until he saw a skunk waddle out of the deadfall.

Matt drew a deep breath. A skunk, or a family of them, called this place home. He gave the deadfall a wide berth. Polecats were known for fearlessness in the presence of predators. This one sauntered away, a black and white creature disappearing in angular shadows and bands of light crisscrossing the forest floor.

Matt picked up the trail. He moved forward one slow step at a time, his footfalls nearly silent on the spongy cushion of pine needles. The shine of glass caught his eye. He saw a whisky bottle on the ground, uncorked and empty—either a careless discard or a trap.

Carelessness, Matt discovered, after advancing another

hundred paces. He smelled smoke, not from tobacco, but a campfire. The prospectors had lost their caution, if they ever had it. Matt suspected he had overrated the pair, and confirmed it when he came up behind two figures in a clearing. One was an unshaven, gray-haired man lying in high grass, snoring, spread-eagle in a drunken posture. The other knelt near the leaping flames, frying beefsteak. Rucksacks lay in the grass nearby.

Matt eased up behind the prospector wearing a floppy-brimmed hat of brown felt, a vest over a flannel shirt, baggy trousers, and clodhoppers. He figured it was a kid, probably a runaway youngster who had thrown in with a graybeard in search of gold. Matt had seen any number of those old-timers who had first come to the territory in the rush of 1859. Few made more than wages, and fewer still struck it rich. But some had, and their legendary discoveries got into the blood of those who hadn't. Caught up in their own yarns of boundless wealth, these modern Argonauts were doomed to a lifetime of endless digging and panning, a life of false hopes.

Matt heard the popping of hot grease when he moved soundlessly behind the prospector. This one was intent on supper, unaware of his presence until the barrel of his Colt .45 revolver pressed against the back of his neck. Or hers.

Matt heard a feminine squeal, and immediately drew back a pace, lowering the gun as the young woman leaped to her feet and whirled to face him.

"You scared me!" she shouted. "You scared me half to death!"

"Keep your hands out where I can see them," he said, glancing at the old prospector. The man was not armed—or alert. He had not stirred from his snoring sleep.

"Who . . . who are you?"

Matt shifted his gaze to the girl. No more than fifteen or

11

sixteen, he guessed; freckles dotted her soot-smudged face. He saw wisps of light brown hair pinned under the brim of her hat.

"You're going to rob us, aren't you?"

He glanced at the rucksacks. "Got anything worth taking?"

"Only our goods," she replied. "We haven't found any gold. Honest."

"Where're you headed?"

"That's a secret," she replied.

Matt smiled.

"What's funny?"

"A placer deposit," Matt said, "a deep one that has never been panned. That's where you two are headed."

She eyed him. "You know about it?"

"I know the tale told by every saloon rat in the territory," he replied. "Most of those yarns start out with a placer deposit big enough to fill a washtub."

"This is no yarn," she said, casting a sidelong glance at the man lying in the grass. His gap-toothed mouth open, he still snored like a steam engine.

"Let me guess," Matt said. "This gent saw it with his own eyes, but through no fault of his own he fell on hard times. All he needs to make a fortune is a grubstake. Just one. Then it's Easy Street."

She made no reply, but doubt crept over her face.

"So you bought rucksacks," he went on, "and filled them with tools and goods. Hope you didn't spend your last dollar in the hardware store."

"Listen, mister," she said, "I don't know who you are or what you want. Just leave us be."

"Can't do that," Matt said.

"What do you mean?" she demanded.

He gestured past her to the campfire. "That's Two-Bar steak you're burning to a crisp."

With a gasp, she spun around. Smoke billowed off the frying pan in the campfire. She rushed to it, snatching it out of the flames. Matt heard her cry out as she burned her hand and dropped the pan into the grass. The meat was little more than charcoal.

"I was doing fine," she said, turning to glower at him, "until you wandered into our camp."

"I'm not wandering," Matt said, "and, no, you were not doing fine."

"Just what do you mean by that?"

"First, you took up with an old codger whose brain's addled by gold fever," Matt replied. "Second, you stole Two-Bar beef."

"No, we didn't!" she said.

"You slaughtered a calf, didn't you?"

"It was a maverick. Mister Smith said so."

"Mister Smith?"

She gestured to the passed-out man. "Mister Smith said an unbranded calf belongs to the finder. He said if we don't make use of it, wolves will get it."

"Your third mistake," Matt said, "was believing one more lie from your Mister Smith."

"Lie," she repeated.

"Branded or slick," Matt said, "that critter walked John Souter's range, which makes it Two-Bar livestock. He expects to be paid for his loss."

She was silent for a long moment. "I don't know whether to believe you or not. I just wish you'd leave us alone."

"Can't do that," Matt said. "You and Mister Smith are coming with me."

"What?" she demanded in a voice not quite loud enough

to raise the dead, but with enough volume to bring Mister Smith upright, bloodshot eyes blinking.

Matt lifted his revolver. "Old John wants to make your acquaintance. Both of you."

The home ranch of the Two-Bar was a man's place, sturdy and unadorned. Over the last decade a cabin and sprawling bunkhouse had been fashioned from peeled logs, chinked with a mixture of mud and straw. Both of the low, dirt-floored structures sported black stovepipes on sod roofs like cocked hats. In the bunkhouse tattered mattresses lined plank beds, cast-iron stoves provided heat, and various pieces of hand-made furniture offered a measure of comfort to men who spent much of their lives in the saddle. Both the ranch house and bunkhouse carried a stench to rival a grizzly den.

By far the finest and cleanest building on the place was the horse barn. In good repair, it was fashioned from thick planks with built-in stalls and a haymow, shake roof tight as a drum. Outside, pole corrals and water troughs were scattered along the banks of a meandering creek. Among half a dozen out-buildings, a cowshed and chicken coop looked ready to collapse under the next snowfall or stiff wind.

Now in the pale light of evening Matt sat his saddle in the ranch yard. He had done his job. With one leg cocked over the horn, he pushed his hat back on his forehead and rolled a smoke.

Old John came out and stood before his cabin like a king before his castle, hands on hips, shirt out, faded red suspenders dangling at his sides. Hatless, his white hair stood on end. That and the fierce expression twisting his weathered face made him look like a man who at some time in his life had been struck by lightning and was forever determined to fight back.

14

"Not so many years ago," Old John said to the sore-footed pair who faced him, "you woulda been strung-up from the ridgepole of my barn. Hanged or horsewhipped, man or woman, didn't make a difference, not before there was law in the territory. You'd take your punishment direct from the man you stole from. That's how things used to be."

"Mister Souter, we admit our mistake," the young woman said. "We'll pay you after we stake our claim."

Old John threw his head back like a Missouri mule and let out a harsh bray.

Matt saw the young woman's face tighten. She was as rash as a boy. Now she was offended. In the past two days of their trek, he had not asked her name. He'd overheard Mister Smith call her Missy a time or two—nickname or given name, he did not know. Mister and Missy. *Some pair of desperadoes, these two,* Matt thought.

"Kind sir," Mister Smith began, "under the circumstances, I don't believe such extreme punishment is warranted. . . ."

Old John cut him off with a wave of his gnarled hand. "Shut up. Both of you. Just shut the hell up."

The young woman drew a sharp breath as though she had expected courtesy from the rancher only to discover she had fallen among barbarians.

Matt fired his cigarette. He glanced at Smith, a shaggy, gaunt man with hollow cheeks and missing front teeth. At first glance Matt had thought the geezer was as frail as a scarecrow. On the way to the home ranch, though, "Mister Smith" had gained strength as he'd sobered, and hiked with the swift stride of a man half his age.

"But kind sir. . . ."

"I done told you to shut up, didn't I?" Old John bellowed. He moved a step closer and spat at the man's feet. "I know

15

your kind. Gift of gab. Hip deep in bullshit. I didn't have you brung in so's you could run your mouth and tell me you're right and the rest of the danged world's upside down. First light, we're headed for Denver. I'll turn you over to the law myself." He added: "I just hope them newspapers write about your trial with as much happy horseshit as they did about rumors of gold in Spruce Creek . . . where no one's found a single nugget, ever."

Old John looked toward Matt. "Herd these rustlers into the cowshed, and twist a wire around the door latch to hold them. In the mornin', hitch the team to the wagon. You're driving."

Matt nodded. He watched the rancher turn and stride into his cabin, kicking the door shut behind him.

Matt held the lines while the wagon rolled along the road to Denver. The day was still and peaceful with a cloudless blue sky, arching overhead. Meadowlarks chirped, and locusts jumped away from plodding hoofs. On either side of the wheel ruts that passed for a ranch road, white-winged butterflies fluttered over green grasses and circled yellow sunflowers.

Mister Smith and Missy rode in the wagon bed, their rough ride cushioned by discarded saddle blankets. Old John himself brought up the rear, riding his brown and white saddle horse. He sat ramrod straight, eyes on the horizon ahead like the pioneer he was.

In its beginnings during the gold rush of 1859, Denver was no more than a tent camp on the banks of the South Platte River, a populace of a few hundred men calling themselves miners. Eager for instant wealth, they yearned to be homeward bound, conquering heroes. Most failed. And most fled after the year's first Arctic blast of winter numbed wet hands

16

and feet. They found themselves squinting into a harsh morning sun rising off the prairie horizon, busted. These "go-backers" trudged homeward, disheartened, possibly wiser, certain never to return.

In the following years the town prospered as bull trains arrived with supplies ranging from barrels of oysters in brine to dry goods in packing crates, from paint to pianos. A steady march of settlers followed, folks who had heard of rich farmland and mile upon mile of stirrup-high grasses. These accounts were a sight more accurate than the fanciful tales of gold-crusted creekbeds lacing the Rocky Mountains.

John Souter came with this second wave of settlers, a Maryland cattleman trailing livestock to the Far Western prairie lands. The native vegetation had supported antelope, deer, elk, and bison for centuries, and this rancher figured the rangeland would nurture his domestic cattle and horse herds, too. He made the gamble of a lifetime, and won. Ten miles north of Denver he carved out his Two-Bar Ranch on a meandering tributary of Spruce Creek, increased his herd, and prospered. Despite appearances, John Souter was a man of some wealth.

Throughout that decade after the Civil War, Denver's population grew from fewer than 10,000 to more than 30,000 souls. By then most folks came to stay, toughing out bone-chilling winters and rebuilding from the damage of spring floods. The town slowly took shape on a grid of streets, acquiring a look of permanence with residential blocks of white-washed frame houses enclosed by picket fences. The business section grew, too, with numerous false-fronted establishments, a few built of sandstone and red brick.

Now on the outskirts of town Matt saw an encampment of Arapahoes on the bank of the South Platte River. Buffalo-hide teepees and brush lean-tos were pitched among cottonwood trees. Naked children played nearby. The boys practiced hunting with small bows and willow arrows. Girls darted in and out of shadows, stealing looks at the ranch wagon and horsebacker passing by.

Of all the tribes west of the Missouri, the Arapahoes were the traders and ambassadors. Most Arapaho clans were intent on living alongside the white invaders while engaging in commerce of one sort or another. This tribe, camped near Denver, moved freely with the seasons while co-existing with whites.

In town, wagon traffic raised dust, and the shouts of teamsters filled the air. Matt drove to the territorial sheriff's office, threading his way through freight and heavy ore wagons to a brick building near the middle of Denver. A star was painted on the window there. He drew back on the lines at the tie rail by a water trough, seeing the raw lumber of a gallows in the vacant lot beside the jailhouse.

Old John reined up behind him and swung down, stiff-legged. Motioning toward the new structure, he said: "Looks like the sheriff's fixing to hang horse thieves and cattle rustlers."

Matt concealed his smile as he set the brake and stepped down. Mister Smith and Missy cast glances at one another, and reluctantly climbed out of the wagon box. Old John shoved the geezer into the sheriff's office. Missy followed, head bowed.

Pulling off his hat, Matt ran a hand through black hair as tangled as a bird's nest. His jaw was darkened by a two-weeks' growth of beard. He looked around for the nearest red and white barber pole, and saw a tonsorial parlor two blocks down and across the street. In need of a shave and a trim with a hot bath, he clapped his hat on his head and stepped into the sheriff's office to tell Old John where he was headed.

The office was empty. Voices drew him to the cell-block. A thick door reinforced by plate steel stood open. He heard the clink of skeleton keys, and entered the cell-block as Sheriff Hiram Ochs locked the two "outlaws" in separate cells. The lawman was lean and wide-shouldered at six feet in height, his long face distinguished by a walrus mustache.

Matt was aware of Old John's plan. The young woman would be released after a day's confinement—a scare tactic. The grizzled prospector, though, would be held for trial. Old John was still intent on making an example of Mister Smith, one that would resound throughout Denver if not the whole territory.

Matt saw the rancher looking on, hands on his hips. In three other cells men lay on narrow bunks. One prisoner stood and came to the barred door.

Matt started to move past this man, but halted. Their eyes met and held. The prisoner was well-dressed and clean-shaven, boots polished. Something about him was familiar. Down the way Matt heard the booming voice of Old John, followed by another protest from Mister Smith as a cell door clanged shut. But still he could not take his gaze from the prisoner. He felt as though a mirror image had come to life before his eyes.

That was it—a mirror. Matt could have been peering into a mirror after a fresh shave and trim. He blinked. This was not a matter of resemblance. The man behind bars was his double.

Dizziness washed over Matt like a hot wave. He staggered and grasped a bar in the door of the cell. The prisoner stared, an eyebrow arched in curiosity.

"What the hell's wrong with you?"

Matt could not find his voice to reply. The whole thing was impossible, a wild, waking dream. Yet there could be no doubt. He saw his own pale blue eyes, cleft in the chin, and high, pointed cheek bones.

"Let's ride, MacLeod," Old John said as he swept past, followed by the lawman.

With his question unanswered, the prisoner looked at Matt quizzically. Clearly he was not stunned by the sight of his double. Matt dragged a hand through his growth of beard, and understood why. The prisoner did not see a double. He saw a rough, dirty cowhand with manured boots, tattered clothes, and his upper face in the shadow of a sagging hat brim. Old John again ordered him to come along, and with a last look back Matt followed his boss and the lawman to the outer office.

"I'm a-looking for a big crowd," Ochs said to Old John. "Been a spell since we had a lynch party. Hangman arrived yesterday. He tested the trap door, knotted the rope, and gave the go-ahead."

Matt overheard the sheriff as though coming out of the fog of sleep. "A hanging?"

Ochs closed the steel-reinforced door and glanced at the clock on the wall. "Son, you was standing eyeball to eyeball with a convicted murderer. He'll hang in less than two hours . . . straight up noon."

"Who'd he kill?" Old John asked.

"He gunned down Miss Augusta Benning with a cut-down shotgun. Point-blank, both barrels. That's the gun over there."

Ochs jerked his head toward half a dozen weapons in the gun rack. "It was horrible, seeing her stretched out over a bed . . . damned near cut in two . . . blood ever'where . . . and I do mean, ever'where."

A chill ran up Matt's back as he looked at the murder weapon. He remembered entering the lodgepole forest in pursuit of prospectors, walking softly as he wished for a Greener like that one. Exactly like it. Both barrels were sawed off to a length of six inches, and the dark walnut stock was cut down to the pistol grip. It was a compact, powerful weapon that could be concealed in a man's duster or overcoat, or even in a pants leg with the barrels thrust into a boot.

"Anyhow, at noon he'll swing," the sheriff said, "and then it'll be over. Over and done with."

Matt cleared his throat. "What's his name?"

"Dunno," the sheriff replied.

Old John asked in surprise: "You don't know?"

"He never gave a name," Ochs replied. "Not during his trial, not even after the verdict came in. Nobody around here knows him. Some folks believe he's sparing his family, wherever they are. What the hell, maybe it's better that way. Name or not, he'll dance at the end of a hangman's rope. You gents gonna stay for the show?"

"Naw," Old John said with a scowl. "I've seen my share of hangings, public and otherwise."

Ochs studied him, but said nothing.

The rancher turned to Matt. "We'll head for the bank to draw the fifty I owe you. I'll take dinner at the Cattleman's Club while you go fill my list over to the Denver Mercantile. Soon as the wagon's loaded, head for the home ranch."

Matt hesitated. "I figured on a visit to the barbershop for a trim and a soak."

Old John eyed him. "You did, huh? And after you're swabbed with some kinda Frenchy toilet water, you'll wanna slug down all the beer in town and turn the wolf loose. Huh?"

Matt managed a smile.

"I ain't completely forgot what it's like to be a young pup," Old John said, drawing a chuckle from the sheriff. "All right, Matt. You don't get to town much. Run free. But I want you back at the home ranch in the morning . . . on your feet and ready to work. Hear?"

Matt nodded. He had never lied to Old John, and now he felt a twinge of guilt even though his silence was not an outright lie. He did not know what he would do after he stepped out of the bank with cash money in his wallet. Still dazed by a strange sensation—the shock of recognition mixed with disbelief—he knew the accused murderer was his identical twin. And he knew he could not let the man die without revealing a truth to explain the impossible.

Chapter Two

More news passes through a barbershop in a given day than the local newspaper in a week. So Matt had once been told, and now he confirmed the theory with a few leading questions. From aproned barbers to the shoeshine boy, from clients to hangers-on, everyone in Dave's Tonsorial Parlor knew the gruesome details of the murder of Miss Augusta Benning.

Twenty-three days ago a shotgun blast erupted in Room 304 in the Inter-Ocean Hotel. A quick-thinking deputy rushed into the back alley, apprehending a man descending the fire ladder. Arrested, he claimed to be chasing the killer, but with blood on his jacket and trouser legs, and no sign of anyone else, there could be little doubt of his guilt.

The accused denied involvement in the killing, yet offered no description of the real killer. He freely admitted to meeting Miss Benning in the hotel room, but gave no reason for it, or even how he, a stranger in town, had become acquainted with her. Miss Benning was well-known, a woman much respected in social circles of a wide orbit. After the deputy, Tug Larkin, offered his testimony, the jurors stayed out long enough to have their dinners paid by the court, and returned a verdict of guilty.

Now with a shave, trim, and hot bath, Matt donned clothes he had bought at the dry goods store two doors away, all new from the socks up. Shaved clean, he worried that he might be mistaken for the jailed killer. The thought was troubling. From an early age values of honesty and truthfulness had been instilled in him by his mother and father. Not only

23

had he been raised to be law-abiding, but also he had enforced laws while serving in the Army.

Matthew MacLeod was an only child—a rarity in an era when farm and ranch families with fewer than five children were said to be small. He had been raised by loving parents homesteading on the windswept plains of Colorado Territory, and lived there until the influenza epidemic of 1868 claimed them. Sixteen at the time, Matt had been on his own ever since. His father had taught him hunting skills. Suddenly alone in the world, he had answered a flyer in the Denver post office and hired on as a civilian scout with General Sheridan's Army of the West. Quickly proving himself, Matt served with infantry and cavalry units from New Mexico Territory to Montana, the blue coats enforcing laws ranging from theft to murder to slavery.

When a squad of cavalry returned stolen horses to the Two-Bar, Old John had observed the scout. He sized up the young civilian riding ahead of the column. The rancher spoke to the officer in command, and then took Matt aside. He offered to double his salary—forty a month—with bonuses for his services as an outrider. With the growing numbers of prospectors and thieves crossing Two-Bar land, the rancher needed a man to patrol his range. Old John warned him the job would be lonely and sometimes dangerous, but Matt needed to hear no more. He made his decision on the spot, and never regretted it. For the first time in his life he rode his own horse under his own saddle, and had money left over at the end of the month. That surplus led to a bank account with his name on the passbook, and hopes for the future.

Now he walked slowly along the boardwalk on Larimer Street with the brim of a new Stetson pulled low on his forehead. Denverites rushed past him. He glimpsed well-dressed businessmen in dark suits, fashionable vests, and starched collars. Women passed by in high-wheeled carriages, many holding parasols over plumed hats. Heavy freight outfits rumbled past, along with water and beer tankers, all of the iron-tired wheels churning dust that hung in the still air like a brown smear.

Everyone in Denver seemed to have a purpose in life, Matt thought, and they were striding toward their destinations. He felt aimless and lost as though sleepwalking. This weird sensation of bodily detachment made him doubt reality, as though he had stepped into a dream—a dream haunted by the face of his twin.

But with gents brushing past him and vehicles leaving him behind to choke in their dust, this scene was all too real. Looking down the block, he was reminded of time's swift passage by the Roman numerals of a large clock on a pedestal at the white-columned entry to the First National Bank. The hour chimed eleven in the morning.

Still not knowing what he would do—or what he could do—about the doomed prisoner, he had driven the ranch wagon from the livery to the mercantile and filled out Old John's list. Covering the load with a tarp, he had secured it by knotting ropes to tie-downs on the sideboards.

Shoppers and clerks in the store, as well as passers-by on the boardwalks, did not give him a second look. Matt relaxed a bit. He realized Denverites had not seen the accused since the trial more than three weeks ago, and, even though most folks had heard of the crime, few had actually laid eyes on the man pronounced guilty of it.

Matt tried to think it through. He alone knew the prisoner was his mirror image. That fact could work to his advantage, he supposed. But how? What would happen, he wondered, if he marched into the sheriff's office right now? Would Ochs stare in disbelief, and think the prisoner had somehow escaped—and then returned to the jailhouse? Or would he arrest Matt on the off chance the wrong man had been convicted? With two identical suspects, would there be another trial?

Matt could not take that chance. Arrested or not, at best he would only delay the inevitable by facing Ochs now. At worst, he would be accused of murder. As an outrider for the Two-Bar, he rode alone. No cowhands or other eyewitnesses could account for his exact whereabouts on the day of the shooting.

Matt felt the pressure of passing minutes, and knew something had to be done. But beyond his ruminations, he drew a blank. Deception was not in his nature. He did not know how to scheme, or how to devise a plan to trick the sheriff into leaving the jailhouse. Yet he knew the only possible avenue to discover the truth was to free his twin—even if that meant committing a crime.

That notion further distressed him, and no less so after he came to an overriding decision: If he managed, somehow, to break his twin out of that cell, he would not turn him loose. He would take him into custody. After the secret of their common past was revealed, he would turn the prisoner over to Sheriff Ochs—and face the consequences himself.

With the gallows completed and tested while the prisoner had watched, his isolation was broken only by the mutterings of the other prisoners and the rumblings of wagon and carriage traffic outside.

He scarcely heard. He had a habit of talking to himself. Not out loud, but an inner dialogue, vivid and silent, as though he was speaking to a spirit. He had done this all of his life, at least ever since he could remember, silently reasoning his way through dilemmas he had encountered.

He was restless but not frightened. In truth, since the day he purchased a granite grave marker for the woman he loved, he had taken each hour—each moment—as it came to him, like cards dealt in a game of chance. He felt empty, numbed, and, if this was his last hour on earth, he was as ready for the end as he would ever be.

The reinforced door squealed on over-burdened hinges. The sheriff came in. He was followed by a heavy-set man, wearing a dark suit and black tie, eyes downcast, black-covered Bible clutched to his chest.

"Need anything?" Sheriff Ochs asked, halting at the barred door to his cell.

The prisoner shook his head.

"If you want dinner," he went on, "I'll fetch it . . . steak and all the fixings."

"No," the prisoner said.

Ochs paused. "Want to talk to this preacher?"

"No," the prisoner said.

The minister cast a darting look at him. Then he stood perfectly still, head bowed, the silence awkward and endless.

"If you've come to pray over me," the prisoner said at last, "save your wind. Watch me hang, and you'll see an innocent man die. Remember that next Sunday when you deliver your sermon."

The minister whispered a prayer as he studied the floor of the cell-block. Then he turned and walked out.

A plan had formed in his mind, but now Matt hesitated as he drove the ranch wagon past the jailhouse. A crowd was gathering in the rutted street by the gallows, a big one, as Ochs had predicted. Men and older boys milled about while a few women stood on the boardwalk across the street, all of them quieted by the knowledge they would

27

soon witness the death of a human being.

Matt drove on, rounding the corner. Half a block farther, he swung into the alley that ran behind the jail. On foot here twenty minutes ago, he had investigated this passageway between buildings.

The alley was littered with rusted tins, barrel staves, and the remains of packing crates. Beer barrels and wooden boxes were haphazardly stacked on either side of deep ruts etched by freight wagons. The rear of the jailhouse could be seen from here, a brick structure with a flat roof, no back door.

No one was here, as Matt had hoped. The best view of the gallows was from the street side. At the rear wall of the jail, he drew back on the lines, halted the wagon, and set the brake. He got down and moved to the wagon bed. Among the provisions for the Two-Bar were cans of kerosene and packets of giant powder, the explosive Old John used to blast out stumps. Those two purchases had inspired Matt's plan.

While his plan was not diagrammed or as carefully thought out as a military attack, he had decided his only chance to succeed was to create a diversion, a big one. That done, he figured he could move swiftly into the jail, free the prisoner, and drive away in the confusion.

Now he knotted his old shirt into a ball, and poured kerosene over the heavy cotton fabric. The first step was to set fire to the gallows. Once the raw pine caught, it would burn fiercely. Constructed in an open lot, Matt figured the flames would not spread beyond those timbers, and other buildings would not be endangered. At worst, if his plan failed, he would buy some time by damaging the gallows.

In the alley he moved beyond the jailhouse to the rear of the gallows, crouching as he glimpsed the swelling crowd on the street. Out of sight behind the base of the structure, he dropped to his knees and struck a match. He touched the sputtering flame to the shirt. Smoke blossomed as the fabric caught fire. Matt stood and nudged it against a six-by-six timber with the toe of his boot. Red-orange flames curled up and licked at wood. He turned and hurried back to the wagon. The flames grew slowly, burning for several long minutes, before someone in the crowd spotted smoke.

"Fire! There's a fire back there!"

Matt lifted a rusted tin out of the wagon. He had packed it with giant powder and fashioned a fuse by weaving strands of twine together and soaking a six-inch length in kerosene. Now he lit the fuse and quickly set the crude bomb on the ground. It would go off with more noise than destruction, he figured, as he climbed up to the wagon seat and took up the lines. He slapped the team. The wagon lurched away amid urgent calls for a bucket brigade. He had driven a hundred feet when the explosion behind him sent out a roaring wind, a hot gust bearing dirt and pebbles.

The horses reared and came down on the run. For the length of the back alley, Matt hauled back on the reins in vain. The team was a runaway until they broke out of the alley. The open street calmed them, and they responded to the lines. Matt turned the wagon and halted. He set the second tin he'd filled with giant powder in the middle of the street, and lit the homemade fuse.

Slapping the team, he drove on. He rounded the next corner where townspeople, eyes wide in terror, rushed toward him. The second explosion erupted, the roar of it driving them back like a flock of sheep. This bomb shattered store windows and sent up a dust-filled cloud mushrooming into the sky. Townspeople ran headlong for safety without knowing where safety was.

Matt managed to drive the frightened team to the jailhouse. He yanked back on the lines, stopping the horses as he leaped down from the seat. The door to the sheriff's office stood open. Drawing his Colt revolver, Matt sprinted inside.

He halted. Ochs stood at the reinforced door. He held the sawed-off shotgun in both hands, chest high. Clearly he had sensed an escape attempt from the start, and had not been lured into joining the panicked townspeople outside.

"Put the Greener down, Sheriff."

When Ochs did not move, Matt took off his hat. The lawman's expression changed slowly from dawning recognition to a look of disbelief and utter confusion.

"How . . . how did . . . how did you get out of that cell?"

"You can figure that one out in your old age," Matt said. He raised the Colt. "If you want to live to an old age, put that scatter-gun down. Now."

Still baffled, Ochs stammered: "What . . . what do you want, mister?"

"There's only one question you have to ask yourself, Sheriff," Matt said, cocking his gun. "Is this worth a bullet?"

A long moment stretched into eternity. Matt was running a bluff, and hoped his eyes did not betray the uncertainty he felt. The moment ended when the lawman bent down and set the sawed-off shotgun on the floor at his feet.

"Turn around," Matt said, hearing more shouts from the street. "Drop to your knees."

"You gonna kill me?"

"Nope."

Outside, Matt heard townsmen cursing and exclaiming to one another about the fire and explosions. The lawman knelt. Matt clapped his hat on his head. With so little time to enact his plan for escape, he was relieved Ochs had obeyed.

Matt crossed the room to the desk. In the center drawer he found wrist-irons and keys. After binding the sheriff's left wrist to his right ankle with the irons, Matt blindfolded him with a bandanna. He unlocked the reinforced door and gave it a shove. Hinges squealing as it swung open, he dragged Ochs into the cell-block.

Shouts outside and two shuddering explosions had sent the prisoner rushing to the window of his cell. He was amazed to see the gallows aflame. Now, hearing the cell-block door open with a squeal, he turned and hopped off the cot. He stared at a man in store-bought clothes and a stockman's hat dragging the blindfolded Sheriff Ochs into the cell-block. The stranger let go of the lawman and rushed to his cell, unlocked the door, and gruffly ordered him to come along.

"Who the hell are you?" the prisoner demanded.

"Come on!"

The prisoner found himself staring at him, mesmerized without knowing the reason.

"Damn it, come on!"

Startled by the sharp command, he followed him out of the cell-block into the sheriff's office. The stranger closed the reinforced door and locked it. Running outdoors, he tossed the keys into a water trough.

The prisoner looked past him. A ranch wagon was out there, loaded and pulled by matched roans bearing the Two-Bar brand. He hesitated only a moment. Then he plucked his hat from a peg on the wall. Scooping up the sawed-off shotgun, he lunged outside.

The stranger leaped to the wagon seat and took up the lines, the wagon lurching away just as the prisoner climbed aboard. He settled in beside him and held on as they barreled down the street with dazed on-lookers scattering before them like birds. No one tried to stop them.

The prisoner inhaled, his first breath of the outdoors in three weeks. One glance over his shoulder gave him a glimpse of the burning gallows. The noose was aflame, twisting like a serpent as it burned. He did not look back again.

The street led to a wagon road paralleling the South Platte River. Two miles out of town the shallow water was spanned by a bridge near the Arapaho encampment. Matt crossed there, hearing the horses' hoofs pound the planks in a mad drumbeat. He looked back, expecting to see a dust cloud raised by a mounted posse.

But there was no cloud of dust or any other sign of pursuers. He had locked Sheriff Ochs in the cell-block and tossed the keys into a water trough with the intent of delaying the organization of a posse. That part of his plan must have worked. The bandanna blindfold, Matt hoped, had prevented the lawman from identifying him as a twin. The longer Ochs was confused on that point, the safer Matt felt.

Beyond the river he covered more ground, fast, not slowing until Denver was long out of sight behind them. Ahead a grove of cottonwood trees marked a pond. Matt guided the team along wheel ruts to a campsite dating back to the gold rush. All that remained now were blackened fire pits littered with bones and tins and broken wheel spokes. The sounds of a horse-drawn wagon sent frogs hopping from the bank, splashing loudly as they leaped into the pond. Overhead, sparrows flew out of treetops, circled, and returned to their perches.

Matt waved mosquitoes from his face as he drove to water's edge and stopped. Sides heaving and tails switching, the horses lowered their heads and drank.

"The sheriff will have a posse on us before long," the prisoner said.

Matt stepped down from the wagon seat. "As soon as the horses are rested, we'll roll."

The prisoner got down and turned to face Matt. In a long silence, the two men looked at one another across the tarp covering supplies in the wagon bed. Matt felt a weird sensation, as though he was looking across the years at his brother.

"Mister, I don't know who you are, or why you cut me loose, but I figure you've got a reason."

Matt nodded.

The prisoner demanded: "What is it? What do you want from me?"

"You don't see it yet, do you?" Matt said.

"See what?"

Matt took off his hat. He shoved his black hair to the side. "You tell me."

The prisoner stared. Recognition seeped into his pale blue eyes. "I'll . . . be . . . damned."

"When I first saw you in that jail cell," Matt said, "I couldn't believe it, either."

"We're . . . we're dead ringers," the prisoner whispered. "How . . . how can . . . where did you . . . ?

"I've got the same questions buzzing in my head," Matt said. "Who are you? Where did you come from?" When his staring twin made no reply, Matt asked: "For starters, what's your name?"

He did not answer immediately. "I've used several."

Matt said: "Start with the first one."

Instead of replying, he stared, his gaze sweeping over Matt from head to toe. "I can't get over it. You . . . you look. . . ."

"Feels like a mirror come to life, doesn't it?" Matt said. "Now, what about your name?"

"That's a long story."

"I'm listening."

He was silent, as though waging an inner struggle. "A gambling man by the name of Hoyt Wilcox raised me," he said at last. "That name mean anything to you?"

"No," Matt said. "Should it?"

He shrugged. "Some folks have heard tell of him." He went on: "Hoyt called me pistol, slick, button, bonehead, meatball, whatever suited him."

"What name were you born with?"

"Hoyt never told me."

Amazed, Matt repeated: "Never told you?"

He shook his head.

Matt asked: "And you never asked him?"

"Not directly."

"What do you mean by that?" Matt asked.

"Like I said, it's a long story."

"This is no time to be cagey. If you never asked this man, Hoyt Wilcox, about your background, you must have had a reason for steering clear of the subject."

"He was quick to hand me a whipping," he said, "whenever I said something he didn't like. That's one thing I learned early. For another, Hoyt always said he won me in a poker game, and, if I caused him a lick of trouble, he'd bet me on a losing hand, glad to be shut of me. I was just a kid, but I learned quick not to give him any guff or ask questions."

"Where is he now?"

"Stoking fires in hell."

"He died?"

Matt's double nodded. "We were staying in a rooming house with me sleeping on the floor, as usual. Middle of the night, and I didn't hear him wheezing and snoring. Thought he was gone, sneaked out on me like he always threatened to. He was gone, all right. I lit a lamp and found him in the bed, dead as a coffin nail. He died with no more to his name than two changes of clothes, a Twenty-Two caliber Derringer with a box of bullets, marked cards and loaded dice, and three hundred and twenty-eight dollars in his money belt." After a silence, he added: "Riley. Riley Wilcox."

"Who is that?" Matt asked.

"You asked me for a name," he said. "After Hoyt died, I've used that one."

"Where did you get it?" Matt asked.

"One time Hoyt called me Riley. Just once. Then he clammed up, like he hadn't meant to say it. Something in his tone of voice made me think Riley could be the name my mother gave me. Or maybe a family name." He studied Matt. "Is it yours?"

"No!" Matt had not meant to raise his voice.

Riley's laugh was a taunt. "How can you be sure?"

Matt answered by describing his upbringing on the homestead claim, assuring Riley that, if another child had been born into the MacLeod family, twin or not, the infant would not have been given away, and certainly not gambled away. Another baby would have been welcomed into the family, and the two of them would have grown up together, brothers.

"The past is a curtain closing on our last act," Riley said with a shrug, "while we stumble across life's stage toward an unknown future waiting in the wings."

Matt was surprised to hear a philosophical statement from him. "Where did you pick that up?"

"Hoyt heard that quote somewhere," Riley explained, "and he liked to use it." He drew a breath and let it out. "Brother, there's only one answer to the mystery. We were adopted . . . separately."

"Adopted." Matt repeated the word as though it came from another language. That notion had never occurred to him. He shook his head, his family background flashing through his thoughts like a series of stereoscopic photographs.

"Maybe they aimed to tell you someday," Riley continued, "and died before they got around to it."

"My mother and father never lied to me," Matt said. "Never."

"Well, somebody sure as hell lied," Riley said, "because we're standing here, eyeballing each other like a pair of jokers out of the same deck."

The rumble of distant hoof beats brought Matt out of a brief search of his memory, a silent hunt for some hint of the truth. He came up empty, no closer to the answer now than the first moment he had laid eyes on his twin. Twin! He still could not believe it, even now as he stared at Riley while the drumming hoof beats grew louder. With no time to wonder, no time for probing questions, he rushed to the wagon and climbed up to the seat.

Riley cocked his head. "Posse?"

Matt nodded as he took up the lines. "Come on."

"We can make a stand in these trees," Riley said, looking around. "If we open up on those town dandies, we'll take the fight out of them in a hurry. . . ."

"Come on!" Matt repeated, backing the wagon.

Riley gazed at him indifferently. "Where to?"

"I know a place," Matt replied, "and I know how to get there without leaving a trail."

"What have you got in mind?"

"I'll tell you on the way. . . ."

Riley interrupted: "We look alike, but I don't know you from Adam's off-ox. I'm not going anywhere until you give me a straight answer."

"The truth!" Matt exclaimed. "I have to find it. That's your answer."

"But how do you aim to . . . ?"

"Riley!" Matt shouted, realizing he had not called his twin by name until this moment. "You coming, or aren't you?"

36

Chapter Three

In the heat of that summer midday Matt drove the ranch wagon across an expanse of loose shale, and then he followed a creek bottom. To anyone but a seasoned tracker, no trail marked either the loose rock or the sand.

Even with a loaded wagon the Two-Bar team of roan geldings was fast. Ochs and his posse never drew close enough to catch sight of the buckboard. By the time Matt drove into the grassy hill country rolling up against the lower foothills of the Rocky Mountains, any dust cloud raised by horsebackers was not visible. The posse, Matt figured, had either broken off the chase, or had followed a false trail.

Now as he topped a grassy rise, an abandoned ranch loomed ahead. His duties as outrider for the Two-Bar had brought him this way a time or two. Drawing closer, he found the sod house to be even more dilapidated than the last time he had passed through here. The rear quarter of the roof had caved in, taking part of a sod wall with it, and the plank door stood open, hanging askew from one rawhide hinge. All that remained of a corral were weathered posts and a few rails.

Every abandoned ranch had a story to go with it, like a ghost ship on the sea or a dark-windowed mansion on a hilltop. This one was no exception. In the Two-Bar bunkhouse Matt had heard of the "white phantom," a big, untamed stallion once confined in this corral.

The rancher's name and brand were lost to local memory, but folks remembered a hostile loner who refused calls for help from his neighbors. In the frontier tradition, entire families would drop what they were doing to aid a neighbor in need, from birthings to branding, from barn raisings to blizzards. This lone rancher answered such calls waving a rusted musket and shouting a warning: "Git offen mah proppity. Go on, git!"

As the story went, he broke his solitude long enough to attend a horse auction in Denver, and placed the high bid on a magnificent white stallion. Standing at eighteen hands, the horse was unmarked and, according to the sing-song tale spun by the auctioneer—"Ain't never been throwed. Ain't never been rode." The rancher led his prancing prize home at the end of a choke rope, determined to burn his brand into that snow-white hide.

He used every technique he knew, from chaining a log around the muscular neck to lashings that drew blood, but he failed to break the stallion's resistance to the saddle. The second week of November of that year saw a hellish blizzard sweep out of the north, the ferocious storm howling like wolves for four days and nights. When the weather cleared, neighboring ranchers sent out cowhands to round up loose stock and count the dead.

Riders ventured into the little valley, bucking snowdrifts to reach the bachelor's sod house. It was empty. Amid broken corral rails, they found him half-buried in snow with a whip clenched in one blood-crusted hand. On his frozen face was the perfect imprint of an unshod hoof. The stallion was gone.

From that day on, winter storms brought new sightings. Cowhands claimed to have spotted a white stallion galloping through the snow, tail high, easily out-distancing pursuers. Known to raid mares from remudas, the white horse on a white plain was never caught, never again strangled by a rope or stung by a lash.

"You believe that one?" Riley asked after listening to Matt's retelling of the tale.

"No reason not to," he replied, dismounting.

Riley swung down. "Have you ever seen that phantom horse with your own eyes?"

Matt shook his head.

"Hoyt used to tell me," Riley went on, "that two breeds of men walk this old world . . . wide-eyed believers and squinty-eyed doubters. Chalk you up as wide-eyed."

"Wide-eyed," Matt repeated.

"You're telling me a horse murders a man," Riley said, "escapes in a storm, and then, out of revenge, cuts mares from ranchers' herds. Nobody ever sees this brute except during snowstorms? And only then from a distance?" He shook his head. "Sounds like a tall one to me. Or maybe cowhands stealing mares dreamed up this tale of the white stallion to cover their crimes."

"You don't trust folks, do you?"

Riley's voice took on an edge when he demanded: "Just what're you driving at?"

"Twelve jurors who didn't trust you."

"Brother," Riley said, anger flaring, "if you're chalking me up as a bad man, I'm calling you out."

"That would be a mistake."

"Not mine," he said. Swiftly closing the distance between them, he thrust his arms out, striking Matt's chest with the heels of his hands.

Matt stumbled back two paces, his boots stirring dust as he caught his balance. When he raised his fists, Riley lifted both arms and came for him in the style of a barroom brawler.

Matt set his feet, legs slightly bent at the knees. He bobbed and feinted with his right. Riley took the decoy jab, and sidestepped directly into Matt's left fist. The hook caught him on the jaw at full force, snapped his head around, and dropped him.

Riley lay on his back, blinking. He rolled over and came up on all fours, pausing long enough for his head to clear. When he stood, he rubbed his jaw. "Should have known. You're left-handed, too, aren't you?"

Fists still up, Matt said: "Want more?"

"Reckon I'd get my licks in," Riley said, eyeing him, "and do some damage before I was done with you."

"One way to find out," Matt said. He had learned the manly art in the Army, and was confident he could handle a brawler.

Riley flashed a quick grin. "What's the sense of us going toe-to-toe, knuckle-busting, eye-gouging, crotch kicking? We're a pair. We'd battle to a tie with both of us crippled up."

"Like I said, there's one way to find out."

"No, brother. Not today."

Matt lowered his fists when his twin backed away. He had won, but did not feel like the victor. Despite the grin, anger lingered in Riley's eyes. Round one, Matt figured, with round two yet to come.

Water was here. The well, hand-dug by the bachelor, produced clean water. Movement caught Matt's eye. In a fringe of grass nearby a diamondback slithered away. He watched the snake disappear among the tall blades of grass. Rather than fear, he felt relief. Rattlers were shy, aggressive only when cornered. The presence of this one was further evidence humans had not trod this ground recently. No roads led here, and neither cowhands nor prospectors had reason to come this way. Gold-seekers favored the main freight road into the mountains to the north, or possibly a short-cut through Two-Bar range to the south.

Matt explained why he was convinced they would be safe here.

Riley surveyed their surroundings. "Paradise."

"You're alive, aren't you?"

Riley grudgingly conceded that point, grimacing as he touched his jaw. Matt's fist had raised a knot, bruised purple now.

As a precaution Matt advised against building smoky campfires. "Keep the cook fires small. I've got a notion folks in Denver won't let Ochs quit on this one, and the posse is still roaming out there. No use in sending up smoke signals."

"There's something you'd better know, brother."

Matt asked: "What's that?"

"I'm leaving this hayseed territory."

"Leaving."

"A lynch-happy jury put the rope on the wrong man," Riley said, "and I'm sure as hell not going to give them a second go at stretching my neck."

"I heard about the murder," Matt said. "What happened in that hotel room?"

"I didn't kill her," he said. "That is a fact, and that's all I'm gonna say about it."

Matt gazed at him. He thought about his earlier decision to return his twin to Ochs's custody after learning the truth about their parentage. It had seemed simple, but, since then, things had tangled. He had not considered the possibility of Riley's maintaining his innocence. Maybe he was a wide-eyed believer, a sucker, as Riley had implied, but Matt trusted his instincts. Something in his twin's voice rang true.

Riley went on: "Thought you dragged me out here to talk about relatives or some such hogwash."

"Hogwash."

"Yeah, hogwash," he said. He hesitated, searching for words. "I'm not much interested in the past. We had some connection somewhere along the line, that's plain. I'm naturally curious about it, and I'd like to know what happened to us, but the fact is, brother, done is done. Clocks don't run backwards. Live in the here-and-now, that's my thinking."

Matt considered his words until a moving shadow caught his eye. He lifted his gaze in time to see a red-tailed hawk swoop out of the blue sky. The winged predator dove to ground level before abruptly sweeping upward, talons clutching a field mouse.

"If I'm reading you right, brother," Riley went on, "you won't let it rest until you find out how we came to be split up. The who and the why . . . that's the truth you were talking about, right?"

Matt nodded slowly.

"Well, I'll tell you everything I can recollect," Riley said, "but don't expect a long tale. Like I say, I'm leaving this hay-seed territory. For good."

Matt drove the ranch wagon across sage and cactus-studded prairie until he reached the well-traveled wagon road leading to the Two-Bar lane. He had left Riley with a box of provisions, promising to return as soon as he could. With no money or mount, no canteen or weapon other than the Greener with a shell in each chamber, Matt figured his twin would not try to walk out. Even if he did, he would track him down.

More pressing problems occupied his mind. He dreaded the prospect of facing Old John. He did not want to quit the ranch, but what else could he do? His life had taken an unexpected turn. He did not know where it would lead. Worse, he would be a fugitive if Ochs ever put two and two together and came up with twins.

Amid the monotonous clip-clops of the horses' hoofs in the shimmering heat of the prairie, he dreamed up tales to account for his decision to draw his pay at the Two-Bar Ranch.

At sundown, day slowly passed into night, and still he had failed to come up with a story that sounded like anything other than what it was—a lie.

Arriving at the home ranch after midnight, Matt was bone-tired when he drove toward the barn. The moon was up, and the barn stood like a great shadow against the sky. He caught sight of dim shapes—horses bunched in the corral. One whinnied, and set off the others.

Matt came out of his half sleep and hauled back on the lines. The roans halted. By moonlight he made out saddle horses in the pole corral, all of them restless in a strange place. None were Two-Bar mounts.

He turned and drove the wagon back the way he had come. A mile away, he left the lane and drove cross-country, guiding the team into a dry gulch. The cleft was deep enough to conceal the wagon and horses. Walking back to the lane by starlight, he obscured wheel tracks with the toe of his boot.

Now it was his turn to put two and two together. Someone in Denver must have spotted the Two-Bar team racing out of town, and the posse had come directly here with Ochs, searching for the driver of the ranch wagon. Old John had put them up for the night.

After sunup Matt was drinking juice from a tin of pears when he heard the distant drumming of shod hoofs. He set the can aside and moved to the team, quieting the two geldings until the posse passed by, unseen. Then he sat in the shade of the wagon and speared the remaining pears with his Barlow folding knife. He waited a full hour to be sure the posse's departure was not a decoy. Then he drove to the home ranch.

He knew what he would do—what he must do in order to live with himself. Lying is for cowards, his father had often said, and his words reverberated through Matt's mind like a voice from the past. Old John had always been square with him—fair-minded, a man of his word. Matt could not lie to him. He would tell the truth, and let the chips fall.

The temptation to lie loomed large, though, when Old John came rushing stiff-legged out of the cabin and greeted him with a welcoming shout. "By damn! Sheriff Ochs told me this-here wagonload of supplies had been stolen! Said an outlaw blew up the gallows, or some such a thing, and freed the killer, and them two stole my goods." He loosened the rope and pulled the tarp aside to inspect the load. "How'd you get it back?"

This was the moment. Old John trusted him. If Matt fabricated a credible story to account for his actions, he would be believed.

"Well?" the rancher demanded as he turned to Matt, grinning. "How'd you do it?"

The door to the cook shack opened. Luther Allen, the cook, came out. A balding man with a watermelon belly bulging under a soiled apron, he waddled toward them with a look of anticipation on his face. Most of this wagonload was destined for his pantry.

"I need to talk to you about that, Mister Souter," Matt replied. "Alone."

"Sounds serious."

"It is."

"Luther," Old John said as he turned to the cook, "unload this wagon, will ya? Come on, Matt."

Allen made no reply. Not out loud. He was a man who did not favor heavy lifting, and Matt saw him scowl at the prospect of doing this job alone.

In the ranch house Old John closed the door. Crossing the dirt-floored room, he sat on the end of a plank bench and planted his hands on his knees. Sunlight streamed in through the south windowpane, illuminating the rancher's white hair. He gazed up at his outrider, a worried young man standing before him, hat clenched in both hands. "You aim to pull the brim off that new hat, or you gonna tell me what this is all about?"

Matt drew a deep breath and launched into his account.

"By damn," Old John whispered after he heard what had happened since Matt MacLeod had first laid eyes on his twin. "Good thing I'm sitting down. This takes a goodly while to soak in, don't it?"

"Yes, sir."

"I recollect seeing you standing by that jail cell," Old John said, "but I never gave the condemned man a second look. He's your twin? Your identical twin?"

"Yes, sir."

"You're dead sure?"

"Yes, sir."

"By damn, you bit a big chaw when you busted him outta the jailhouse. A big chaw." Old John ran a gnarled hand through white beard stubble. "Hell, reckon I'd have did the same, was I in your boots. Glad I ain't."

"You're a fool's fool for telling him."

Matt eyed Riley. "Old John won't say a word. . . ."

"You trust him?"

"That's right."

"No, that's the difference between us," Riley countered. He explained: "Say Ochs finds that wagon and team at the ranch. Will Old John protect you if he's arrested? No, he'll turn on you the minute Ochs pulls a pair of wrist irons out of his saddlebag."

"Yeah, I see the difference between you and me."

On the Two-Bar Old John had refused to accept Matt's resignation. The rancher had told him to come back after he got "this here thing straightened out."

Returning to the abandoned bachelor's ranch astride his chestnut mare, Matt found Riley waiting. He led a second mount from his string, a speckled gray gelding with the Two-Bar brand. Six months ago he had purchased the aging cow horse from Old John. Now he had accepted the loan of a saddle, blanket, bridle, and saddlebags for Riley's use. Matt had been reluctant to take the gear. More than a friendly loan, it made the rancher an accessory to a crime. But when Old John made up his mind, "augurin' " was pointless.

Suspicious of the man's motives, Riley would not let it go. "When a reward's posted for us, you can be sure that old-timer will be first in line to collect. That's why he's stringing you along . . . so he'll know where to find us."

Anger surging through him, Matt said: "You don't know the man."

"I know human nature," he insisted. "If things don't go his way, he'll turn on you."

"And if manure was gold," Matt said, "you'd be filthy rich." With Riley glowering at him, he went on: "Save your jawing for something you know about."

"Meaning my family tree?"

Matt nodded.

Riley folded his arms across his chest. "You brought the deck, brother. Turn up the first card."

How does a man put his life into words? Matt had never attempted to do this before. In the cuss and discuss of bunk-house life, he had never mentioned his back trail, and no one had ever asked. His life experience was a tangle of memories—good, bad, indifferent—and now, as he stumbled through a disjointed account of his upbringing on a remote homestead, visual images filled his mind: running his hands through the sun-warmed sand of a dry wash; his first dog; tracking game and hunting with his father; the sweet smiling face of his mother as she stood in the doorway of their soddy to watch her son at play.

Matt had never given much thought to the isolation of their lives on the homestead. Scattered neighbors lived the same way, rarely visiting, traveling to town two or three times a year. But now he realized his parents had spoken of relatives only in vague terms—deceased grandparents in Delaware, an uncle in Virginia—and they had never received mail in town, at least no letters he was aware of. Maybe Riley was right. Details of his lineage could have been withheld.

The thought was disturbing. Matt had never, in any way, mistrusted his parents. They had loved him. Their deaths from influenza contracted during a visit to town marked a turning point in his life. From then on he had been on his own. After selling the family possessions, the milk cows and laying hens, he had outfitted himself, and later signed on with the Army as a civilian scout.

"You figured you were born into the MacLeod family," Riley said, "because no one ever told you different."

Matt nodded. Of course, he believed that. What else would he believe?

"Well, none of what you said rings a bell with me," Riley said. "Not one word. Far as I know, I never lived on a lonely homestead. If I did, it was so far back that I have no recollection of it."

"What memories do you have?"

Clearly pained, Riley did not answer for a long moment. "I'm thinking on it." When he finally took a stab at autobiography, Riley described bits and pieces of his early years as little more than a servant boy. His life with Hoyt Wilcox amounted to chattel, and his youthful dependency on the man was underscored by a fear of abandonment. Even long after he was old enough to fend for himself, he stayed with the gambler off and on, loyal to the only father he had ever known. By then Hoyt Wilcox was ravaged by consumption, and needed him.

Riley's earliest memories involved running errands for the gambler on riverboats plying the Mississippi and Missouri Rivers, endless rounds of five-card draw and blackjack in mining camps from Colorado to Montana. Hoyt gambled in railroad towns on the Union Pacific line. Many of Riley's memories were laced with violence, for men who lose at poker sometimes have nothing more to lose, and attack out of desperation. In high-stakes games the Derringer was never far from Hoyt's hand, his gaze taking the measure of poker faces across a field of green felt.

He had once shot an adversary to death across that green expanse and run into the night with young Riley pounding at his heels. For several harrowing days they hid from friends and relatives of the murdered man, all of them armed and sworn to kill the gambler. Riley remembered the sharp sting of powder smoke in his nostrils as they had fled that gambling hall. They had spent a long night in a cemetery, hiding in a newly dug grave among the tombstones. Riley remembered his recurring nightmares, too, vivid scenes of being chased, caught, and buried alive.

One vivid memory ignited another. While Riley rediscovered the past, Matt began to understand his twin's make-up. Small wonder Riley trusted no one. When Hoyt Wilcox landed in a new town, he was not the prince of the pasteboards. He was a merchant, banker, undertaker, teacher or a mine owner or a doctor. The only profession he had never claimed, he once confided, was posing as a veterinarian.

Folks were picky about the doctoring of their livestock, and Hoyt knew he could never run that bluff.

With his silver tongue, Hoyt made friends quickly. He had a knack for professing an interest in the well-being of the town, in time allowing himself to be drawn into friendly games of chance. Whether it was the course of several days or a few weeks, Hoyt squinted as he threw dice or shuffled cards clumsily. He lost more than he won until the pot swelled, ripe for the picking. That was when he "got lucky."

Whether pursued by an outraged citizenry or dogged lawmen, they always escaped before the chickens knew they had been plucked. Hoyt Wilcox never deviated from his dictum. Run before dawn was the gambler's legacy to the nameless boy, and the bastards will never catch you.

Out of the nightfall came silence, and from silence came quietude. With a flickering campfire between them, the twins stretched out on blankets, boots off and hats tossed aside, mirror images of one another as they each leaned back on an elbow to meditate over dying flames. They had wearied of re-membering, wearied of talking, and certainly Matt had long since wearied of countering Riley's oft-repeated opinion: "Our quest for an answer is futile. The shining key to unlock the mystery of our births is not to be found in our memories."

At times Matt wavered and was inclined to agree with Riley, although he never gave him the satisfaction of saying so aloud, for he was determined. In the great stillness of the starlit prairie, he figured there was more to know, more sub-stance to their life experiences than the fragmented incidents and childhood memories portrayed in their halting words and stumbling phrases.

Like fish surfacing from murky depths, more memories slid into their minds the next day. Still, in all their talking and reminiscing, all their digging into the past, they found nothing in common—no dates, names, or specific places to link their births to the circumstances of their lives, two lives that could hardly have been more different. They were left with the only possible answer, the one Riley had raised from the first. Their mother had either not survived childbirth, or for some compelling reason she had relinquished her twin sons, separately, in infancy.

This was not an answer that rang true to Matt. His parents would have gladly adopted both boys, if the existence of a twin had been made known to them. Beyond doubt, he knew that much, and said so. Riley countered with a reasonable explanation—twins would be a burden to parents who were not wealthy, so it was sensible for the babies to be adopted separately. If prospective parents saw them together, choosing one over the other would be well nigh impossible. Better not to let anyone know.

Matt conceded that it was possible for his parents to have adopted him without knowing he had a twin brother. His thoughts drifted. As he gazed at his twin, he was troubled by another unknown.

"Who was Miss Augusta Benning?" Matt asked.

He glowered. "I told you all I'm gonna."

"But if you're innocent," Matt said, "why won't you talk about it?"

"I told you."

"You haven't told me anything," Matt countered. When Riley did not respond, he pressed him. "I risked my neck to save yours. You owe me an explanation."

Riley glowered. "Playing your ace-in-the-hole?"

"Whether it's an ace or a deuce," Matt replied, "seems to me you'd want to prove your innocence."

"Face it, brother, we've ridden into a box cañon. We've gone as far as we can go."

50

Matt studied him. "Run before dawn . . . is that your plan?"

Riley replied with half a grin at his twin's reference to the gospel according to Hoyt.

"But if you're innocent . . . ?"

"What I know," Riley interrupted, "and what you think doesn't matter. Get that through your thick head. I was tried by a glorified lynch mob. Every man, woman, dog, and cat in Denver wanted to see me hang. There's no way in hell to prove to them that I'm innocent."

"You didn't even know her well enough to call her by her first name?"

"Hell, I didn't know her, period. Never laid eyes on her before that day."

"Then how did you come to meet her in the hotel?"

"I had one of Hoyt's IOUs bearing her name and a Denver address," he replied. "I wrote her a letter, telling her about Riley Wilcox, and signed Hoyt's name to it. I figured if Miss Benning didn't know he was dead, I'd collect the money. Sure enough. She wrote back, telling me where to meet her." His voice trailed off as he thought better of confessing details of a fraudulent claim.

"What happened then?" Matt asked.

Riley shook his head, jaw clenched.

"You owe me," Matt said again.

Riley drew a deep breath. "All right. I knocked on the door. I heard a shotgun blast. Should have turned around and walked away. But I eased open the door and went in. A stout woman was sprawled across the bed, blood splattered all over the bedspread and up on the wallpaper behind her. The cut-down shotgun was on the floor by the open window. Heard an uproar behind me in the hallway, and I knew what folks would think if I backed out of that doorway. So I left through

51

the window. Got blood on my clothes as I crawled out. A deputy nailed me in the back alley." He added after several moments: "Reckon I made a hero out of Tug Larkin."

"Go on."

"That's the whole story . . . not that it matters a single damn."

"Why do you say that?"

"Like I told you, I'm leaving," Riley said. "You can keep your spare horse and gear."

Matt said: "How far can you go on foot?"

Riley cast an ironic smile at him. "I'll catch that phantom white stallion, brother, and gallop over the far horizon to freedom."

Where the Colorado prairie rumbled up against the foothills of the Rocky Mountains, a cool dawn with dew-moistened grasses belied the coming of a blistering hot day. Matt MacLeod had awakened in cool darkness before the dawn, shivering as he splashed water over his face. He dressed, shook out his boots, and pulled them on. By the time the rising sun cast its red glow across the eastern horizon, he was kneeling in the damp grass at Riley's side, revolver in hand. He thumbed the hammer back, cocking the gun.

Riley stirred at the sound of a metallic click. His eyes opened. "I figured you had some notion of stopping me, brother." He came up on one elbow, rubbing his face with his other hand. "It won't work."

"You sure know a lot," Matt said.

"You won't shoot me," he said. "Not your own flesh and blood."

"You're wrong about that," Matt said.

"Am I?"

"Think about it," Matt said. "The only way I can be sure the sheriff won't come after me is to take you back to the jailhouse. If I have to wing you to do it, I will."

"A bullet or a hangman's noose . . . some choice."

"You have another one," Matt said.

"Such as?"

"Prove your innocence."

"I told you," Riley said. "I can't prove it."

"You owe it to me to try," Matt countered.

"Owe it to you?"

"Look at us," he reminded him. "I live in these parts. If you're guilty, I'm guilty."

Riley eyed him. "Say I go along. Just how do you aim to clear me?"

"I don't have answers yet. Only questions."

"Such as?"

"What was the connection between Miss Augusta Benning and Hoyt Wilcox?"

"She owed him over a thousand dollars," Riley said. "That's all I know."

"Hoyt never mentioned her by name?"

"Not to me," he said.

"Weren't you with him?"

Riley shook his head. "I was on my own, more or less, until he took sick and needed my help just to get through the day. He must have met that woman when I was not with him. Why are you asking?"

"Maybe she was a link to his past," Matt said, adding, "to the Riley name."

Riley shook his head. "I'd say she's linked to a gambling debt, that's all. Maybe her son or husband made the mistake of underestimating Hoyt. He held a lot of markers, most of them worthless. Occupational hazard."

"Won't hurt to dig up the whole story," Matt said.

"Won't hurt!" Riley repeated. "Are we going to ride into Denver big as day, politely tap folks on the shoulder, and ask who killed Miss Augusta Benning?"

Matt held back a smile. "Something like that."

"And while we're at it," Riley went on, "we'll ask those high-minded citizens to rebuild the gallows."

"We?"

Riley scowled. The moment of good humor passed. A long silence followed as they regarded one another.

"I might tag along," Riley conceded at last, "except for one thing."

"What's that?"

"I get the feeling you're not leveling with me."

Matt studied him. "What do mean?"

"If I read you right, you have some wild hope of uncovering our past if you keep me on a short leash."

Matt made no comment. He eased the hammer down and slid his revolver back into his holster.

"I'm right about that, aren't I?"

"The notion might have drifted through my head."

"Thought so," Riley said. He rubbed a hand against the black beard stubble shadowing his jaw. "Look, brother, you saved my life. I owe you. I don't deny that. Truth is, I'd like to clear myself so I don't have to live out my days looking over my shoulder." He inhaled. "So I'll go along with you. For now. Just remember one thing."

"What?"

"I've been handed a second chance at life," he said, "and I aim to live a long time."

"So you'll be looking out for yourself?"

"First and foremost," Riley answered. "You might say it's the way I was raised."

★ ★ ★ ★ ★

Through the remainder of that week and all of the next, Riley let his beard grow. Matt shaved his jaw and grew a thick black mustache. The disguises were unsophisticated, hardly foolproof, but they might keep them from being spotted immediately as twins—or a clean-shaven killer. Neither of them was known in Denver. Matt was counting on that and on the fact that the town was bursting with newcomers. Men arrived daily by coach. Most were eager beavers passing through on their way to easy fortunes in distant mining camps. With some caution, Matt figured he and Riley could move freely.

Meanwhile, they passed the time by repairing the sod house and rebuilding the storied pole corral. The ranch house was empty except for a den of rattlesnakes that had taken up residence under a section of the collapsed sod wall. Coiled with tails vibrating, their mad buzzing sent Riley sprinting to the corral.

Matt feared diamondbacks only when he was on horseback. The sudden buzzing of a rattler inspired a saddle horse to new heights, dumping the rider before galloping to hell-and-gone. More than once Matt had hiked to the home ranch in boots meant for riding, arriving gimpy and blistered, only to find his unrepentant horse waiting at the barn door. "Boys," Old John was fond of saying in a mournful voice, "the saddest sight in nature is a cowhand afoot. Yes, sir."

Now Matt built a small, hot fire, dropped a handful of green grass into the flames, and used his hat to fan smoke into the den. Eight or ten rattlers, young to full-grown, slithered away to escape unfriendly neighbors. With the fire out, Riley had to be convinced he could safely set foot on the ground.

"Best mousers you'll ever see," Matt said.

"Mousers!" Riley eased down from the top pole of the

corral. His eyes darted left and right as he walked gingerly through the high grass.

"Keep a few rattlers around," Matt explained, "and you won't have a lick of trouble with mice, prairie dogs, or any other flea-bit rodents."

Riley gave that some thought. "Fleas aren't so bad."

In the following days they chased down a wild turkey, and trapped two prairie chickens, but after the third week their provisions were gone. Worse, a fierce boredom gnawed at them. Their moods ranged from silent edginess to tempers openly flaring. After a hot argument over who would gather firewood and who would cut it nearly exploded into a fist-fight, they looked at one another, and grinned.

No words were needed. The twins knew the time had come. Under a hot afternoon sun, they saddled their mounts and swung up, turning the horses toward Denver.

Chapter Four

Riley's gut tightened into a hard knot as they rode down Sixteenth Street and passed in front of the Inter-Ocean Hotel. Polished reflectors of kerosene lamps illuminated patriotic bunting. In anticipation of statehood designation next year, red, white, and blue banners framed the hotel entrance, and American flags decorated the corners at every floor.

Men in business suits lounged in the portico there, gents smoking cigars while debating affairs of the day in the cool of the night. Standing among them was a chunky, barrel-chested man. Riley recognized Tug Larkin when the nickel-plated badge pinned to his vest caught a flash of lamplight.

Relieved when the deputy did not look their way, Riley spoke to Matt in a hushed voice: "What the hell are you doing?"

If he heard, he gave no sign. Riley could see that Matt had not spotted the deputy. Left and right, darkened shops lined the street. Matt turned in his saddle as he gazed up at the hotel like an awed country bumpkin. The Inter-Ocean, as imposing as a great square-rigger in harbor, stood out among the shops like a flagship in a fleet, flags flying, sails struck.

They rode past the front of the four-story structure and rounded the corner. The Inter-Ocean occupied a quarter of a block, by far the largest building in Denver. Matt guided his horse into the alley behind it, the site of Riley's arrest, and drew rein.

Closing the distance, Riley halted beside him. "I said, what the hell are you doing . . . ?"

"I heard you," Matt said. He pointed up to darkened win-

57

dows on the third floor. "Which one is Three-Oh-Four?"

"Up there by the fire ladder," he said. He looked around, spooked by the dark familiarity of this place—all the more so now that he had caught sight of Larkin hobnobbing with well-heeled gents.

"I've been thinking about it ever since you told me what happened," Matt replied. "Wanted to see this stretch of alley for myself."

Riley cast a furtive glance back to the side street. "All right. You've seen it. Let's ride."

Horse prancing when Riley started to turn his mount, Matt held a tight rein. "Ochs said you told the deputy you were chasing the murderer."

Riley looked at his twin's face shadowed in darkness. "That was the best I could come up with on short notice."

"But the truth is you never saw anyone?"

"No one."

"That's what I've been thinking about."

"Thinking what?"

Matt did not answer. "When you heard the shotgun blast, how long did it take you to get from the door to the window?"

"Hell, I don't know," Riley said.

"Half a minute?" Matt prompted.

Riley shook his head. "Not that long. Like I told you, I saw the body and all that blood, and heard folks coming down the hallway. I knew I had to get out of there, fast. I ran across the room, climbed out through that window, and leap-frogged down the fire ladder. That's when the deputy nailed me." He asked: "What're you driving at?"

"I keep wondering where the killer went," Matt said. "Either he was hiding under the bed in that room, or he left through the window and climbed up the fire ladder."

"Up?"

"You were looking down, weren't you?"

"Reckon so."

"That would explain why you didn't see anyone."

Riley craned his neck. "I'll be damned. The killer could have been on the roof when that deputy jabbed a gun into my back."

"Or," Matt said, "in Room Four-Oh-Four."

Riley considered that possibility, nodding slowly. "Wish somebody had thought of this sooner."

"Folks figured you did it," Matt said, "and you did not give them much reason to look further."

Riley swore in disgust. "So in this hayseed territory I have to prove I'm innocent . . . is that what you're saying?"

"I'm saying," Matt explained, "that you did not give the jury much to go on."

"I told my side of it," he said stubbornly. "Truth is, when those jokers looked for somebody to hang, they looked at me."

Matt did not argue. He turned his horse. They rode, side by side, out of the alley. Turning onto the street, Riley announced he had suffered long enough with campfire cooking, sleeping on hard ground, and checking his boots in the morning for rattlesnakes. He craved a meal in a café and a night in a real bed.

"We'll camp beside the pond in the cottonwood grove outside of town," Matt said. "It's safe, and the price is right."

"You do what you want, brother," Riley countered. "No more star-gazing and mosquito-slapping for me. I tell you, I want a big steak for my supper, and then I want a roof over my head when I stretch out on a nice, soft cotton mattress. . . ."

Matt broke in: "What do you aim to use for money?"

Riley halted the saddle horse. "Hell, I forgot. Ochs cleaned me out."

Matt drew up. He patted his wallet. "We'll have to squeeze fifty dollars as tight as we can. . . ."

Now Riley broke in: "Give me twenty."

Matt stared at him in the dim light cast by the hotel lamps half a block away.

"Give me twenty dollars," Riley repeated, "and I'll bring back two hundred. One for you, one for me."

"Big talk."

"Wager small, win small," Riley taunted. "I'll deliver. Care to place a side bet on it?"

"Not with a man who doesn't have a cent to his name," Matt replied, "and rides a borrowed horse under a saddle that doesn't belong to him."

"Damn, I hate to be a beggar," Riley said. He shrugged. "But what the hell . . . it's all in the family."

Riley pointed to lamplight streaming through a plate glass window three doors away. **Rocky Mountain House** in gold letters marked a café with upstairs rooms to let.

"Get yourself a bite of supper, brother," Riley said. "Order the best cut of beef on the menu, and don't forget dessert . . . a big slab of pie under a mountain of whipped cream. Not a hill . . . a mountain. Take your time. I'll be along shortly with your twenty. Plus interest."

Matt hesitated.

Riley added: "The world will look like a better place when your stomach's full." He watched Matt grimace, as though a tooth was being yanked, when he dug out his wallet. Snatching twenty dollars from his hand, Riley gave him a careless salute and rode away.

Matt watched Riley fade into the night shadows. He wondered how many times Hoyt Wilcox had sharped a trusting victim with the extravagant promise of a quick return on an investment, a sure thing. And he wondered if he would ever see Riley again—or his saddle horse and Old John's outfit.

At this late hour the café was nearly empty. Matt was seated at a small table with his back to the kitchen door. The waiter handed a menu to him, and stood by. Dressed in a black swallowtail jacket over a white ruffled shirt and creased black trousers, he wore his thin brown hair slicked back, shiny with oil. Matt did not like the looks of this strange bird, any more than he liked wasting money. With the waiter looking on, he took a deep breath, disregarded his better judgment, and followed his twin's advice. He ordered sirloin steak with a baked potato, carrots, squash, and a fist-sized biscuit with a dollop of butter. And pie. With extra whipped cream. The waiter nodded and quoted the total amount due, and waited.

Half a minute passed. Matt took the hint. He looked more like a rough cowhand off the range than the prosperous gents who took their suppers in a sit-down café. He pulled out his wallet and paid in advance—$1.15. Money in hand, the waiter uttered a—"Very good, sir."—and turned away, striding into the kitchen.

Everybody's after my dollars, Matt thought.

He was the last diner in the café when the grand meal arrived, steaming food served on white china with silver utensils. Expensive as it was, he cut through the glistening steak and chewed slowly, enjoying every bite of his best meal in weeks. Afterward a slice of apple pie topped by a Long's Peak of whipped cream arrived at the table along with coffee. When Matt raised the cup of hot brew to his mouth, he glimpsed a shadow. Outside, a figure passed by the window. The front door swung open.

Riley came in. He crossed the café, smiling broadly. He sat down and shoved two twenty-dollar gold pieces across the tablecloth.

"There's your hard-earned *dinero,* brother . . . with interest."

Matt looked at the coins, then at his twin. "How did you manage to rob a bank after hours?"

Before Riley could reply, the waiter came to their table and looked down his nose as he spoke to him. "Sorry, sir, but our kitchen is closed for the night. . . ."

Riley produced a five-dollar gold piece. He held the coin out and dropped it into the waiter's palm the moment his bony white hand came up. "Waiter, I'll choke down the same cut of beef and trimmings my friend just et. Keep the change."

"Yes, sir," he said, backing away. "Very good, sir."

Matt had never seen money so casually discarded. When the waiter left, he leaned closer. "Where did you get that cash?"

"Blackjack table in the Ace High," he said. "I'd have raked in more, but a pair of Ochs's deputies trooped in. I slipped out, one step ahead of those law dogs."

"Blackjack," Matt repeated.

"Know how to play?"

"Yeah."

"You a card counter?"

"I can count to twenty-one."

Riley laughed. "That's not what I'm talking about."

"What are you talking about?"

"Crooks like Hoyt Wilcox are card counters," he said. "He always knew which cards were out. Shifted the odds in his favor. The trick is to avoid winning too much, too fast. Play the dealer, that's what you have to do. Play him like a fish on a line."

"One of Hoyt's sayings?"

Riley shrugged. "Hoyt said a lot of things."

"Such as?"

"Lose before you win," Riley said. "And make your opponent think you're a sucker before you clean his damned clock."

"And run before dawn."

Riley grinned. "That's right. Run before dawn."

"Hoyt Wilcox was strong on proverbs, wasn't he?"

"He was a talker," Riley agreed. He paused. "Bet you thought I wasn't coming back."

Matt shook his head in silent denial.

"Question is," Riley added with a glance past him, "who's that watching us?"

Matt turned in his chair and looked at the kitchen doorway. He caught a glimpse of a sandy-haired young woman in a long, white apron the moment before she ducked back.

"Saw her looking you over when I came in," Riley said. "Cook's helper, likely. The way she was staring, I do believe she's taken a shine to you."

"Never saw her before," Matt said. "Have you?"

"I'm new in town," Riley replied with a grin. He thought about that and added: "Reckon if I shaved my beard clean down to a mustache like yours, the girls would flock to me, too?"

"A sure bet," Matt said, "until they get to know you."

Riley chuckled.

When they left the Rocky Mountain House, both had eaten their fill and then some. Walking to their horses at the tie rail, Matt had to admit this part of the world seemed a little better now. He untied the reins and looked across his saddle. Framed by bright lights, the Inter-Ocean Hotel loomed out of the darkness like a stilled presence.

"Now what are you thinking?" Riley asked in a voice edged by dread.

"I wonder who checked into Room Four-Oh-Four the day of the murder," he replied. "If we're going to find evidence to prove you didn't shoot that woman, there's our starting place."

"Brother, I'm not moving one step closer to that establishment," Riley said. "Before you start scheming, we need to board these horses, and then we need to locate a decent rooming house to board us. . . ."

Instead of picking up their argument over where to spend the night, Matt reached for his revolver and half turned. Movement had caught his eye. Someone was standing in the shadows between two buildings, the café and a darkened shoe and boot repair shop next door.

"Come out."

Now Riley spun around in surprise, following his twin's gaze.

Matt drew his gun, cocking it as he brought the barrel up. "I said, come out of there."

A slender woman stepped out of the near-darkness, halting on the boardwalk.

"Who are you?" Matt asked.

She moved closer, eyeing both men in the half light before turning to Riley. "I thought so."

"Thought what?" Riley demanded.

"I saw you in the jail," she said, adding: "One of you."

Now Riley echoed Matt's question: "Who are you?"

Matt recognized the young woman from the Rocky Mountain House kitchen. She had exchanged her apron for a waist-length jacket, and she wore a simple cotton hat tied under her chin by a scarf.

"Anne Marie Painter," she replied, and moved a pace closer. "Sheriff Ochs put up a two-hundred dollar reward. 'Dead or Alive for the Murder of the Beloved Miss Augusta

Benning' . . . that's what the poster says. 'Name Unknown,' it says, with a description."

Matt said, "Hold on, Miss Painter. . . ."

She broke in: "You don't want more trouble from the law, do you?"

Riley snorted. "You're out-numbered, out-sized, and out-gunned. You're in no shape to be making threats."

"If I scream for help," she said, "men will come running. When the night deputy gets here, you'll both be under the gun."

Matt stepped around his horse, peering at her in the dim light. "Missy? Missy? Is that you?"

Riley said: "Thought you didn't know her."

Matt eased the hammer down and holstered his gun. "Last time I saw her she was in a jail cell, wearing a plug-ugly miner's get-up."

Anne Marie waved a hand impatiently. "That's enough chatter."

"For a little wisp of a gal," Riley said, "you've got a big, bossy mouth."

Her gaze swept past Riley to Matt, and back again. "Oh, my!"

Riley said: "Oh, my what?"

"Oh, my . . . now I see."

"See what?" he asked louder.

"You're twins, aren't you? Yes . . . if you'd both shave properly, I'd say you're identical twins."

Riley turned away.

"Will the sheriff sort all of this out," Anne Marie asked, "or just hang the both of you?"

"Miss Painter . . . ," Matt began.

She interrupted him again: "Let's get down to business."

"Business," Matt repeated.

65

"I need you," she said, "and you need me. That's business, isn't it?"

"Don't call me Missy. That isn't my name."

Matt listened, hearing Anne Marie Painter's voice quake with anger when she spoke of her "awful confinement among drunken, stinking men in cages." Her one-night sentence to a jail cell was "the longest of my life," and she heartily blamed "that narrow-minded, mean old rancher, John Souter."

Sheriff Ochs had cut her loose the next morning. She returned to her job, working for the restaurateur who regularly purchased cream and butter at the Painter farm. Her daily routine was a three-mile hike from the farm to the Rocky Mountain House, and back home after closing.

Anne Marie informed them every mattress in every flophouse in Denver held at least one man, some two or three, at this late hour. They might have found unoccupied rooms in the Inter-Ocean, but Matt was too tight to pay the fare, and Riley was too jumpy to set foot in the place. Anne Marie offered the use of a haymow for the night as long as neither man smoked in her family's barn.

"I'll fix your breakfast," she added. "No charge."

"You aim to collect the reward," Riley said.

She eyed him. "No, I don't."

"Then what is your game?"

"Why are you so suspicious?"

"Because you're up to something," Riley insisted. "Has to be the reward." He turned to Matt. "I figure Ochs emptied out my money belt for that damned reward. Hell of a thing, my own money doled out to the joker who brings me in."

She said evenly: "I don't want your money."

"What other reason would you take up with a couple of notorious criminals like us?" Riley asked, and then answered his own question: "When we're asleep, you'll fetch the law. Collect an easy two hundred."

"I heard what you two were saying just now," she said. "You didn't kill that poor woman. If you had, you wouldn't be in Denver, trying to find out who did."

Matt turned to Riley. "Sounds like she's straight up."

"She said business," Riley reminded him. "That means she wants something."

Matt turned to her. "Why are you offering to take us to your home?"

"In the morning after breakfast," Anne Marie said, "I want you to listen to what I have to say. Both of you. We'll go from there."

Riley shook his head. "You're not calling the shots for me."

"You don't trust anyone, do you?" Anne Marie said.

Riley took Matt aside and whispered: "Told you this hare-brained scheme of yours wouldn't work, brother. We haven't been in town two hours, and we're spotted. Now she's leading us on like sheep to slaughter."

Matt eyed him. "I believe her."

"You would," Riley muttered.

Matt moved around his horse and thrust a boot into the stirrup. Grasping the saddle horn, he swung up. He reached down for Anne Marie. He clasped her hand and pulled her up behind him, noticing how small and fine-boned it was.

"You coming?" Matt said to Riley.

He glowered, unmoving.

Matt shrugged. He touched his spurs to the horse and rode away with Anne Marie holding on, her hands lightly on his waist above his gun belt.

Riley watched them, at fierce odds with his instincts for survival until heavy footfalls sounded on the boardwalk behind him. A group of five gents came through the shadows from the hotel, jovial and talkative as they headed for the saloon district. One gruff voice sounded familiar. As they drew closer, Riley made out the stout figure of Tug Larkin.

Riley turned and leaned close to the horse's neck. He reached for the brim of his hat. The townsmen passed by with Larkin no more than six feet away. When they were gone, he exhaled slowly, recalling the sight of the burning hangman's noose, a rope that seemed to squirm as it was consumed by fire.

Loco, he thought as he untied the reins. *This whole thing is loco.* Mounting then, he urged the horse down the street and rode after his twin at a high lope.

Matt expected to see a real barn, a weatherproof, cavernous structure like the fine horse barn on the Two-Bar Ranch. But now, in the starlight, Anne Marie pointed to an over-size shed next to a battered Conestoga wagon. Constructed from sawmill cast-offs, the barn was built of warped pine boards, all of them nailed together without benefit of a carpenter's square.

The farmhouse stood a short distance away from the barn, near a small, star-reflecting pond at the base of a rise. Little more than a twelve-by-twelve box made of squared cottonwood logs, it was flat-roofed, stout as a fort—an impractical design in snow country. Cottonwood logs were subject to dry rot. In time the roof would leak, or a wet spring snowfall would cave it in.

Matt figured this place was in compliance with the minimum requirements of the Homestead Act, President Lincoln's Public Land ownership law requiring annual improvements and continuous residence on a registered claim. He wondered, though, if this poor-man's farm would ever meet approval from an inspector.

Anne Marie's two younger brothers slept in the wagon. At the sound of horses, they climbed out of the wagon box in their nightclothes, rubbing sleep from their eyes as they approached in bare feet,

"Who . . . who are these men?" one asked.

By the light of the stars, Matt made out two blond-haired, scrawny youngsters. The tallest was introduced as Micah, the other Samuel. Both spouted questions while their sister shooed them back to the wagon with a promise to answer every query first thing in the morning.

"I would have introduced you," she said, when she came back, "but I still don't know your names."

Matt felt a wave of hot embarrassment. He had been raised better. His father often said criminals hid their identities; honest folks were proud of their names. He gave his name, and after a long moment Riley did the same. With introductions made, Anne Marie showed them to the barn.

By lamplight Matt could see the mow was obviously too weak to hold any more weight than the hay bales and feed sacks already up there. He looked around. The same snowfall that would cave in the farmhouse roof would flatten this place. He heard Riley cough and saw him raise a hand to his mouth and nose. The dirt floor in here was rank with cow urine.

After Anne Marie bid them good night and went into the farmhouse, the twins stepped outside. Riley spread his blankets and stretched out, grumbling about having to sleep on hard ground again.

Matt lay down. He stared up at the starlit heavens, and pondered the events since he had first laid eyes on his twin. The changes in his life since that moment were dramatic, but the most disturbing was this sense of losing control of his destiny. As an outrider for the Two-Bar life had been straightforward and simple by comparison to the tumble of events he had experienced since then. Now, drifting into sleep, his thoughts turned to Anne Marie. He wondered if Riley was right about her motives.

Dawn was announced by an insistent rooster. Smoke drifted out of the rusted stovepipe sticking out of the flat roof. Anne Marie had not sent for lawmen during the night, a fact Matt cheerfully noted while he and Riley washed up at the pond. Riley swatted insects and answered with a grunt.

When Anne Marie announced breakfast, her brothers leaped out of the wagon. After a detour at the outhouse, they raced into the cabin. Anne Marie met Matt and Riley at the door. Showing them in, she introduced them to her father.

Paul Painter was seated in a wicker armchair when he greeted two strangers in a growling voice. "Who've you drug into the house this time, Annie? First, it was that crazy prospector. What now? Saddle tramps?"

"Father, that's no way to welcome two gentlemen," she said with a pained glance at Matt and Riley. Her brothers stood off to one side, heads ducked in shyness in the presence of strangers. Matt saw the boys cast darting glances at his holstered revolver.

"How do you know I wanna welcome them?" he demanded.

"Common courtesy," she replied.

"Common," he repeated. "Everything out here in the wild waste is common. Bone dry, and common."

His skin paper thin, his voice weak, Paul Painter was clearly unwell. Not old, he was bald, his scalp pink, eyes bloodshot. He did not shake hands with either Matt or Riley, but made no further objections when they all gathered around the table for a breakfast of eggs, biscuits, sausage, and hot tea.

Afterwards, Paul Painter sent the boys outdoors to their morning chores, and retired to his bed. He slept beyond a partition fashioned from moth-eaten blankets hanging from the ceiling. Anne Marie touched a finger to her lips and led the way outside, closing the door after Matt and Riley. The day was bright, already heating up, and the elongated patch of shade under a cottonwood tree was welcome even at an early hour. The three of them stood in silence until Anne Marie lifted her arm and pointed to a murky pond fringed in green grass.

"Spring's over there," she said. "After milking, the boys will herd our cows to it." She turned and added: "You'll have to forgive my father. He lost his dream. Nothing is left in his heart but bitterness."

Matt and Riley listened as she recounted a family history that was at once unique and typical of westering emigrants—typical in the place of origin, unique in their predicament. Twice a widower, Paul Painter had uprooted his family from Ohio to seek prosperity and a new life in Colorado Territory. Keen to leave behind everything that reminded him of personal tragedies, he made "the bold leap to prosperity on the American Frontier" advertised in the brochures of land agents. The bold leap was an ill-conceived stumble into the unknown. The rigors of the westward journey, as well as rough conditions in the territory, had broken Painter's health.

"The wild frontier trapped us," Anne Marie said, "and now we're stranded."

The Conestoga wagon had barely made it this far, she went on, and upon arrival in Denver their oxen had been traded for milk cows. Her father was too weak to make the return journey to Ohio, and poverty ruled out any hope of traveling home by coach. "We were never poor until we came out West," she said.

Anne Marie and her half-brothers earned some cash from the sale of cream and butter, and the family survived by hand-watering the garden and by gathering eggs from laying hens. Eggs were bartered to a neighbor in exchange for summer sausage and to a miller for flour. Matt noted both the vegetable garden and chicken coop were fenced with chicken wire with the base covered by scraps of fabric—protection from predators ranging from hopping locusts to hungry rabbits, from clever coyotes to raiding red foxes, and the great birds of prey of the West, hawks and eagles swooping out of the sky.

Matt had guessed right when he had first met "Missy." She had spent precious dollars outfitting herself and Mister Smith in their search for gold. All of her gear, from hats to boots, shovels to gold pans, had been returned by Sheriff Ochs upon her release from custody. She had sold those items at a loss.

"You were right about Mister Smith," Anne Marie said to Matt. "Sheriff Ochs told me so."

Unreported by the *Rocky Mountain News,* the old-timer had been declared destitute after a judge had found him guilty of cattle rustling. He was set free when he had served out a five-day sentence. Invigorated by the regular meals in the jailhouse, he had made for the nearest saloon where he caged drinks until he was expansively drunk. Once again extolling his claim of a fortune in gold that lay just beyond his grasp, he bent every ear in range. All he needed was a grubstake.

Anne Marie held no grudge against Matt for thwarting her plans for prospecting. Instead she made a curious comment: "Fate brought you to me."

Matt figured her rambling history of the Painter family was her way of working up to the unanswered question of last night. However, rather than state what she had meant by *business,* she fell silent.

Matt observed Micah leading a cow out of the barn to the spring at the base of a nearby ridge. "A homestead claim with water is valuable."

"By law, we can't sell until we prove up," she said. "My father's too weak to do the work." She repeated: "We're trapped here, all five of us. . . ."

"Five?" Riley broke in. "I count four."

With a glance toward the farmhouse, Anne Marie said: "Father has renounced my older sister, Sarah. He won't allow me to speak of her in his presence."

"Where is she?" Riley asked.

"Valmont City. Have you been there?"

Their answer was unrehearsed, but both Matt and Riley shook their heads in unison.

From back issues of newspapers left behind in the Two-Bar bunkhouse, Matt knew Valmont City was located high in the Rockies, west of Denver. It was a mining camp that had swelled and proclaimed itself a "city" after the discovery of gold deposits. Prosperity came quickly in the form of brick-paved streets, the construction of the largest opera house west of the Mississippi, elegant hotels, and two-story residences of granite trimmed with snow-white Colorado marble. All that was lacking was a rail line to Denver.

Residents of "the richest square mile on earth" had petitioned the federal government to name Valmont City the capital of Colorado Territory. Mine owners had even traveled to Washington, D.C. to make their case and grease political wheels with numerous dinner parties for senators. But on the eve of statehood Denver won that designation, and despite protests from a higher altitude everyone knew the decision from higher powers in Washington was final.

"Sarah's working off a debt to Mister Eldon Collier," she said. "In her first letter, she said he was a wonderful man, an important man. He helped her borrow money, enough for our passage back home, but it was stolen from her . . . every penny of eight hundred dollars. Now Mister Collier won't allow Sarah to leave Valmont City, not until the debt is paid in full."

"Collier," Riley repeated.

"You know him?" Matt asked.

"He's a wealthy man," Riley said. "So they say."

Anne Marie reached into her pocket and brought out a tattered letter. "Sarah wrote about mineral claims and buildings owned by Mister Collier . . . Valmont City Mining Supply, Collier Mercantile, half a dozen saloons and dance halls, and . . . a house."

Riley let out a harsh laugh. "Not a home."

"House?" Matt asked.

"Sarah wrote in this letter," Anne Marie explained, "no sign is on the door, but all the men know about Maude Riley's Sporting House. The letter was addressed to me, but Father read it . . . and that's how he found out. . . ."

When Matt and Riley exchanged a glance, she added quickly: "Sarah is imprisoned just as surely as if caged in a jail cell. I have to see her. She needs help, but I've heard it's dangerous to travel to Valmont City alone." She paused. "I don't have a saddle mount. Or money for coach fare."

"What good will it do to see her?" Riley demanded.

She whispered: "It's a family matter."

When she did not elaborate, Riley glowered.

Matt said: "It's your father, isn't it?"

Anne Marie ducked her head to hide her tears.

Matt remembered the day he drove his flu-stricken parents in a farm wagon from their homestead to the doctor in town. It was a horrible journey to a bad end.

Anne Marie's voice choked when she said: "It's hard to ask for help, but . . . if you help me, I'll try to help you. We can make a fair trade."

"Trade?" Riley asked. "What kind of trade?"

She lifted her head. "You wanted to know who was checked into Room Four-Oh-Four in the Inter-Ocean Hotel the day Miss Benning was murdered. My friend, Martha Hayes, works there as a maid. She can have the bellman look it up in the hotel register. If you want me to ask her."

"In return for an escort to Valmont City," Matt said.

She nodded. "Yes."

Jaw clenched, Riley said: "Count me out."

Matt glanced at him, and turned to Anne Marie. "We're in business."

Chapter Five

Riley watched Anne Marie head for the cabin, and wheeled to face his twin. "I know what you're thinking, brother. I know exactly what you're thinking."

"How long have you been reading minds?"

"This is no parlor game," he said. "It's written all over your face."

"It is, huh?"

Riley nodded. "Plain as day."

"Read it out loud then," Matt said, "so I'll know what I'm thinking, too."

Riley ignored the sarcasm. "You're riding to Valmont City with that girl because of a madam going by the name of Riley. You figure I'll tag along like I did last night. That's about the size of this deal, isn't it?"

"You wanted to get out of Denver," Matt said.

"Not on some wild-goose chase," he replied.

"How do you know it is?" Matt asked.

"Riley is dirt common. Probably a dozen folks right here in Denver wear that Irish name. You have to admit that."

"I admit it," Matt agreed.

"Just what the hell do you aim to gain?" Riley demanded.

"You're the one who said it a while back," Matt answered. "Straight out."

"I say a lot of things," he said. "Habit I picked up from Hoyt. What are you recollecting this time?"

"You figure we were adopted separately," Matt replied, "and our mother probably had a strong reason for giving up her twin babies. Maybe she didn't survive childbirth. Maybe

76

she did." He paused. "Maybe she was a lady of the evening with no place in her life for children."

"Lady of the evening?" Riley repeated scornfully. "Where do you get that kind of talk? Day or night, a whore's a whore. Whores usually owe debts to the madam of the house," he went on, "for liquor, opium, clothing, jewelry, loans, you name it. Sometimes a madam loans money, and steals it back. It's all a way of keeping her ponies in halter."

Matt gazed at him, wondering how he knew that for a fact, and mystified by the tone of anger in his twin's voice.

"What's the matter?" Riley demanded.

"I'm trying to figure out what lit your fuse," Matt replied. "Is this getting too rough for you?"

"What're you talking about?"

"The notion of a woman in a whorehouse giving birth to us," he said. "Is that too rough for you?"

Face flushed, Riley stepped toward him. "Brother, I don't know what it is about you, but you have a damnable way of raising a man's anger. I ought to knock you flat on your ass."

"You mean," Matt said, "you ought to try."

In sudden fury Riley clenched his fist and drew his arm back. He lashed out with a roundhouse punch.

Matt ducked it. He came up with an uppercut to the chin. The swift, short blow snapped Riley's head back. Eyes rolling, his knees buckled. He went down.

Matt stood over him. "Next time you throw your Sunday punch, don't telegraph it from last Thursday."

"One of these days," he said, "I'll take you apart."

Matt threw a taunt at him: "Today or tomorrow?"

"Tomorrow I'm leaving," he said. He got to his feet and brushed dirt from his clothes. "I held up my end of the deal by riding to Denver with you. Now you're off on a wild-goose chase. Not me. You're on your own."

"You said you wanted to clear your name."

"Your loco idea," he reminded him. "I told you I'm leaving. Two close calls are enough."

"Close calls," Matt repeated.

Riley told him about the near-miss with Tug Larkin.

"So you aim to run before dawn?" Matt asked.

Riley cast a severe look at him. "I don't need your horse, if that's what you're getting at. After a few hands of poker, I'll be a passenger in the next coach rolling out of Denver. North, south, east, or west, I don't care where it's headed as long as it takes me out of here."

Matt said: "Wait an hour."

"For what? To give Tug Larkin a good look?"

"So Anne Marie can find out who was registered in that room in the Inter-Ocean."

"Another wild-goose chase," Riley said.

"Could be," Matt said. "But you'll never know if you don't wait long enough to find out."

Riley hesitated.

"Want to place a bet on it, gambling man?"

"Hate to take your money," Riley replied. "I know how it pains you to part with pennies."

"One silver dollar says we're not chasing a wild goose."

"Brother," Riley said, "I don't know where we were born, or even when, but you're a born cheapskate." He paused. "What the hell. One hour. No more."

The three of them rode to Denver, arriving an hour before Anne Marie's shift in the Rocky Mountain House. The twins watched her cross the street and enter the big hotel by a side entrance.

They waited in the alley behind the café. Half an hour dragged into an hour. Riley paced, jaw clenched. Halting abruptly, he turned to Matt. "What if she brings the law down on us?"

Matt shrugged. "If that was her plan, she'd have done it before now."

Riley scowled, but did not leave.

Minutes later Anne Marie joined them in the alley, alone.

Riley listened to her account. "Wild goose," he muttered, and strode away without so much as a parting handshake, much less collecting his one-dollar bet.

In addition to asking the bellman to look up the Room 404 guest's name on the day Miss Augusta Benning was murdered, Anne Marie and her friend Martha Hayes spoke to maids on duty. As might be expected, a great deal of discussion among the staff was devoted to the shocking event, and even seven weeks later memories of it were vivid.

That day Room 404 had been occupied by Ruth Burlingame, a schoolteacher who had been burned in a kerosene stove fire. She was in bed, recovering, when she and a nurse heard the roar of a shotgun blast from the room below. Moving cautiously to the window, the two women were too frightened to open it and peer out. They saw no one until two figures in the alley came into their line of view. One marched the other away at gunpoint. In those moments immediately after the murder, no one had climbed the fire ladder past their window. One of the maids had posed that very question, and Ruth Burlingame was certain of her answer. So was the nurse.

"Wild goose," Matt said, watching his twin walk away in long strides.

Riley shuffled clumsily. He dealt like a thick-fingered yokel who rarely touched the pasteboards. He fanned his cards. Luck of the draw brought him a strong hand, pairs of sevens and jacks, but the pot was light. He folded. In previous hands he had used clumsiness as a cover when he creased the corners of all four aces and nine face cards with his thumbnail. Forty-three dollars up, now was the time to lay back.

A new horsehide valise at his feet held store-bought clothes as well as the Greener. In a gunsmith shop, he had purchased ammunition and a Derringer, a two-shot .22 with pearl handles. Keeping the little gun in reach now in his left coat pocket, he sized up the other players, four men seated at a round table covered by dirty green felt. One stocky gent smoked a two-cent cigar, and the scowling man next to him drew on a blackened corncob pipe. Both exhaled clouds of smoke while mulling the hands they had been dealt.

Time dragged, and Riley's mood turned as foul as the smoke that hung like a pall in this low-ceilinged room. The game was far too slow, giving him far too much time to reflect on recent events. He found himself thinking about Anne Marie. The weight of the world bore down on her. He understood that more than he had let on. Despite his comments, he felt a measure of sympathy. She was too young to be thrust into such circumstances, yet she had no choice but to shoulder them. You play the cards you're dealt, Hoyt often said, unless you're holding the deck.

While troubled by his decision to leave the territory, Riley felt justified. What else could he do? If he crossed trails with either Tug Larkin or Hiram Ochs in full daylight, he was a dead man.

The players seemed to pray over their cards while weighing two choices—add to the pot, or cut their losses and take a chance on fresh cards. Quiet here, this was not a raucous gambling hall alive with the click of chips. The back room of the Long's Peak Saloon was well beyond the heart of Denver's saloon and gaming district. No poker chips, cash only.

Riley was here because he figured this place would not draw the attention of the law. After leaving Matt and Anne Marie in that alley, he had stepped into a barbershop for a shave and a bath. Glad to be rid of that itching beard, he kept the full mustache. He liked the way it looked on his twin even though he knew a shave increased his risk of being recognized. The gambling halls in town were patrolled, so he came here, his instinct for survival overriding a desire for quick cash.

Riley's goal was modest. He intended quietly to win about a hundred dollars. With cash for coach fare out of Denver and beyond, he would have enough left over for a fresh start in a new place.

Exactly what he would do for employment in a town beyond Colorado Territory, he did not know. Gambling was the trade he knew. He knew it all too well. Perhaps the adage was true—familiarity breeds contempt—for he found neither thrills nor satisfaction in games of chance. Over many years he had watched Hoyt practice his profession with polish and a flare, a proud knight of the round tables engaged in go-for-broke contests as he bluffed and bullied adversaries. More than that, as Riley came to understand, Hoyt Wilcox had relished their defeat at his hands.

Riley saw the cheating and fakery of it all. From a young age he had understood the workings and had known the odds of games of chance from faro to craps, from draw poker to blackjack, and even sucker games like the wheel of fortune. Ever since he had been on his own, he had fallen back on gambling as an easy way to make money—never great sums, but enough to meet expenses.

Now he idly considered heading east to the Mississippi for a tour of riverboats. The professional gamblers on board who had known Hoyt would not recognize "Pistol" as a grown man. He could pose as a bumpkin from Colorado, and clean their damned clocks, as Hoyt used to say, before any of the dandies in their string ties, brocade vests, and long-tailed coats caught on. With a stake, he could buy a business, or seek other gainful employment, some line of work that required minimal deceit and only an occasional look over the shoulder.

Worthy adversaries? In this back room Riley faced amateurs. The man with the scowl on his face, whether he won or lost, never uttered more than a word or two, as if he could prevail by force of will. The other two players were young store clerks, their jackets tossed aside. They wore white shirts with open collars and sleeve garters, a pair of friends just drunk enough on beer and shots in the saloon to talk themselves into winning a fortune at the poker table here. Each dollar won cost them four, and they winced at one another every time they lost or tossed a weak hand down on the table. Yet they stayed the course, convinced stubbornness would be rewarded.

Riley knew the type. The greater the loss, the more determined they were to stick it out, believing their luck would turn, and they would win back their money and more—the timeless allure of the games. Riley could almost hear Hoyt's voice: "Gambling is for suckers, and greedy suckers deserve to be plucked clean." Hoyt had revealed tricks of the trade to Riley as a tradesman to an apprentice. Riley learned one overriding principle from his mentor: Never trust in luck. Hoyt had been a practical businessman. He had left little to chance.

Now one of the clerks folded. Riley looked on while the stocky man across the table called. The other young man tentatively showed a pair of fours. He swore when his stout opponent tossed three deuces to the felt and grinned as he raked in eight dollars.

Ante-up, wager, draw, fold. The next few hands went that way with none of the players willing to run up the pot. Riley's pile of coins and wadded bills dwindled, along with his determination to hang on. Staying in this smoke-filled room had deteriorated from a test of patience to an exercise in futility.

He was ready to risk a confrontation with lawmen in a bona-fide gambling hall, when he drew four eights. He casually raised the bet once, twice, three times, and still the stocky gent did not fold. Interest growing, Riley knew where the aces were, as well as five face cards. The other players sat this one out—one scowling while the two youngsters watched in silent fascination.

Riley dug into his wallet to keep up the pace in a two-man contest. When he replaced the billfold in his left coat pocket, he palmed the Derringer and put it on his leg under the table. The pot swelled, exceeding eighty dollars when Riley called. Sweating now, the big man placed five cards on the felt, face up.

"Three gentlemen, two ladies," he said with an air of confidence. His confidence in kings and queens evaporated and color drained from his face, when Riley showed his cards.

The stout man cleared his throat as though strangling. "A feller . . . a feller can play a long while . . . without seeing four of a kind." He cleared his throat again. "A long while."

Riley fixed him with a stare learned from Hoyt Wilcox. Scooping up the money, he shoved coins and bills into his pocket. He slid his left hand under the table.

Silence followed. The others watched. At last Riley tossed in his ante and nodded to the clerk on his right. The young man picked up the deck, hands shaking as he shuffled and dealt. As a matter of courtesy, Riley played that hand out. He lost two dollars, and shoved his chair back, palming the Derringer again.

"You ain't gonna give us no chance to win that money back?" the stout man asked. He was still pale, mouth sagging open as if the enormity of his loss had hit him like a punch to the gut.

"Sir, how long would you have me stay?" Riley asked, quoting a line from Hoyt Wilcox. A professional gambler often faced irate losers, and Riley well remembered Hoyt's techniques in handling them.

"You cheated us, mister. How, I dunno. But somehow you cheated us."

"Funny thing is," Riley replied cheerfully, "I won that pot fair and square. Damnedest thing, the way those cards fell." He paused. "But, mister, you go ahead and believe whatever in the hell you want to believe."

Puffy hand stabbing to his waistband, the stout man froze when Riley leaned across the table and shoved the two-shot Derringer into his face. The weapon seemed to come out of nowhere.

"Mister, I believe we can agree on one thing," Riley said, quoting Hoyt again. "Five cards aren't worth dying for. Not in some hot little room stunk up by smoke from the fires of hell. We agree on that, don't we?"

The stout man nodded once, face white as flour now.

"But there you sit," Riley went on, "one breath away from the great beyond."

The man swallowed.

"Take out your piece," Riley said. "Slow. Set it on the table, butt first."

The gun was short-barreled, a .32 revolver. Riley pocketed his Derringer and picked it up. Pressing the release, the cylinder swung out. He ejected all six rounds, the brass-jacketed bullets rolling across the table. With the other players watching in a silence born of fear, Riley bent down and picked up his valise. Backing away, his gaze swept past them.

"Too bad every show has to end, gents," he said with a grin, "because you've been a great audience." Holding up the empty revolver like a dead rat, he added to the stout man: "You'll find your popgun outside."

Riley turned and left the room. He hurried through the saloon, and left the batwing doors swinging behind him. In the harsh sun-glare of mid-afternoon Riley tossed the gun into the middle of the rutted street. Half a dozen passers-by stopped and stared, trying to make sense of what they saw. One was staggering drunk, a gap-toothed old-timer Riley recognized from the jailhouse. Now the graybeard caught his balance, staring at Riley as he was obviously trying to place where they had met.

Can't seem to get away from folks who have laid eyes on me in this hayseed town, Riley thought. He walked two blocks and turned on Fourteenth Street, heading in long strides for the telegraph office and stage stop. He should have felt good about his good fortune in that smoke-filled room, but, after another close call, all he could think about was leaving. No doubt that old drunk would go after Ochs's reward if he ever cleared his boozy brain long enough to know when and where they had seen one another.

Riley's thoughts returned to his twin brother. He felt a twinge of regret. Matt was something of a bumpkin, a loner who rode the range. His tracking skills and survival instincts were ill-suited for town life. As long as he stayed on Two-Bar Range, Riley figured, he would be all right.

Not my worry, Riley thought as another name edged into his memory—Nell. Nell Bloom.

Even though she was gone, her loving smile and resonant voice were never far from his thoughts. Tangled memories of lost love surged into his mind, deep currents of raw emotion he had not confided to his twin, or to anyone else. Now with anger and anguish stirred anew, he was glad to be away from probing questions.

He had told Matt the truth—as far as it went. The claim of theft in that letter from Anne Marie's sister might have been true. Or it could have been an excuse she used to justify staying in Valmont City. Most whores were drunks, and every drunk was a liar. And he had told the truth when he said he had never met Maude Riley. He could not say the same for Eldon Collier.

It was Hoyt who had known the man. Collier was big, slow as a turtle. He suffered from a facial tic. The twitch tugged at his upper cheek and lower eyelid, a holdover from the war, folks said. In a murderous battleground known as The Wilderness, Major Eldon Collier had plunged his saber deep into the right eye of a charging Reb. The moment he slew a teen-aged boy wearing a butternut uniform was when that twitch came upon him.

Hoyt Wilcox had posed as a banker from Kansas. Claiming he had sold his share of the business at great profit, he had slipped into Collier's circle of rich friends. In one round-the-clock marathon poker game, he took them to the cleaners, every blessed one of them. Riley had assisted the wheezing gambler. Physically weakened, Hoyt's eagerness for this high-stakes game sharpened his wit as never before, as if a lifetime of practicing the gambler's art had reached its peak. He had played his role to the hilt—an ill and slightly befuddled banker coughing into a silk handkerchief. The white cloth facilitated his sleight-of-hand techniques.

Riley remembered the game not only for the sight of a rich man tormented by that tic or the great sums of cash on the table, but the setting—Collier's furnished railroad car on a siding near Cheyenne, Wyoming. Paneled in cherry wood, the interior was furnished with leather-covered chairs and soft fabric couches custom-made for the space. A chef and servants were housed in a second car, along with a fully stocked wine rack, pantry, and kitchen. Servers came and went as they answered whispered requests from the man who turned and tilted his head to hide the constant twitch in his face.

That long day into night was memorable for a mighty scare. An hour after the last hand had been dealt, Riley waited with Hoyt in the stone Union Pacific dépôt for a passenger coach. The gambler was recognized by a patrolling deputy. As the lawman sprinted to Collier's private car to confirm his suspicion of a rigged, high-stakes poker game, Riley helped Hoyt down the tracks. The day was just dawning when he hefted him into the empty boxcar of a departing freight train, and scrambled in after him, cutting their escape close.

Later they heard Collier had vowed to kill "the lying, thieving card sharp, Hoyt Wilcox," and had put a price on his head. As it turned out, Hoyt had only weeks to live, not enough time to be run to ground by bounty hunters, or enjoy the rewards of his coup, either.

But that was . . . what . . . almost two years ago? Riley silently debated the spirit within. What difference did it make now? He knew one thing. If asked, Matt would insist he could take care of himself. *Well, he'll have to,* Riley thought as he strode by posted Wanted flyers bearing his description. He stepped into the Missouri & Platte River Overland stage station, and headed for the barred ticket window. *He'll have to.*

Matt stood in the sun-drenched doorway, framed by cottonwood logs. Before him was a tableau of a father protesting his daughter's decision to leave home and hearth, an argument lost even before it had begun. The grim fact was unspoken, yet obvious even to an outsider: Anne Marie had grown stronger as her father had weakened. Of age now or not, she made her own choices in life, and her father was neither strong enough nor persuasive enough to sway her.

Matt watched Anne Marie listen patiently to her father's objections, her manner much like a mother attending to her child, not listening so much as waiting for him to finish. Paul Painter begged her to stay, and then cursed her sister for shaming the family.

"Don't bring Sarah here! Hear me?" Painter breathed raggedly, eyes closing. When his teary eyes opened again, he fired one last broadside to the heavens: "And don't take money from her! Not a cent! It's the devil's pay!"

Anne Marie tried to calm her father. When he again protested that she could not leave, not today, she assured him the boys would tend the chores and everything else in her absence. Her job at the café was being held for her, and their lives would return to normal when she came back. She avoided using the word home, Matt noticed, when referring to this small farm. Ohio was home.

She leaned down and tenderly kissed her father on the cheek. Picking up her threadbare carpetbag then, she turned and said she was ready. Matt lifted a hand to Painter, hoping to signal him that his daughter would be safe during their journey to the high country. The man did not acknowledge the gesture. Seated in his wicker armchair, he was a gaunt, hollow-cheeked figure covered by a blanket, shivering on a hot summer day. Matt left without knowing if his parting wave was a comfort, or even noticed.

From prairie lowlands to lightly forested foothills, the

freight road twisted through steep-walled cañons. Matt led the way through this rugged maze with Anne Marie astride the gray gelding. He thought of Riley. Short of gunning him down in that alley behind the Rocky Mountain House, he'd had no way of stopping him. Riley had been right, after all, when he had boasted Matt would not shoot him, not his own flesh and blood.

No, he could not shoot Riley. Now he faced a weird dilemma, unlike any he had encountered. First, he had become a fugitive himself by setting Riley free. Second, he could be mistaken for a convicted murderer and shot by any citizen determined to collect the reward posted by Sheriff Ochs.

Twin or not, Matt had saved a man from the gallows, a man he now believed was innocent of murder. Yet he found little pleasure in the triumph of justice over hysteria. Proof was missing. Who would believe him—particularly in view of the fact that since Riley's earliest childhood years he had been under the influence of a man who had lived by concocting lies.

Matt looked back. Anne Marie wore a divided skirt, much patched and repaired, a cotton duck jacket, and her face was shaded by a wide-brimmed straw hat. Carpetbag and bedding tied behind the saddle, she grimaced in her constant search for a comfortable riding position.

The mountain road to Valmont City was nearly as crowded with traffic as a Denver street. Matt and Anne Marie encountered a variety of bull trains and freight outfits, passenger coaches, and horsebackers. Cowhands drove cattle to slaughter in Valmont City. Sore-footed from sharp rocks, bawling cows congested the road and slowed passage. Prospectors led burros with bulging panniers lashed to the backs of the nimble animals. Everyone knew prices were cheaper by one-third in Denver, and mining men loaded up—and overloaded—their beasts of burden for the trek to the high country, a gain in elevation from 5,000 to 10,000 feet above the sea.

Teamsters bunched for protection against robbers. For them, there was a cycle to it all. Loaded wagons headed west with harnessed or yoked animals straining upslope through the countless cañons. They hauled goods from the Denver railhead to loading docks in Valmont City or on to mining camps such as Damndifiknow and Gawdawful. On the return trip empty rigs rattled through the cañons as fast as conditions allowed. The sooner those cursing, whip-cracking men reached Denver, the sooner they would collect pay—and load wagon boxes with goods for the return trip behind a fresh team.

The fastest and by far the most elegant of all the vehicles Matt and Anne Marie encountered was a custom-built Concord. The big coach had been converted to a vehicle for private use, painted in black lacquer with pale yellow trim and wheel spokes, and pulled by six black horses. Two armed men followed on horseback.

Matt had never seen anything like it. The glossy black coach bore no lettering or outward indication of ownership. Windows were tightly battened in sail canvas. The coach rounded hairpin turns with warning blasts of a bugle, a brass horn clenched in the hand of a red-haired man, riding shotgun beside the driver. The great, rocking coach churned dust and tossed up stones in its passing.

In quieter moments Matt heard breezes whispering through pine boughs, soft sounds against a background of a creek crashing against granite boulders. Drop by drop that numbing cold water flowed from glaciers and snow banks high in the mountains, tumbling downslope to the plains. Pooling brooks not only refreshed man and beast and provided native trout for suppers, but lulled tired travelers to sleep under starry skies.

Evenings, Matt and Anne Marie camped at water's edge. Matt kept both his Colt and Winchester in reach day and night. Vivid accounts of attacks by highwaymen on this route were legion. Travelers were known to carry cash, and the robbers, preying on them, were said to be ruthless, lusting for gold and as thirsty for blood as pirates plying the high seas.

Abandoned campsites were everywhere. These gulches had been picked, poked, and panned in the decade and a half since the rush of 1859. Placer gold had been discovered in creekbeds, driving men to higher altitudes until at last one lone prospector, Mike O'Donnell, stumbled upon an outcropping of gold-bearing quartz.

According to the folklore of the region, it was O'Donnell's runaway burro that did the stumbling. Named Boy, the burro kicked over a rock, exposing a vein of gold to the pursuing prospector. A mundane event was momentous. Not only was that tundra-like mountaintop a geographic watershed, a physical divide between the Atlantic and Pacific Oceans, but the burro's hoof, dislodging a piece of nondescript country rock the size of a dinner plate, marked a watershed in American history.

Word of the discovery rippled through Colorado Territory and spread across the continent with the impact of a boulder dropped into still water. In the following year more outcroppings were discovered. For each claim, an official-looking parchment prospectus promised mineral deposits to stagger the imagination. Ore deposits were called "gold fields" to imply vastness and ease of recovery as a way to tantalize investors from here and across the Atlantic—England, France, Germany. Hard-rock miners knew better. Every ounce of gold hammered from the earth was hard-earned, and most diggings led only to more country rock. Yet aristocratic families of old Europe sent representatives to sink their money into deep shafts and long tunnels, gold coins financing a frantic search for gold ore.

The fate of that first prospector to strike gold was entered into the lore of Colorado mining, too. Mike O'Donnell had staked a claim and sunk his prospect hole. He mined gold near the surface of his Lucky Boy Mine, ore that he extracted himself and lugged to a Denver crushing mill on the back of the errant burro.

Even though assay reports were supposed to be confidential, rumors sent buyers to Mike O'Donnell. At first turning them all away, he agonized over an offer of $3,000 for his claim. Finally rejecting it, he was immediately regretful, fearing he had lost his only opportunity to attain a measure of wealth, the driving force behind all prospectors. When an English investor mad with gold fever made another offer, O'Donnell snapped it up. He sold his Lucky Boy Mine for $10,000, more money than he had ever dreamed of possessing. Wearing a new suit, shoes, and hat, he returned home by coach and by railcar to Worcester, Massachusetts to live out his days in comfort. Boy went with him, a mouse-gray, long-eared critter with big brown eyes, traveling in its own cattle car. Upon reaching the destination, the burro promptly ran off, never to be seen again, at least not by Mike O'Donnell.

In the first full year of operation the Lucky Boy produced $4,000,000 in gold. When the vein petered out, that hole in the ground was sold again, this time to Blue Knight, Ltd, a group of British investors said to be fronting for the Royal family.

Whoever was behind the name had money; $2,000,000— cash—bought the Lucky Boy Mine, a number so large as to strike awed disbelief into the minds of prospectors who heard it. Renewed hand drilling and giant powder charges shattered granite and quartz, exposing webs of gold locked in stone. In the first three months after the purchase, concentrate production of gold ore from the Lucky Boy reached $947,000. If this figure held up for the year, the Blue Knight's expenditure was not so large, after all.

Unfortunately these and other statistics from the burgeoning Valmont district in Colorado Territory were published in both the *New York Times* and *Boston Globe*, the latter newspaper faithfully read every evening by Mike O'Donnell.

Chapter Six

Matt's estimation of Anne Marie Painter changed a great deal in a short time. She was small in physique, but strong and unafraid. Obviously saddle sore, she grimaced but did not complain. Sudden rainstorms slinging hailstones brought no protest from her. Neither did the glaring sun high in clear blue skies. She worked diligently to make the tasks of the day go smoothly, from meal preparations and camp clean-up to tending the horses and gear.

Early morning found Anne Marie kneeling by the rushing creek. In stolen glances, Matt saw her hold a small, oval mirror, slanting it left and right, up and down, to examine her face by the light of the rising sun. She washed, and then vigorously combed her light brown hair before pinning it up.

Hat on, she stood and walked gingerly to Matt as he held the horses, saddled and ready to ride. Such was their routine, the two of them exchanging a smile every time the scene played itself out. He no longer saw Anne Marie Painter as a tomboy or a cattle thief, but a young woman intent on keeping her family together.

Valmont City was the highest town in the United States, platted on a flatland 10,120 feet above sea level. Sturdy buildings of brick and stone made a business district, and fine residences lined brick-paved streets radiating out from the town center. Beyond clean streets stood a hodge-podge of shacks and log cabins on random lanes, the tracks often muddied by the rains of summer afternoons. In the distance, head-frames and heaping piles of rust-colored tailings marked the mine sites. The most prominent was Lucky Boy, but other well-known mines were in the region— Thunderation, Blue Knight, Good Buy, Sunrise, American Heritage.

Matt rode through town with Anne Marie at his side, their shadows lengthened by the light of a red ball of fire sinking into the western horizon. The horses wheezed. Breath was short at this altitude, and the air quickly chilled at sundown. Even in mid-summer, shaded exposures still held pockets of snow. As the old joke went:

"How long does winter last in Valmont City?" asked the newcomer. "I don't know," replied the miner. "I've only been here for three years."

Matt looked left and right. Shops, hotels, liveries, and other buildings were starkly cast in the light of evening. The largest was an opera house with playbills posted on either side of double front doors.

Horses boarded, Matt and Anne Marie checked into separate rooms in a small roadhouse on the edge of Valmont City. They paid ten cents extra for hot baths in a tub in the back room. Donning clean clothes, they ate supper in the Cornwall Café on Front Street. Servings were plentiful, but priced exorbitantly at $2.40 a plate, nearly a day's wage. Mounted paintings pictured scenes from Cornwall, homeland to the hard-rock miners who had emigrated from the English peninsula. Copper and tin mines in that region of England dated from antiquity, well known to traders of ancient Greece. Cornish miners new to America brought their hammers, hand drills, and their skills. True to their tradition, they were proficient hard-rock miners, much in demand. Frequently asked if they knew of anyone else in Cornwall who could

come to work here in the mines, their standard answer was—
"Well, I have a cousin named Jack."—and thus became
known by the nickname "Cousin Jacks."

When Anne Marie discretely asked a waitress for directions to Maude Riley's, the aproned woman assumed she had
come to Valmont City seeking employment in a house of ill
repute. Taking her aside, the woman warned of contracting
running sores and lesions that oozed yellowish pus, not to
mention diseases of the brain, promising madness—at best a
life of enduring violence at the hands of filthy, drunken men.
The cautionary words were whispered by an older woman intent on dissuading a young one from a foolish decision.

"It is hell on earth to hate yourself," she whispered.
"You'll have to find someone else to send you there."

In the morning they found the place. Directions had come
from a liveryman. The saloon district stretched along a
murky creek on the south side of the business district, the
red-light establishments farther away still. On foot Matt and
Anne Marie came upon facing rows of shacks and cribs beyond a treeless rise, all of them just far enough away from
town to be out of sight and out of the minds of proper folks.

Even from a distance Maude Riley's was clearly the best of
the lot. A simple two-story clapboard with flowerboxes at the
windows, the house was painted white with a white-washed
picket fence and knee-high gate. It stood beyond a row of
squat log structures with canvas roofs, some connected by a
network of plank walks, others with nothing but a beaten path
to the door. Quiet now as Matt and Anne Marie walked past
the establishments, this morning hour was too late for yesterday's revelers and too early for today's.

Matt opened the gate for Anne Marie. They followed the
walk, mounted three steps, and crossed the porch. The windows were heavily curtained. An oil lamp with a red chimney

beside the door was unlit.

Matt watched Anne Marie hesitate before stepping forward. She reached out and twisted the brass handle in the door. A bell chimed on the other side. With a glance at Matt, she held her ground, her instincts clearly urging her to flee. She took a deep breath and rang the bell again. No one answered. Matt stepped closer and pounded on the door with his fist.

The door opened far enough to reveal a gray-haired woman in an ankle-length gown of purple velvet. She was thin, her doughy cheeks wrinkled. The dark fabric, draping from bony shoulders, made her look like a cadaver come to life.

"Closed," she said, her gaze shifting from Anne Marie to Matt. "We're closed until six this evening."

"Are you Maude Riley?" Anne Marie asked.

She turned to her. "Do I know you, honey?"

Anne Marie introduced herself.

"Either you aim to work in my establishment, Miss Painter," she said, "or you're hunting someone."

"I'm looking for my sister . . . Sarah."

Maude Riley gave her a self-satisfied look. "Never heard of her."

"But she told me she works here," Anne Marie said. "I came from Denver to visit her."

"Can't help you, honey," Maude Riley said. With a brief, sympathetic smile, she stepped back a pace. "You might as well run along back to Denver. This is no place for you." She closed the door.

Matt heard a deadbolt shoved into place. "You figure your sister's in there?"

She nodded.

Matt thought about that. "She could be going by a different name. Maybe she doesn't want to be found."

"That's why I didn't write. She doesn't know I'm here."

Matt asked: "Still want to talk to Maude Riley?"

"Yes," she said. "But she won't come to the door."

"Reckon she will," Matt said. He knocked hard enough to rattle windowpanes. Then he backed away and kicked the door, once, twice, and again, harder. Presently the lock was released from inside. The door swung open. An angry Maude Riley appeared there.

"Meet Philip," she said, and stepped aside for a burly bouncer. Bald as a cue ball, Philip was thick-necked, dressed in boots and a long nightshirt with pink piping at the seams and lace trim at his hairy throat.

"You was axed polite to leave," Philip said.

Matt gave him the once-over. "You make some sight."

"You was axed polite," Philip repeated. "Now, I'm telling you. Move along."

Matt grinned. "Is that some lady's gown you're wearing? I've never seen a grown man in a dress before."

Anne Marie darted away as the big man bulled through the doorway, fists knotted, right arm cocked back.

Matt ducked a clumsy punch, spun away from his charge, and hit him squarely on the temple as he went by. Staggered, the bouncer drew up on the edge of the porch. He shook his head like a dazed bull, and turned in time to be kicked in the crotch. Mouth opening in agony, the big man doubled over, his nose meeting Matt's knee in an upward thrust. He went down heavily, legs drawn up as he lay on the porch, gasping.

From the doorway, Maude Riley stared at the downed man in amazement. She lifted her gaze to Matt. "If you've hurt Philip," she said, "you'll pay. There's men in this town who'll hunt you down for what you just done to him."

"Ma'am," he said with another look at him, "if that's some

lady's dress he's wearing, there's men in this town who'll hunt me down to buy me a drink for what I done to him."

"We keep things peaceable around here," Maude Riley said. "Now, I want you to leave. Both of you."

"I'm peaceable," Matt insisted. "I had a notion. If Anne Marie gives you a description of her sister, you'd know if she's here."

"The only notion I've got," Maude Riley said, "is to see you walk away."

Matt barely heard as he stared at her. The possibility, remote as it was, that he had been born of this woman filled his mind.

"Did you ever give birth to twins?" he asked.

The question clearly caught her off guard, and her doughy face stiffened like putty. "I'm only going to say this one more time. Leave. Both of you."

"I'll leave," Matt said, "when I'm ready."

In a voice as low as a cat's growl, she cursed him.

"Please," Anne Marie said as she stepped between them, "please. We don't want trouble. All I want is a chance to talk to my sister."

Maude Riley gazed at her, lips pursed. For several moments it seemed she would say nothing. On the porch floor, Philip groaned. Blood dripped from a nostril. At last the madam spoke. "Honey, girls appear at my door every week," she said. "They've all heard about my establishment, and they know there's only one sure-fire way to earn a fortune in mining country. And gents know I run a high-class place. Any man craving Charlotte-the-Harlot or Sweaty Betty won't find them here."

Maude Riley cast a critical look at Matt, and turned to Anne Marie. "I do recall a certain young woman at my door a while back. She was your size, hair long and straight, same wheat color as yours. . . ."

"Where is she now?" Anne Marie blurted.

"I'm fixing to tell you." The older woman drew a deep breath, as though trying to fill out the heavy garment clinging to her bony shoulders. "Now, I don't know if this young woman is your sister or not. No promises. But I can tell you she's not in my house. . . ."

"Where is she?" Anne Marie interrupted.

"I said I'm fixing to tell you, didn't I?" She glared. "Eldon Collier. I sent her to him."

"Where is this gent, Mister Collier?" Matt asked.

"Damn it, I'll tell you, if you give me half a chance." The madam gestured toward town. "You'll see his house on the third cross street from here, off Front. Biggest house in town. Red brick. Hard to miss. Tell his man I sent you."

"His man?" Anne Marie asked.

"You will be met at the door by a manservant. He's a tall red-haired dude. Name's Jimmy."

Matt studied her. He wondered if she was telling the truth about Sarah Painter. Something in her manner raised a suspicion in his mind. But whether she was truthful or not, she was hard-headed. Deciding to let it go for now, he turned and followed Anne Marie. They stepped around Philip. The man sat up, eyes slowly blinking. Blood trickled down his chin.

"Cowboy."

Matt realized Maude Riley was speaking to him. He halted at the top step of the porch, and turned.

"Cowboy, I don't know what you meant," she said, "when you asked me about bearing twins. But I warn you. Don't start baby-killer rumors about me. You do, and I'll come after you. I mean it."

In town, Matt found Maude Riley had been right—the

Collier mansion stood out. Occupying a large lot, the structure stood two-stories high with a brass-trimmed cupola stretching skyward. The carriage house was bigger than most residences. Matt noted black horses in the corral, ten draft animals tended by three armed men. One was roped and thrown, being broken to saddle. He paused on the stone walk and cast another look at the carriage house. The sliding door stood open. He saw the black Concord coach inside.

Riley hated Concords. The fore-to-aft rocking motion of the high-wheeled Missouri & Platte River Overland stagecoach sloshed bile in his gut. He worried he would vomit directly into the lap of the stoic passenger facing him, a bearded drummer whose knees banged against his own.

As the miles slowly rolled by, Riley felt bilious, green as gall, and ready to welcome the Grim Reaper, anything to escape this misery. Worse, after two hours of torture, his journey to North Platte, Nebraska was cut short when the wheel horse pulled up lame.

The driver halted the coach. Spouting curses, he swung down and unhooked harness straps and loosened the lines. Pulling off the collar, he set the animal free. Despite vigorous complaints from six passengers, he turned the coach in a wide semicircle through clumps of sagebrush and pear cactus. He regained the road and headed back to Denver with the limping horse following.

Eyes closed while trying to keep his breakfast down, Riley recalled Hoyt's words: *An omen is nothing more than the sign a man sees when it is too late to duck the consequences.* Riley took the lame horse to be an omen. That, along with the Wanted dodgers posted in Denver.

Back in town, he cashed in his ticket and bought another. Two hours later he boarded an open coach, a surrey mounted on leaf springs with plenty of leg room in the cabin. The four-passenger vehicle was bound for Valmont City.

Matt had never set foot in a house with twelve-foot ceilings before, and now the sheer size of the foyer of Eldon Collier's mansion struck him silent. With the quiet Anne Marie close at his side, he watched the uniformed manservant walk away. The red-haired dandy in tails had asked for their names and the nature of their business with Mister Collier, and now he was off to fetch the man of the house, his footfalls silenced by a thick multi-colored Persian carpet.

Matt gazed at the gold-framed oil paintings hanging high on floral papered walls. One showed a foxhunt with riders in red coats mounted on impossibly sleek brown horses in full gallop, men and mounts seeming to float effortlessly above the dale bordered by a stone fence. Another painting portrayed women picnicking on an ocean shore, scarves wind-borne. Matt's gaze shifted to his left. Over the great fireplace hung a life-size portrait of a spade-bearded gentleman. Matt stepped back, eyeing the painting of this gent who seemed to stare down at him. The artist had captured his subject's expression, he thought, about halfway between the squinting grimace of constipation and the look of a man who owns everything from here to as far as the eye can see. Stepping closer, Matt read the name engraved on a brass plate centered on the bottom of the gilt frame: **Eldon James Collier III**.

He heard a door open. The manservant came in, halted, and stepped aside to stand at attention. Then, as though striding out of the portrait, the man himself entered and lumbered across the room. Spade beard and all, he was heavy-set, breathing hard by the time he reached them.

"Mister Collier?" Matt asked, holding his hand out to

shake the beefy paw of the man standing more than six and a half feet tall.

Eldon Collier ignored the gesture. He seemed to wink as he turned his attention to Anne Marie. She explained her reason for coming to Valmont City, or started to.

"Young lady," Collier broke in, "I shall give you the best advice of your life. Listen carefully."

Anne Marie stared up at Collier.

"Leave Valmont City," he said. "Today. Do not come back."

Anne Marie drew a sharp breath.

Matt studied him. The man's florid face was stirred by a facial tic below the eye. That involuntary twitch tugged at his upper cheek, a muscle clenching and relaxing in an endless cycle. It gave his broad face an oddly slanted look, as though the man was constantly attempting to compensate for a deformity.

"Mister Collier," Anne Marie said, "I must talk to my sister. It is a family matter. . . ."

"Rest assured," Collier interrupted again, "she is not here."

"But Miss Maude Riley told me. . . ."

Collier interrupted and finished her sentence: "To give her name at my door. It's our code, you might say."

"Code?"

"Yes, yes," he replied with a glance at Matt. "Trouble-makers in her establishment are either sent to me, or a runner comes to notify me. It is my signal to take control of the situation. As I am now."

"By booting us out of town?" Matt asked.

"If necessary, yes," he replied. He gave Matt a more measured look, clearly sensing his resistance to an ultimatum. "That is why I am informing the young lady that she will be wise to take my advice. Return to Denver, and we shall all go on about our business."

Matt stiffened. "We'll head back down the road after Anne Marie talks to her sister."

"Perhaps you fail to understand," Collier said. "Maude Riley wants nothing to do with either of you. She would not have sent you here if she had. The lady you are seeking is not in my home. See that door? Now is the time for you to walk out. Do you understand?"

Anne Marie grasped Matt's arm. "Come on."

"We'll leave Valmont City," Matt said.

Collier smiled. "Excellent."

"After Miss Painter talks to her sister."

The smile faded. "What did you say your name is?"

"I didn't. I'm Matthew MacLeod."

"Mister MacLeod," Collier repeated slowly, his facial tic growing more pronounced, "when I first saw you, I thought you looked familiar. Have we met before?"

"No, sir," Matt said.

"Are you certain? I travel a great deal."

"I don't," Matt said.

Collier eyed him. "Even so, I think we have met somewhere, sometime."

Matt shook his head in a curt reply. At once, though, he recalled Riley's reaction to the name Eldon Collier when spoken by Anne Marie. Riley had volunteered the information that the man was said to be wealthy. Now, as Matt met Collier's gaze, he suspected Riley knew him—most likely through Hoyt Wilcox.

"Jimmy will show you to the door."

Anne Marie tugged at Matt's sleeve.

Matt eyed the manservant. Jimmy was long-faced with a thin red mustache. Matt was ready to fight, but knew it would be a mistake to give Collier time to figure out when and where he had seen his twin. He knew Hoyt Wilcox had rarely, if ever, left friends in his wake.

With Anne Marie at his side, Matt followed the manservant through the foyer. When Jimmy reached for the door handle, his coat opened far enough to reveal a small pistol in a shoulder holster.

Outside, Matt and Anne Marie followed the stone walk to the fence. He opened the gate. Instead of passing through it, she turned and looked back at the house. "Look!"

Matt followed her gaze to an upstairs window. He saw a curtain move, settling into place.

"Sarah," Anne Marie whispered.

"What?" Matt asked.

"Sarah!" she repeated urgently.

"What about her?"

"She was standing up there, watching us!"

Matt had seen no more than the curtain drop into place at a second-floor window. He looked at Anne Marie, her upturned face bright with anticipation. He did not doubt she had seen someone. But he wondered if wishful thinking had presented an apparition to her mind's eye. When she lunged toward the house, he reached out and grasped her arm.

"What . . . what are you doing?" she demanded, and indignantly pulled away, or tried to.

Matt held on. "Wait."

"Wait!" she exclaimed, face reddened. She struggled against his grasp, but failed to pull free. "Wait for what?"

"I don't know what's going on here," he said, his gaze moving from the mansion to the carriage house.

"What do you mean?"

"Every man on the place is packing a side arm."

"I don't care!" Anne Marie exclaimed. "Let me go!"

Their eyes met and held as they stared at one another in a tense silence. Her defiance reminded him of the time they had first met, a determined expression in a youthful face.

"I'm trying to help you," he said. "I'll let go after you've listened to me."

Breathing hard, she nodded once.

"Think it through," Matt said. "If your sister saw you. . . ."

"Not if!" she snapped. "Sarah saw me!"

"Then why doesn't she come running out here?" Matt asked. "Why didn't she raise the window and call out to you?" When Anne Marie did not answer either question, he asked: "Why did Collier lie to us?"

"I . . . I don't know! But I have to talk to her!"

"You will," Matt said. "But right now the smart thing to do is make Collier think we're leaving. Then we can figure out what to do next." He let go of her arm.

Instead of running to the mansion door, Anne Marie gazed searchingly at him. "I don't understand."

"Your sister won't stay in that house day and night," Matt said, "if she's free to go."

Eyes widening, Anne Marie whispered: "She's being held against her will. Is that what you think?"

"Right now I don't know what to think," Matt replied. He turned and opened the gate. "All I know is we'd better find out what's going on before we come back."

Chapter Seven

The driver of the surrey donned a yellow rain slicker at the first rumble of thunder. "These here mountain storms," he called back to his passengers, "they gits a leetle loud and flashy, but they blow through purty quick, most usually."

Lightning flashed out of the sagging underbelly of the thunderhead. Moments later the storm hit with a thousand times the explosive force of giant powder. One great boom followed another in deafening blasts, each one reverberating off cañon walls like cannon fire from a fortress stronghold. Then a drum roll of wind-driven rains charged through the cañon.

Riley and the three other passengers glanced at one another. If the driver's words had been meant to reassure them, another too-close lightning strike cast doubt on the authority of his meteorological observations.

Seated in the surrey across from Riley, a mother managed to smile at her young son. The fourth passenger was at his side, a well-dressed woman of middle age who clutched a beaded handbag in her lap. At the driver's instruction, the passengers had hastily unrolled the side-curtains. Pulling each one down, they tied the waterproof oilcloth snugly to keep the rain out, or most of it.

Another lightning bolt flashed and cracked overhead. Instead of blowing through as predicted, the storm intensified. The driver yelled. His words were lost, but his tone of voice betrayed alarm. With the creek rushing out of rocky banks to flood the freight road, the driver shouted again, louder. Riley heard the whip pop, and knew the driver was searching for safe ground now.

The driver called to his horses. The coach rocked as he hastily turned off the cañon road, wheels splashing through shallow, but swift, waters. Riley opened the side-curtain a few inches. He peered out as the driver guided his frightened animals up a slope to a clearing in the pines. He glimpsed a mine site, an abandoned tunnel at the base of a towering granite formation. On level ground the driver shouted: "Whoa!" Halting the coach, he set the brake and jumped down from the seat.

Riley saw him stride to the team, a lone figure in yellow standing in the pouring rain as he attempted to calm the spooked horses. Riley considered going out to lend a hand. His slicker and gear were in the horsehide valise stowed in the boot, a covered storage compartment at the rear of the coach. He would be drenched by the time he got there.

The roar of the storm covered hoof beats. From their seats inside the coach none of the passengers knew they were surrounded by highwaymen until shouted curses from the driver were cut off by a gunshot. The young mother shrieked and reached out to grab her son. The older woman was silent, eyes widened by fear as she looked to Riley.

He pulled open the left side-curtain far enough to see a pair of horsebackers outside the coach. Both were full-bearded men, sopping wet in rain-soaked clothes and shapeless hats, guns drawn. On the muddy ground lay the driver, his yellow slicker funneling rain while blood streamed from his chest. Riley turned, leaned across the woman, and opened the right side-curtain a few inches. Two more gunmen rode past, mounted on restless horses.

"Come outta there!" shouted one of them. "Hand over your valuables. Hand 'em over, and you won't get hurt none."

Riley untied the side-curtain. The woman grasped his

arm, and just as quickly let go when he opened it to a wind-driven blast of rain. The four gunmen had bunched, horses side by side and fidgeting as the riders trained revolvers on the coach passengers. The man who gave orders was older than the others, his iron-gray hair plastered to his neck, his beard streaked with white.

"Please don't shoot!" Riley cried out. "Oh, Lord, please don't shoot me!" He grabbed at the handbag in the woman's lap beside him. She glowered and pulled back. After a brief tussle, he yanked it from her hands. He turned and tossed it outside. The handbag landed in the mud at the horses' hoofs. The woman said nothing, but stared at Riley, her expression showing both fear and disdain.

Climbing out of the coach with his hands raised, Riley begged for his life. "Take the money! Take all of our money! Oh, Lord, just let me live!"

"Helpful citizen, ain't he, Dad?" the nearest gunman said to the older man on his right.

Dad spat a stream of tobacco juice into the rain. "Shore is."

"Hand over that lady's bag," a third robber said.

Riley dove to his knees and came up with the muddy handbag, offering it to them in both hands like a supplicant. Soaked by the relentless rain now, Riley gestured toward the boot at the rear of the coach.

"Jewelry is in the ladies' luggage!" he shouted over the roar of the storm. "I've got five hundred dollars myself. Take it! Take everything! Please, please! Just don't shoot me!"

"Tell you what, mister," another gunman said. "You can just fetch that 'ere loot fer us. Go on. Soon as we get our due, we'll move on. Ain't that so, Dad?"

"We ain't gonna cut down nobody," the older man said. "All youse folks gotta do is foller orders."

They eyed the two women, and glanced at one another. Riley did not miss the wordless exchange. He knew what it meant. This surrey was in a clearing away from the road, out of sight of passers-by. Rain had erased wheel and horseshoe tracks. Riley knew these men would gun him down in the next few minutes—the boy, too, probably. Then they would have their way with the women, here or in the tunnel of the abandoned mine.

Hands raised high, Riley sobbed as he staggered toward the rear of the coach. He glimpsed the other passengers. The boy sat close to his mother, fear in his eyes, while the older woman cast a hateful look at Riley. All of them were soaking wet and bone-deep scared.

Each gunman held his horse under a tight rein. Riley noticed the pair closest to him had leaned back in their saddles, guns drawn, but lowered. The element of surprise was good for a heartbeat or two, he figured, no more. Riley knew he would have to take out that pair first, grab his Derringer, fire it, and reload.

"Hurry it up," Dad said.

"Yes, sir, yes, sir!" Riley said.

At the boot, Riley loosened and untied the straps. He pulled back the wet canvas cover. His horsehide grip was on the left side, on top of larger pieces of hard leather luggage. He opened it, plunging his hands in as though eager to do the bidding of the outlaws. He did not come up empty-handed.

Too late, the gunmen spotted the Greener, their eyes bulging in sudden terror. Before they could aim and fire their revolvers, one .12-gauge blast knocked the nearest man out of his saddle, blowing off one side of his face, and the second load of buckshot killed another as he raised his gun. Rocked back, the body tumbled out of the saddle, landing in the mud.

Horse rearing, the man addressed as Dad squeezed off a

shot while trying to control his mount. The bullet went wild. Riley pulled his coat lapel aside and drew his Derringer. With quick aim, he fired both barrels at him, driving him back, but not killing him. The remaining robber, a youngster, had lost his taste for a fight. He turned toward the rain-shadowed pines, frantically kicking his horse.

Riley broke open the shotgun. He pulled out the two spent shell casings, and shoved fresh loads into the smoking chambers. Dashing after the two fleeing outlaws, he halted at the tree-line and squeezed off both barrels in a great blast. Riley did not know if he had hit either one, but he felt certain the one called Dad had been struck by a round from the Derringer.

Riley walked past the two dead men when he returned to the rear of the surrey. Hastily reloading his weapons, he waited in the driving rain in case the two surviving highwaymen regrouped for an attack. Then he heard cries from the coach.

The woman who had been seated beside him climbed out. Introducing herself as Greta Schumann, she lunged toward Riley. "I thought you were a terrible man, the worst of all cowards. But you saved our lives. You're very brave." Suddenly she embraced him. She wept, her body shuddering against him.

"I was too scared to be brave," Riley said, as she pulled away, chiding him for false modesty.

The next voice he heard came from the direction of the team. With Greta following, he turned and hurried past the coach. The driver was on the ground by the horses, sitting up now as he gazed down at the dark powder burn on his slicker.

Riley and Greta knelt at his side. She unbuckled his slicker, pulled open his shirt, and unbuttoned his woolen underwear. The wound was superficial, a fine slash across his

111

chest that bled in a long line. Greta pulled off her cotton scarf for use as a bandage.

"I musta turned away jest as he pulled the trigger," the driver said, grinning wildly. "My lucky day."

"With that kind of luck," Riley said, "I wouldn't want any that was bad."

"Anybody else hurt?" the driver asked.

"All of us passengers are wet but unhurt," Greta said. "Two bandits paid with their lives . . . thanks to this courageous gentleman."

"Obliged, much obliged," the driver said to Riley when he had heard her account of what had happened after he was gunned down. "This is the fourth time I've been robbed. I've been shot at before, too, but this is the first time I got hit. I asked fer a man to ride shotgun, but the company won't spend the money."

Riley helped him stand. "Maybe somebody'll listen to you now."

Greta grasped his other arm and steadied him. "Or perhaps you shall find another company to work for."

"Yes, ma'am, maybe I will at that," he said, nodding slowly. He looked at the two dead men sprawled on the muddy ground. "Wouldn't wanna press my luck no more than necessary, now, would I?"

The worst of the storm had passed by the time Riley finished burying the two men in rocky ground near the mine. Standing in sprinkling rain, muddy to his knees, he became aware of Greta watching him.

"I won't apologize to you again," she said, "or embarrass you more than I already have. But I want you to know something."

"What?" Riley asked.

"My brother owns the Home Café in Valmont City," she

said. "Come through the door, and you will be well fed. Your money is no good there, not one dime."

Even though she agreed to leave, Matt had fairly to drag Anne Marie through the gate. They walked from the Collier mansion as if departing. Across the street Matt noted a lady inside a red brick house. She watched them from a front window half covered by a curtain. When her view was obscured by another house, he turned and led Anne Marie into an alley. A quarter of the way down the block, they stopped behind a cowshed and pen. Leaning out from the corner gave them a partial view of the Collier mansion and carriage house.

"Now what?" Anne Marie asked.

"We'll wait," he replied.

"How long?"

"If your sister is in there, she will come out sooner or later."

"I saw her," Anne Marie insisted. "I know I saw her."

Horse flies buzzed around them. The milk cows in the shed grew restless in the presence of unseen strangers. Matt heard the big animals nervously bump against their stalls. He looked across the alley at a small barn. A fenced area next to it indicated someone had raised horses or mules there. But not now. The over-size door stood open. He crossed the alley and looked in. As he had guessed, it was empty. Judging by the thin odors inside, the barn had been unoccupied for a good long time. Outside, he walked the length of it and edged around the corner. Dandelions grew in the footpath to the house. With no window coverings, he could see that it stood empty—a property for sale, he supposed, or perhaps abandoned. For whatever reason, no one lived there.

Matt backtracked. He lifted his gaze to a block-and-tackle

suspended from the end of a timber at the access door to the barn's mow. A rope and two pulleys up above gave a man enough mechanical advantage to lift hay bales and sacks of grain from the alley to the mow for storage. He gestured to Anne Marie.

With a questioning look in her eyes, she crossed the alley. "Where are you going?"

"Into that barn," he replied. "If we stay in this alley like a couple of vagrants, those cows will bust up the shed, and the neighbors will send for the law."

He led the way into the empty barn. In the half light he found what he was looking for on the far side—the ladder to the haymow was bolted to the wall. He climbed it. Anne Marie followed.

A layer of straw covered the floor of the mow he found, when he reached the top rung. No hay bales or feed sacks were stored here. Movement caught his eye. Mice silently scampered away like tiny shadows. With Anne Marie behind him, he crawled to the access door by the block and tackle. He took off his hat, and lay on his stomach to look outside.

Annie Marie scooted in beside him. This position gave them a bird's-eye view of the Collier property. Lifting his gaze, Matt saw distant mountains. Here the sky was blue, but down range storm clouds spawned lightning flashes over a stand of aspens.

They lay side by side in silence for a long time, peering out of the shade over the sun-bathed roofs to the imposing Collier mansion. Rhythmic blows from an unseen woodcutter's axe came to them. A dog barked when three boys, brandishing wooden swords, ran headlong down the alley to the street. Their battle raged until a mother's shout imposed peace. Later a carriage passed by, heading for the business district of Valmont City.

Aware of Anne Marie's gaze, Matt turned his head to find her studying him.

"My father. . . ." Her voice faltered.

"What about him?"

"Guess I was thinking aloud," she said, embarrassed.

"Thinking what?" Matt asked.

After a long pause, she said: "My father believes Mister Collier is a white slaver who turned my sister into a prostitute. Sarah gave into temptation and fell from grace. That's what he said after he read her letter . . . a private letter to me."

Matt remembered the tattered stationery in Anne Marie's hand. "What do you think about her?"

She paused before answering. "After seeing her in that window today, I don't know what to believe. That is part of the reason I have to talk to her."

"What's the other part?"

"A legal matter," she replied. "I am not of age."

"Age?"

"The Homestead Act requires a family member to be of age, twenty-one or older," she explained. "If Father dies, my brothers and I will lose the property." She drew a breath. "To a cowman like you, I know our claim doesn't amount to much."

"I'm a hired hand riding for the Two-Bar Ranch," he said. "I was raised on a homestead that didn't add up to much more than hard work."

Anne Marie cast a smile at him, clearly interested in this insight into his past.

Matt had not thought about this for a long time, but he remembered the MacLeod homestead had reverted to the territorial government upon the deaths of his parents.

"My brothers and I have made the improvements required by law," she went on. "If Father . . . if he dies, we'll lose everything. And if we can't sell the land, we won't have the means to go home."

"Sarah is twenty-one?"

A look of child-like cunning crossed her face. "She can pass for twenty-one. There's no official record of her birth. If she swears she was born in the spring of Eighteen Fifty-Four, then we'll be able to prove up and sell the place in two more years."

She rested her chin on crossed wrists as she looked at the Collier mansion. Neither of them spoke. Matt thought she seemed older now than the first time he had seen her. At first he had pegged her as little more than a kid. Now he looked at her honey-colored hair, the curve of her chin, her small nose, and a scattering of freckles. He discovered he liked lying close to her, and wondered about her feelings toward him.

Lost in her thoughts, he figured, as she gazed wistfully at the Collier place. He imagined magnificent furnishings arranged in spacious rooms there, and reckoned Anne Marie craved elegant clothing from a seamstress, fancy hats from a milliner, patent leather shoes imported from Italy, a multitude of servants at her beck and call. Matt knew he could not provide luxuries for her—and at once felt amazed such a thought had entered his mind. Luxuries!

As though awakening, Anne Marie blinked rapidly and turned to him. "I've answered your questions. Will you answer mine?"

"What questions?"

"I'm wondering about that woman . . . Maude Riley."

"What about her?"

"Is she your mother?"

Riley twisted the brass bell handle in the door. After a long wait, a gaunt woman answered. Her robe of purple velvet cascaded from narrow shoulders to her ankles.

"You're Maude Riley?"

A scowl deepened the wrinkles in her face like an over-size white prune. "You know damn' well who I am."

"No, I don't."

Pursing her thin lips together, she cursed him. After demanding to know why he had come back, she did not wait for his reply. Half turning, she called out: "Philip! Philip!"

Bald and shirtless with a residue of shaving cream on his jaw, a heavily muscled bouncer appeared in the entryway behind her. Without warning, Philip charged through the doorway like a bear. He grasped Riley's coat by a lapel and drew his right arm back, hand knotted into a fist.

"You boke mah node," he said, and punched Riley in the jaw. Letting him sink to the porch, he stood over him, hands on his hips.

The woman cleared the doorway and kicked Riley. "Get out of here, cowboy! Get out! Don't ever come back!"

Riley stood. He gingerly touched his jaw. "I wish to hell someone would give me one good reason."

"Good reason for what?"

"Why folks in this hayseed territory are so unfriendly," he replied. "Not enough air up here? Can't catch a good breath? Is that what makes you so blamed cranky?"

"Get out!" the woman repeated, and kicked at him again. "Get out before I turn Philip loose on you!"

"Sic your pet on me again," Riley said, "and I'll put him out of his damned misery."

Philip took the challenge and advanced until he saw a pearl-handled Derringer. The gun seemed to appear magically in Riley's hand. Philip halted, hands fluttering to his face like birds. He retreated into the entryway, leaving Maude Riley to fend for herself.

117

Riley noted the bent and darkened nose in Philip's broad face. His gaze went to Maude Riley and lingered long enough to draw another curse from her.

"How many times do I have to tell you, cowboy? Get out!"

Shaking his head, Riley pocketed the Derringer. He turned and descended the porch steps.

Matt answered Anne Marie's question: "I don't know."

"You don't know who your mother is?"

"I know who raised me," he replied, "and I know the mother and father who loved me and cared for me." He paused at the question that still sent a chill through him. "What I don't know is who gave birth to me, where, or when."

"I've heard twins pine for one another if separated," Anne Marie said. "When you were a child, did you think you had a brother, someone lost to you?"

Matt shook his head. He had thought of this before, almost from the moment he first laid eyes on his twin in that jail cell. The answer was always the same. If he had yearned for a brother, no memory of it lingered in his mind.

"Tell me about that homestead," she said.

Memories surged through his mind. A strange sensation swept over him as he told Anne Marie about his upbringing. For the first time since he had stood over the newly carved grave markers bearing the names of his parents, he wept. His tears were sudden, not so much sorrowful as simply a release, an inner dam that cracked and burst, freeing emotions impossible to hold back. Matt turned his head. He pulled a wadded blue bandanna out of his hip pocket. Wiping his face, he apologized to her.

"There is nothing wrong with being sorrowful," Anne Marie said. She seemed older than her years when she reached out and put her arm around his shoulders. Their eyes met, faces drawing close. He felt the warmth of her body alongside his own.

"Sometimes we cry," she whispered. "We have to. All of us."

Her gaze left him suddenly as she looked outside. She drew a sharp breath. "Look!"

Matt followed her gaze. From her excited tone, he expected to see a young woman emerge from the Collier mansion—Sarah Painter. Instead he saw a lone figure standing outside the gate. It was Riley.

Chapter Eight

Too late, Riley wished he had trusted his instincts. He passed a magnificent carriage house, his eyes drawn to a shiny black lacquer coach and eight or ten black horses confined in the adjoining corral. With two horses saddled, the others were draft animals, all of them tended by a trio of armed stable hands.

Instead of hurrying on as his instincts had told him, Riley paused at the iron gate. He looked at the brick mansion with its tall cupola, awed by a hotel-size residence that was imposing and at once forbidding. He stood there too long.

Shadows moved behind windows on either side of the front door. A moment later that door swung open. A tall, red-haired manservant came out. He beckoned to Riley. Eldon Collier stepped into the doorway behind him, arms folded over his chest.

When Riley did not comply, the manservant obeyed a barked command from Collier and rushed off the porch. He sprinted down the walk to the gate, drawing a pistol from his shoulder holster as he closed the distance. He brought the weapon to bear on Riley. The three men from the carriage house answered a shout from Collier. Drawing their revolvers, they headed for the gate on the run.

After losing his Derringer during a quick search of his pockets, Riley entered the mansion at gunpoint. Face twitching, Eldon Collier sized him up. Then without a formal greeting, he led him into a library off the foyer. At his signal, the stable hands left. The red-haired manservant lingered by the door that remained half open.

"I don't know why you came back," Collier said to Riley.

Riley watched the big man lower himself into a leather-covered armchair. He breathed hard from the exertion. A narrow shaft of sunlight was cast from a side window filled with dust. The room was musty and close, bearing a vague, dry odor of disuse. Riley looked around. This place made him think of an exclusive gentleman's club, one that had been locked and long unoccupied. He saw heavy armchairs and ottomans, claw-footed tables bearing oil lamps, and a world globe on a swivel base. Dark paintings mounted in elaborately carved gold frames hung on two walls. Thick, leather-bound volumes lined the other two. In the far corner stood a floor safe with a combination lock in the door. The door was decorated with a painting of a corvette on storm-tossed seas, sails bulging, bow crashing into foaming waves.

"Arrogance, I suppose," Collier answered his own question.

The pot calling the kettle black, Riley thought. *If anyone in this territory is arrogant, it is this man.*

"You must have believed I would not remember you," Collier went on, "but after you left I recalled where we previously had encountered one another. The occasion was a poker game in my railcar on a Cheyenne siding." He added: "You were a gambler's lackey."

Riley did not reply, but he well remembered Eldon Collier. The size of the man, his overbearing manner, the facial tic—all these traits made him a figure that loomed large in the memory.

Riley had headed back to town after he left Maude Riley's Sporting House in the red-light district. His jaw was sore, but no damage had been done by the bouncer's punch. He had gotten directions to the Collier place from a passer-by and had come here because he knew of no other place to look for

Matt and Anne Marie. Now from Collier's comment, he knew he was on their trail. His twin must have been led here in Anne Marie's search for her sister, and clearly Matt had been mistaken for him by Eldon Collier. The question was, where had Matt and Anne Marie gone?

"Smooth as oil," Collier went on. "Slick and slimy, that's Hoyt Wilcox. He claimed to be a banker or some such, and rather easily made a fool out of me and half a dozen of my associates." His voice rising in anger, he demanded: "Where is the cheat now? Preying on the citizens of Valmont City?"

"He died," Riley replied.

A look of skepticism crossed Collier's twitching face. "Sounds like a tale he concocted to duck retribution. He sends you around, I suppose, to make his victims think it's true."

Riley met his gaze. "It *is* the truth."

"Truth!" Collier drew a heaving breath. "The man's a liar, through and through! More than money lost to a cheat, it is the act of betrayal that drives a cold spike into the chest. The man who turned out to be Hoyt Wilcox was introduced to me by a friend, and I believed his every word. I welcomed him to an inner circle of trustworthy gentlemen. That damned outlaw did more than merely rob us. He betrayed our trust."

Riley eyed him. He knew how Hoyt would have replied to a high-minded speech about trust and betrayal. Fact was, Hoyt had flashed a bankroll, and every man in that rail car had lusted for it. The money was the reason he had been dealt into the game. It had nothing to do with some gentlemanly standard of trust.

Riley smiled. "Hoyt said something about that."

"What, exactly?"

"He said an honest man can't be cheated."

Collier leaned forward in the chair, his face darkening as

more dust stirred sluggishly around him. "That's a hell of a remark, coming from the only man among us who hid behind an assumed name and lied about his profession. Nobody else was waving a handkerchief around while dealing cards. That's right. After we learned his identity, it was obvious he had used sleight-of-hand and false shuffles to slant the odds in his favor. I don't believe he was sick then, any more than I believe he's dead now."

The bell in the front door rang. The manservant left to answer it.

Riley changed the subject. "I'm not here to tell tales about Hoyt Wilcox. I'm looking for a woman by the name of Sarah Painter."

"I know, I know," Collier replied impatiently. "If you think I'm going to change my answer now that you're here alone, think again."

"That black Concord with covered windows," Riley said, "is used to transport women, isn't it?"

"What crime are you accusing me of now?"

"I think we both know the answer to that one."

"I'm not a white slaver, if that's what you are suggesting," Collier said evenly. "I protect the girls who work for Maude Riley. My coach assures anonymity in their travels. None is held against her will."

"What about the women who are in debt to you?" he asked.

Collier glowered, the side of his face twitching, but then he shrugged as though none of it mattered.

In the next moment Riley heard muffled sounds from the direction of the entryway, or thought he did. He could not identify them, other than a vague disturbance.

"Girls make money by plying their trade," Collier said. "When they have as much money as they want, they leave

Valmont City, usually in the privacy of my coach. Most of them marry, bear children, join churches, and lead respectable lives. What we do here in Valmont City, well, it's business, that's all . . . and none of yours." Collier paused. "Fact is, a savvy businessman can calculate the financial well-being of a burg by the number of whores in residence. I don't know how many sporting houses are in full swing here now . . . fifteen, maybe twenty . . . but I can tell you we had more last year, and even more the year before that. I don't have to pore over assay reports to know gold production is in decline. Those cribs south of town will point the way long before all the accountants tally their columns of dreary figures."

Riley heard a muffled curse and then a quick scuffle of feet from the direction of the front door. He glanced over his shoulder, but his line of vision to the entrance was blocked by the library door, standing open.

Preoccupied by his own analyses, Collier went on: "First, Valmont City failed to get the railroad spur from Denver. Second, Denver was named capital of Colorado Territory. When that news hit, I didn't have to pay a Gypsy to read the tea leaves. We'll see boom-and-bust here, like all the other mining towns in the West. That's why I'm pulling out, as most of my friends already have."

The man was talkative, waving a manicured hand in an expansive gesture. "You may believe I live in the lap of luxury, but the fact is, I make ends meet by selling off my holdings . . . properties, mine claims, even let go a Pullman car. My Concord coach is next." He leaned back in the chair. "Now you know my secret."

Riley doubted that was much of a secret. The Valmont district covered thirty-odd square miles, and a man in Collier's position would be well-known from one end to the other. Proven ore deposits were not difficult to sell. Gold mines attracted investors, adventurers, and fools alike, just as gaming tables attracted bettors. Before Riley could reply to Collier, a familiar voice came from the library doorway behind him.

"What about your other secret, Mister Collier?"

Riley swiftly turned at the sound of his twin's voice. He saw Matt standing there with Jimmy, a deep bruise on the manservant's cheek bone, marking the place where he had been hit. Matt had subdued Jimmy, and had one of his arms twisted behind his back. A pistol was shoved into Matt's waistband. Riley figured the weapon had been stripped from Jimmy's shoulder holster. Anne Marie edged into the doorway, her face tightened by the anxiety of the moment.

"Turn Jimmy loose!" Collier bellowed.

"First, tell the truth," Matt said.

"What are you talking about?" Collier demanded.

Riley stood, wondering the same thing. He left the chair and moved behind Jimmy. Patting down the manservant's pockets, he recovered his Derringer as Matt replied to Collier's booming question.

"You lied," Matt said. "You lied when you claimed Sarah Painter was not here. Now I want the truth."

Matt hoped Anne Marie had been right when she claimed to have caught a glimpse of her sister in the upstairs window. He knew she felt certain. But he had doubts about what she had seen, or thought she had seen. Doubts aside, everything came to a head when he saw Riley marched into the Collier mansion at gunpoint.

"I'll be damned," Eldon Collier whispered now. His gaze moved from one to the other. "You two are dead ringers. Twins, aren't you?" He thought about that, clearly mystified by his discovery. "You both work for Hoyt Wilcox?"

Anne Marie pushed her way through them. "Where is she? Where is my sister?"

When Collier did not reply, Matt drew his Colt for emphasis.

"I can offer an attractive deal," Collier said, his cheek muscle twitching rapidly.

"No deals," Matt said.

"She's upstairs!" Anne Marie exclaimed. "I saw her! You've got her locked in a room up there, don't you?"

Collier did not answer immediately. "Turn Jimmy loose. Turn him loose, and I'll permit you to walk out."

"No!" Anne Marie shouted.

"Not without Sarah Painter," Matt said.

"If I alert my men outside," Collier said, "there will be bloodshed."

"Yours spilled first," Matt said. He shoved Jimmy forward and moved closer to Collier. "Get out of that chair. We're going upstairs."

Collier glared at him. "No man gives me orders."

"This one does," Matt said. When the big man made no move to comply, he added: "If I have to, I'll hog-tie both of you gents and leave you here while I kick in every door until we find her."

After a long moment, Collier leaned forward. He came up out of the chair, red-faced with the effort. Matt released Jimmy's arm, but kept him at gunpoint. Collier led the way out of the library. With Jimmy at his side, he slowly mounted the staircase to the carpeted hallway of the second floor. Matt, Riley, and Anne Marie followed. Collier halted at the first door to his left, and paused to catch his breath. Then he drew keys out of his pocket, unlocked the door, and opened it.

With a sharp gasp, Anne Marie lunged past him. "Sarah!"

Matt saw Anne Marie embrace a young woman dressed in wrinkled nightclothes, her blonde hair tangled and uncombed as though she had awakened from a restless sleep. He overheard the sisters' quick whispers. To ensure their privacy, he leaned past Collier and eased the door shut. Then he heard Riley's voice.

"That's her."

Matt turned to find him gazing at a portrait mounted on the wall at the staircase landing. Life-size, the round, full-cheeked face of a woman stared at all who came this way. Her hair was swept toward the top of her head in a fine, rounded form, turban style, and two strings of pearls looped over the ruffled front of her black dress.

"That's her," Riley said again, his voice hollow.

"Who?" Matt asked.

When Riley did not reply, Matt stepped closer to the portrait. He took his eyes off Collier and Jimmy long enough to read the name engraved into the frame: "Augusta Collier."

"Who is she?" Matt asked again.

Riley pulled his eyes away from the portrait artist's rendering of a perpetually stern countenance. He said: "Miss Augusta Benning."

Matt stared at him, and then turned to Eldon Collier. "Your wife?"

Collier nodded once. "We were married for a time. Then we divorced." He gazed at the portrait with a certain wistfulness. "I should take it down, I suppose."

"She took back her maiden name of Benning?" Matt asked.

Collier nodded, adding: "It is none of your affair."

"That's where you're wrong," Matt said. "Somebody gunned her down in Denver. An innocent man was arrested and convicted of her murder."

The big man shrugged. "I was in Philadelphia when I received word by telegraph of Gussy's death. I was informed

127

the murderer had been caught." He fell silent. "Even though we parted in rancor, I was saddened to learn of her death, very saddened. She did nothing to deserve such a violent end."

Matt exchanged a glance with Riley. He was surprised to hear a note of compassion in the man's voice. A moment later his twin asked the question looming in his own mind: "Why was her signature on a marker held by Hoyt Wilcox?"

Collier's face registered surprise. "I assure you, I have no idea."

"You assured us Sarah Painter was not here, too," Matt reminded him.

Collier stiffened. Hushed voices came from the bedroom. "You represent yourself as an honest man, MacLeod. If you take that girl out of here, you're no better than a thief."

Matt said: "Sarah Painter owes you money, doesn't she?"

Collier nodded curtly. "She borrowed eight hundred dollars. Said it was for expenses and coach and rail fare to Ohio for her family. Next day she claimed the money was stolen. Maude asked her to work off the debt. The girl refused, even after admitting she had left her family behind in Denver to work in the finest sporting house Valmont City has to offer." He paused. "I gave her an opportunity . . . time to think about how she could repay her debt."

"You mean," Matt said, "you locked her up like some runaway dog."

"This isn't Denver," Collier retorted. "In a mining town lawmen have their hands full, day and night, with crimes ranging from saloon fights to claim jumping. For minor offenses, we administer justice in our own ways."

"Whose justice . . . yours?"

"Keep your half-baked opinions about law and order to yourself, MacLeod," Collier said. "In Valmont City, sir, we honor the tradition of miners' courts. We do what must be done to keep the peace."

Riley stepped between them. "In the tradition of fair and square, let's make a trade."

Collier cast a look of skepticism at him. "What kind of trade?"

"The gambler's marker of eleven hundred dollars from your wife," he said, "for Sarah Painter's debt. Straight across."

Collier snorted in disgust. "I told you, I know nothing of that marker. Gussy was on her own after we parted. A settlement was arranged between us. I cannot be held responsible for her debts. Besides, if Wilcox is dead, as you claim, all bets are off." Collier studied the twins again. "I suppose Wilcox uses both of you as shills in his schemes to defraud honest folks. Now you aim to rob me again, don't you?"

The question went unanswered as the door to the bedroom opened. Anne Marie stepped out into the hallway with Sarah a pace behind her. She had dressed. Now she carried a battered valise, averting her eyes from the men who watched her move to her sister's side.

"MacLeod," Collier said, "you're a thief."

"I reckon that's true, Mister Collier," Matt allowed, "if you're in the slave trade."

With bright flames leaping toward a star-filled sky, Matt looked across the campfire at Anne Marie and Sarah. The air had chilled since dark, and the sisters huddled together under a blanket from Anne Marie's bedroll. Wavering shadows and bright firelight played across their stilled faces. They were not twins, but their resemblance to one another was striking.

At sunset, Matt had found this campsite in a stand of white-barked aspen trees at the base of a ridge. He had seen this grove from the mow of the empty barn in town, and, as a man who camped often, he had made a mental note of it. Aspen trees needed water, and he had expected to find a creek here. After a brief search, he heard a tiny brook gurgling through the high grass. The grove stood untouched by loggers. The wild flames of the campfire reminded Matt that aspen wood burned like paper, hot and fast. Too soft for log structures, aspens were also too weak to be ripped for boards. Pine and spruce were superior for fuel and construction purposes. Among barren, treeless slopes—the proverbial "Stump Towns" surrounding mountain settlements—this grove had escaped the bite of loggers' axes. And with no mines in this immediate area, the brook was diamond clear, unsullied by tailings.

"How was it stolen? When? Where?" Riley's gruff questions were thrown through the flames at Sarah.

Matt was surprised to hear a harsh tone in his twin's voice. Sarah ducked her head. She made no reply. Anne Marie gazed at her sister. Then she turned to Riley, looking at him across the fire. "The money?" she asked.

"The money," Riley repeated.

"Sarah told me it was stolen from her valise," Anne Marie replied. "Stolen the same day she borrowed it."

"Can't she talk for herself?" Riley demanded.

With a cautionary look at him, Anne Marie said softly: "Give her some time."

Riley persisted: "Who robbed you?"

Anne Marie reached out to brush strands of hair from her sister's forehead. "Sarah had been drinking tea, not knowing it was laced with laudanum. She's been drugged all this time, and does not know what happened. . . ."

"A trumped-up debt," Riley interrupted, "is an old trick in the oldest profession."

Sarah straightened. "Trick?"

"A kindly madam loans out cash," he replied, "and then steals it back."

"But why?"

"Sooner or later," he said, "the time comes for one soiled dove to be kicked from the roost to make room for another. Hurt feelings are smoothed over when the madam generously forgives the debt."

Sarah said nothing, but Anne Marie eyed him. At last she said: "Are you speaking from experience?"

Instead of answering, Riley stood. He turned his back to the fire and walked away, disappearing among the starlit shadows cast by the trees.

Matt went after him, his fire-dazed eyes adjusting to the forest darkness. After a brief search, he found him. His twin knelt at the edge of a small clearing, a hidden place that was still and wild-smelling from rains. Starlight shone on the high grasses. Around the clearing, aspen trees stood like silent, white-clad sentries. They might have been guarding the ant-lered creature emerging from the timber. Across the way a bull elk moved ponderously along the tree-line, grazing, alone in the shadows of the night.

Matt watched the big animal saunter into the cover of trees. He pulled the makings out of a vest pocket, built a smoke more by feel than sight, and fired it. Exhaling, he said: "I've been wondering."

Riley did not acknowledge the implied question.

Matt went on: "When you offered to trade Augusta Benning's marker for the debt owed by Sarah, I wondered how you aimed to get that piece of paper. Ochs took every-thing from you, didn't he?"

Riley shrugged. "Forging a marker is not much of a trick."

"Reckon not," Matt said thoughtfully. He paused. "Something else I've been wondering."

131

Riley still did not rise to the bait.

"Why did you come hunting for us?" Matt asked. "You were leaving the territory. This hayseed territory."

Riley made no reply.

"It has something to do with Sarah, doesn't it?"

"No," he said immediately. "Not her."

"Who?"

Riley did not answer.

"Something's got you on a short fuse," Matt said. "What is it? Or who? Some woman?"

Riley stood. He faced him. "Are you planning to shut up, or do I have to shut you up?"

Matt dropped his cigarette and ground it out under his boot. He motioned toward the clearing. "Step into the ring, and we'll have us a go-around."

Riley drew a deep breath and let it out. "Ever since that day you saved me from the hangman's noose, I've been getting knocked on my butt."

"It's your own fault," Matt said.

"Huh?"

"You drop your shoulder before you throw a punch."

Riley eyed him in starlight. "I do?"

"Yeah," he said, and demonstrated with his right shoulder moving downward before his left fist lashed out.

"I do that?" Riley asked. He shook his head. "What the hell? No, brother, I'm not going to fight you."

"Then tell me about her."

Riley did not reply.

"I won't give you any peace until you do."

Half a minute passed before Riley answered. "Her name was Nell Bloom. We met in a cemetery."

Hoyt Wilcox had no funeral service, not the "proper burial" af-

forded to most folks upon their deaths. Amid elaborately carved marble and granite headstones festooned with angel figures and flowers in relief, the graves were fenced within rectangles defined by wrought iron. The gambler was buried in a pine box, his final resting place unmarked, his life uncommemorated.

Standing over the freshly turned soil of the grave, Riley searched his thoughts. For weeks he had known this day would come. Hoyt had lost strength since his grand performance in a private rail car stocked with wealthy gents ripe for the picking. A last triumph, Riley had thought at the time. He had been right. Death had come, casting silence into the small room of that boarding house where Riley slept on the floor.

He did not feel grief. His feelings were numbed, buried, too.

A woman moved quietly among the elegant grave markers. Riley saw the down-turned brim of her hat and a bouquet of sunflowers clutched to her breast in gloved hands. Her gaze came out from under the wide brim and found him. She was pretty, jet-black hair brushed to a sheen, her dark eyes large enough to hold a man. Impeccably dressed in a maroon skirt reaching down to high-button shoes, she wore a jacket buttoned snugly over her starched white blouse.

That was the moment he first saw Nell, a fragment of time fixed in his memory, forever vivid.

"So here we are," she said easily, "pondering life's ironies as we wander among the dead, you and I, the living."

Riley stared. Hoyt was one to spout quotations, and for a dream-like moment it seemed the gambler had sent her. Impossible, of course, and later Riley would learn she was here because she found peace in cemeteries. But that day Nell's voice stirred him. Later her intimacy opened a wellspring.

Strange as it was, the moment his heart opened to love, grief came fully upon him. He shed tears over the death of the only father he had known, an emotional storm that cleansed his spirit.

With Nell in his arms, he felt attuned to life, to sorrow, and to joy, as never before.

The whinnying of agitated horses drew Matt and Riley back to the campfire. Stepping into the wavering light cast by the flames, neither of them caught the significance of the stricken looks on the faces of Anne Marie and Sarah. In the next instant a lanky, red-haired figure stepped into the firelight behind the sisters. Matt reached for his Colt.

"Pull that gun," Jimmy said, "and you'll see these girls die."

Three men appeared out of the darkness. They were clean-shaven and well-dressed. Matt recognized them from the carriage house on Collier's property. Two were armed with cut-down shotguns, the third brandishing a pistol. Both Greeners were trained on Anne Marie and Sarah.

Chapter Nine

"We saw you leave town," Jimmy said, "riding double and headed this way. At nightfall you stoked up your campfire. A mistake. Easy to find you."

Matt's hand eased toward the grips of his revolver. "What we have here," he said, "is a stand-off."

"No, we don't," Jimmy countered. "What we have here is an escort."

"Escort," Matt repeated.

"An armed escort," Jimmy said. "We brought a spare horse, and we'll escort this chippie back to Mister Collier. Then she can settle her debt."

"You mean, settle a phony debt," Riley said.

Jimmy eyed him across the flames. "Phony debt. What the hell are you talking about?"

"Maude Riley stole that money from her," he replied. "You know that as well as I do."

"Can't say I do," he said. "Better take that up with her. Right now, we're escorting the girl back to Valmont City so she can set things right with Mister Collier."

Sarah covered her face with her hands.

Anne Marie reacted strongly. "No, you're not!"

"You're not the one who's giving orders, girlie," Jimmy said.

Matt grasped the grips of his Colt.

Jimmy turned to him. "Mister, I told you to leave that gun holstered. Do as I tell you, and we all walk away. If it's a fight you want, well, that's what these gents"—he indicated his cohorts with a twist of his head—"get paid for."

135

Anne Marie looked up at Matt, a pleading and fearful look in her fire-lit gaze.

"Let Sarah go," Matt said.

"Mister Collier sent me to do a job," Jimmy said. "I can't let him down, now, can I?"

Riley stepped forward. "Let her go. I'll cover her debt . . . in gold."

"Gold," Jimmy repeated, suddenly interested. "Just how do you aim to do that?"

"Give me a couple of days," Riley said, "and I'll bring enough gold ore to satisfy the debt, twice over."

"Big talk," Jimmy said. "You own a mine?"

"You could say that."

"Reckon I could. Where is it?"

"Not far from here."

"In the Valmont district?"

Riley shrugged. "Close to it."

"Cagey, aren't you?" Jimmy said. He studied Riley. "How I see this, if you've got gold ore, you jumped a claim. That's the only reason for keeping your site a secret."

"It's not your business."

"I'm right, though, aren't I?" Jimmy said.

"Could be."

Jimmy grinned.

Matt gazed at his twin. Riley was playing this man.

"Gold, silver, liquid sunshine," Jimmy went on, "I don't care what the hell you've got or where it comes from. Pay the debt, or this chippie works it off in a bed. Understand?"

Sarah sobbed.

Anne Marie put her arm around her sister's shoulders, and cast a desperate look at Matt and Riley. "I'm going with her."

Now Sarah protested: "No!"

"You can't stop me," Anne Marie whispered to her.

Jimmy moved closer. "Now, hold on here. This wasn't part of the deal. . . ."

Anne Marie cast off the blanket and stood. "If I have to walk back to Valmont City, I will. She's my sister, and I'm going with her. The only way to stop me is to shoot me."

Jimmy studied her while Sarah sobbed quietly. "What the hell. I'm sick of that whimpering. Maybe you can stop her from crying her brains out day and night." He gestured to Riley. "Bring your ore, mister. I'll see if you're a bag of wind like the other damned fools claiming to have discovered the next Lucky Boy."

Jaw clenched, Matt watched the girls and men leave the campsite. Presently the sounds of departing horses drifted to him. He slapped his hands together in frustration. By stoking up a campfire to warm Anne Marie and Sarah, he had sent out a beacon to Jimmy. That was one mistake. Now he felt like he had compounded it by letting him ride out without a fight. Giving up ran against his nature. But at once Matt knew he had had no alternative, no way to have prevented Collier's men from carrying out Jimmy's threat. If he had drawn his gun, he would have knocked down Jimmy in an eye blink. But he could have done nothing to stop the others from blazing away.

He turned to Riley. "You've got a gold mine up your sleeve?"

"Something like that."

"Something like what?"

"Just leave this to me, brother."

Matt cast an exasperated look at him. "That's what I was afraid you were going to say."

"Haven't let you down yet, have I?" Riley said.

They boarded their horses in a Valmont City livery. This

time Matt did not argue when Riley told him to wait while he toured the local saloons and gambling halls. He pointed out the Home Café on Front Street.

"I'm off to purchase ore and a few ounces of placer gold from some miners," Riley explained. "We'll meet in the café. You're in charge of buying a spool of twine and a couple of miner's candles in Collier's store, and we'll be set."

"Set," Matt repeated. "Set for what?"

He shrugged. "When I know, you'll know."

By Matt's standards, straight talk meant honesty, and plain speaking meant a clear head. Riley's habit of muttering vague terms made him wary. Jaw tight, Matt was silent, figuring nothing could be gained by challenging his twin now.

The Home Café was a squat, low-ceilinged building squeezed between two larger shops, **Collier Mining Supply** and **Valmont City Furniture & Undertaker**. Long dining tables were covered by blue-checked oilcloth, and the sidewalls were decorated with framed illustrations of pastoral farm life and domestic scenes in idealized villages. A menu posted on a chalkboard by the door offered meatloaf, venison steak, rabbit stew, eggs and bacon, and biscuits under sausage gravy—simple fare to evoke memories of home, he figured. Pulling off his hat, he briefly studied the menu, and then moved along a plank bench to the nearest table.

A sudden, joyous shout from the kitchen in the rear of the establishment caught him off guard. With two-dozen customers looking on, a middle-aged woman came striding toward him, arms spread wide as she reached for him. Before Matt could mount a retreat, she closed the distance and embraced him.

"I was hoping you'd show!" she exclaimed. "Hungry? Eat your fill! Your money is no good here! Not one dime!"

Matt had no idea where she had met Riley, but clearly she

was mistaking him for his twin. The more he protested, the more insistent she became, cheerfully accusing him of false modesty. Her name was Greta, and she gave him no choice but to sit down and follow orders. Within minutes she lugged platters of food from the kitchen and placed them before him, urging him to eat, eat, eat.

Matt ate, ate, ate, and more. He was nursing a cup of coffee when Riley came striding through the café door. Matt heard Greta gasp. He turned to see her gaze darting from him to his twin.

"I tried to tell you," Matt said.

With that realization full upon her now, she clasped her hands together and laughed aloud. "You did for a fact, didn't you?"

Matt added: "I'll pay for all that food meant for Riley. . . ."

"Oh, no, you won't!" she exclaimed. "The joke is on me, and so is the food. Twins or not, my offer holds for the both of you. Your money's no good, not one dime."

Riley sat across the long table from Matt. Greta brought a platter with meatloaf and mashed potatoes awash in a sea of dark brown gravy bearing creamy white islands of congealed grease. Between bites, Riley recounted his clash with the highwaymen on the freight road to Valmont City. He tried to cut the story short, but Greta kept interrupting to add her version of the events. Not only had her life been spared, she said with tears welling in her eyes, but the lives of a mother and her young son had been saved, along with the coach driver's life, thanks to Riley.

"I reported the attack to the Valmont City marshal," she went on. "He knew all about that gang of robbers. Dad Anders and his sons are skunk mean . . . robbers who leave their victims for dead. This is the first time they've been shot up." Greta drew a breath. "The marshal hopes Dad Anders was run out of the district. Nobody wants to tangle with a mad dog, and the marshal has never been able to find volunteers to posse-up and go after him and his sons."

Matt listened as he finished his coffee. He had never said so, but he had often wondered if Riley was all talk, if his twin would hold up his end when bullets were flying. Now he knew.

On horseback the twins followed Front Street out of town to the heavily traveled freight road. It led past the screaming saws of a lumber mill into a mountain cañon. Matt asked where they were going.

"I'll know it when I see it."

Matt shook his head. Another vague reply. He noticed Riley frequently looked back to make certain they were not being followed. Matt kept an eye peeled, too. The usual wagon traffic congested long stretches of this road, but no horsebackers were in sight behind them.

Their destination turned out to be a set of wheel ruts curving off the freight road, upslope, through a stand of pines. The ruts ended in a meadow five hundred yards off the main road. Matt saw blackened fire pits among the scattered débris of old campfires. A pile of granite rocks and quartz shards marked a mine site.

Matt's saddle mount shied suddenly. He held a tight rein to regain control of the animal. Ahead, he saw Riley halt. Before him, a narrow tunnel had been blasted into the base of a granite cliff, dislodging the gray rock laced with bands of white quartz. Matt's eye passed over the mine, caught by a gruesome sight. His horse pranced away from a human forearm and hand sticking out of the earth. The flesh had been chewed by animals, leaving skeletal fingers stretching skyward, stiffened by *rigor mortis*. The claw-like hand seemed to be grasping for some means of escape from a shallow grave.

"Outlaws . . . those robbers," Riley explained matter-of-factly. "I buried these two in the mud. I didn't have a pick and shovel. I covered them as best I could."

Matt watched as Riley dismounted. He threw the saddlebags borrowed from Old John Souter over his shoulder, and grabbed the .12-gauge Greener taken from Sheriff Hiram Ochs's office.

Riley turned and looked up at Matt. "You carry a pocket knife, don't you?"

Matt nodded.

"Let me borrow it."

"Why?"

"Ochs stripped me clean," Riley replied. "He lifted the Barlow knife I've lugged around for years. It's probably in his trouser pocket right this minute."

Matt still made no move to dismount.

Riley said impatiently: "Well?"

"Just what the hell are you up to?" Matt asked.

Riley raised the shotgun and gestured to the mine tunnel. "I'll use the scatter-gun to salt this old mine."

"Salt?" Matt asked. "What're you talking about?"

"It'll take longer to tell you than to do it," he said. "You brought the candles and twine?"

Matt nodded. "If you aim to make a fuse, you'll need kerosene. . . ."

"I'm not making a fuse," Riley broke in. "Quit your jawing, and maybe you'll learn something. Now, loan me that knife."

Matt studied him. "You've got a way of rubbing a man's nerves raw."

"You're not exactly a piece of cake yourself, brother," Riley said. "Now, climb off that horse."

141

Angered enough to do battle, Matt swallowed hard and kept his mouth shut. He swung down. Tying his horse, he followed Riley to the mouth of the tunnel. He tossed his pocket knife to him.

"A Barlow just like mine," Riley said with a quick smile of discovery. He looked at his twin. "Reckon we have the same taste in knives without even knowing it."

Riley used the point of the knife blade to open the ends of two shotgun shells. He poured out the buckshot. Then he drew a leather pouch from his trouser pocket, explaining that he had won the poke in a blackjack game in Valmont City. Loosening the drawstring, he poured placer gold from the pouch into the two shells, and closed up the ends. Then he opened the shotgun and shoved both rounds into the chambers.

"Light those candles," Riley said, closing the shotgun, "and follow me."

The tunnel opening was man-wide, not an inch more, a tunnel typical of Cornish miners. With hammers, drills, and chisels, they had followed a vein of gold, removing just enough rock to allow passage. Forty yards into the mountainside, the vein petered out and the narrow tunnel ended.

Matt held the candles up to cast light. Riley knelt. By candlelight he placed the cut-down shotgun on the rocky floor of the mine. Aiming the weapon slightly upward at the rear corner of the tunnel, he piled heavy stones on the shotgun. He cocked both hammers. Then he looped the twine around the triggers. They retraced their steps to the mouth of the tunnel with Riley feeding the thick line from its spool.

Outside, Riley glanced at his twin with a wild look in his eye. "Here we go, brother."

Matt watched as Riley slowly pulled the twine taut and gave it a tug. The report was instantaneous, the explosions from both barrels reverberating off the granite walls underground.

They waited for a while. Then, with candles held aloft, Matt entered the tunnel behind Riley. They moved slowly through powder smoke clouding the dead air. At the end of the tunnel, the light of the candles illuminated gold ore, or so it seemed.

Matt stared, amazed. He stepped past Riley, reached out, and touched the "ore" with his fingertips. Placer gold had been blasted against the rough surface of granite by the force of the gunpowder charges. Now it caught the light of candle flames like a newly uncovered lode.

"A trick you learned from Hoyt Wilcox?" Matt asked.

Riley grinned. "Not exactly."

"What exactly?"

"One of the few times the wool was pulled over Hoyt's eyes," he replied, "was the night he won a gold mine in Montana. Turned out to be salted. The trickster had been tricked. Hoyt went after the gent. Mad as hell. Forced him at gunpoint to tell how he did it."

"You aim to sell this mine to Eldon Collier?"

Riley shook his head. "All I have to do is convince him it's real. Then we'll make a swap . . . Sarah's debt for the mine site."

"And run before dawn?"

"Now you're getting it," he said, heading for his horse.

"Riley."

He drew up and turned to him. "Yeah?"

"Why are you doing this?"

"Doing what?"

"Paying off Sarah Painter's debt."

Riley did not answer immediately. "Let's just say I'm evening the score before I leave this damned place."

Matt watched him turn away and stride to his horse. He secured the saddlebags, grabbed the horn, and swung up. The horse cantered out of the clearing.

Matt jogged to his mare and mounted, neck-reining her around. No touch of spur was needed. She hopped once and trotted after the gelding, eager to leave this place.

If a mansion was no more than a monument to what had gone before, as Hoyt Wilcox often claimed, Riley figured Eldon Collier was on a downhill slide, and a steep one at that. Like an aging monarch ruling from his throne, the big man stirred fine dust from his overstuffed armchair and professed no interest in the ore Riley showed him.

"I don't want those rocks," Collier said, his eyelid and upper cheek twitching. "I'm not in the milling business. I can't crush that ore to find out how much gold's in there. And I sure as hell don't want to buy another stinking mine."

Riley pulled the sack away from him. "Jimmy said you would accept payment in gold."

"Jimmy needs to be reminded he's not the boss around here," Collier said. He gestured to the black safe in the far corner of the study. "The only gold I want from you is coined. Bring eagles to me . . . eight hundred dollars' worth. And one silver dollar."

"One silver dollar," Riley repeated.

"The debt goes up," Collier said, "every day that chippie refuses to work."

Riley asked: "Where is she now?"

"That's none of your affair, is it," he replied, "until the debt is paid. In full."

Riley struggled to hold his temper, knowing the arrogant man was horsing him around. The sporting house was a business, Eldon Collier had once said, and it must be a lucrative one for he had assumed the rôle of both banker and lawman for Maude Riley.

"What about that twin of yours?" Collier asked. "You two trade off working as shills for the gambler?"

"I told you," Riley said, "Hoyt Wilcox died."

"And I told you," he said, "Hoyt Wilcox is a liar."

"No one lies to the Grim Reaper," Riley said.

Eldon Collier scowled. He abruptly called out to Jimmy. The manservant appeared in the doorway and moved toward him like a well-trained guard dog. "Show the man out," Collier said.

Riley did not wait to be escorted. He picked up the sack and strode out of the library. Crossing the foyer, he went out, leaving the front door standing open.

What went wrong? Everything was in place to hook a big fish. Collier had no way of knowing the gold ore was high-graded, purchased from miners in an alley behind a saloon. Anyone could see it was gold-bearing. An opportunist would jump at it, and if ever there was an opportunist, it was Eldon Collier.

In the parlance of hard-rock miners, "high grade" meant stolen. The practice was common. After a charge was detonated underground and the smoke and rock dust cleared, the first men to see the results were miners, not supervisors. With owners increasing their wealth daily from the dangerous and back-breaking labors of men earning $3.00 a day, workers felt justified in their small-scale thievery. Gold ore was hidden in an over-size boot, the false bottom of a lunch bucket, or even a pouch sewn into the crotch of a man's underwear. To combat theft, some owners instituted a policy of body searches after every shift. The larceny may have been slowed, but when a vein ran as pure as the urine of the gods, even hard-nosed inspectors could be bought off.

Riley heard the door to the mansion close. He was un-aware someone had come out behind him until he approached the front gate. The scuff of a boot heel on stone made him turn. He saw Jimmy striding after him.

"I'll have a look at that ore," he said.

Riley halted. He was unprepared for Jimmy's taking the bait intended for Collier.

"Let me have a look," Jimmy repeated after a furtive glance toward the door of the Collier mansion.

Riley opened the burlap sack. He watched Jimmy reach in and take the ore out, briefly examining each piece in the sunlight before dropping them back into the sack.

"Mister Collier told me about you," Jimmy said. "That gambler who cheated him is dead, huh?"

Riley nodded.

"Mister Collier doesn't believe you," Jimmy said.

"I don't give a damn what he believes."

Jimmy grinned. "Me, I've got a hunch you're telling the truth. Otherwise, you'd still be with him."

"What're you getting at?" Riley asked.

"How I see this," Jimmy said, "you don't like me, and I sure as hell don't like you or your ugly brother. We're on opposite sides of this thing because Mister Collier got himself cheated a while back, a year or so before I went to work for him. He's still riled over it." He eyed Riley. "But we don't have to like each other to make a profit, do we?"

"Profit," Riley repeated.

"How I see this," Jimmy said, "we put our differences aside and make some money off this mine of yours." He eyed him. "Legal or not."

"Reckon you've got me pegged about right," Riley said.

A triumphant expression crossed Jimmy's face. "I figured

your mine wasn't legal, or you'd ship ore instead of trying to pawn it off."

"What're you driving at?" Riley asked.

"That ore looks good to me," he replied. "If it assays out, I'll buy the mine, registered or not. I can ship ore to the mill in Denver, no questions asked."

"How do you aim to do that?"

"Mister Collier's selling off his holdings," Jimmy replied, "but he still owns a played-out mine or two. If I say the ore was extracted from one of them, no one can prove otherwise."

Riley nodded slowly. "What about Collier?"

"He's not invited to this party," Jimmy said. He folded his arms over his chest. "Now, are you going to take me to that hole in the ground, or aren't you?"

"I'll take you," Riley conceded, "on one condition."

"What's that?"

"It's just you and me."

"Meaning?"

"Meaning Collier's gunmen stay in Valmont City."

"Fair enough," Jimmy said. "You do the same. Leave your trigger-happy brother in town."

"Trigger-happy," Riley repeated.

"You two look alike and you dress similar," Jimmy said, "but you sure as hell don't act the same. Every time I see that son-of-a-buck, he's either reaching for his Colt, or he's waving it around and giving orders. Between the two of you, I figure you're the one who can be trusted."

Matt heard them before he saw them. Lying prone on a prickly carpet of dried pine needles, he pressed the butt plate of his Winchester against his shoulder as he peered over the sights. The clatter of shod hoofs coming up from the freight road to the mine site gave ample warning of approaching riders.

He had been here since sunrise, long enough to select his spot. He had heaped dead pine branches over a lightning-struck pine, now a log split open, darkly weathered. When he had finished, the deadfall was a seemingly random pile of timber. It concealed his position while allowing a view of the clearing and the mouth of the tunnel.

Matt was skeptical about Riley's scheme to deceive Jimmy. Collier had not bought into it. Why should Jimmy? Riley had not had a glib answer for that one, but he had allowed one fish was as good as another. The deception would not be known until later, and the crime would not be reported to the law. If Jimmy said anything, he would be forced to explain why he claimed ownership of an unregistered mine, one that was salted, and why two corpses were on the property.

Run before dawn.

Some scheme, Matt thought now. He should have trusted to horse sense. If he had, he would not be here. His mare had tossed her head and reared at the strong scent of death wafting up from two shallow graves. A tight rein had held her while Matt had studied the soft ground. Tracks around the site indicated a cougar had been feeding there. During the night the big cat had tugged at the clothing and gnawed the flesh of two half-buried corpses. During the day, as Matt saw for himself, ravens and jays pecked at the carrion.

He felt nauseated from the sweet-sour stench hanging in the air like an invisible cloud. He was here because Riley did not take Jimmy at his word, and Riley figured Collier's gunmen would trail them. So far Matt had not seen anyone. He was desperate to escape the stink of rotting human flesh, and was considering how much longer he would stick it out when the metallic ringing of horseshoes on rocks reached his ears. Moments later two riders came into the clearing—Riley and Jimmy.

Immediately agitated, Jimmy covered his nose and swore. He demanded to know where the stench came from, his voice carrying to the deadfall. Riley pointed out the exposed corpses in the two shallow graves.

Jimmy stared. "How I see this, you and that trigger-happy brother of yours killed two miners and jumped their claim. You figure on busting rock and selling ore on the sly."

Riley swung down. "You want to see the mine, or don't you?"

Jimmy eyed him. "You and your brother, you're a couple of hardcases."

Peering through the branches, Matt watched his twin tie the speckled gray gelding. Riley dug two candles out of the saddlebags, and headed for the mine. Jimmy dismounted. With a scowling glance at the half-buried corpses, he hurried after him, fingers pinching his nose as he sprinted into the mine.

Matt was observing the dark mouth of the tunnel when again he heard horses coming. He looked to his right. Two riders slowly entered the meadow, guns drawn. They halted and looked at one another wordlessly. At first Matt thought they were Collier's gunmen, and figured Riley had been right not to take Jimmy at his word. But this pair wore tattered clothes, and they rode broken-down horses under beat-up saddles. One, a kid of twelve or thirteen, was mounted on a sway-backed plug. The other was much older with shaggy gray hair sticking out under his hat brim like weeds. A blood-stained sling supported one arm across his chest.

Chapter Ten

Inside the mouth of the tunnel Riley lit the miner's candles. He handed one to Jimmy, and held the other aloft as he led the way in. At the end of the tunnel he halted. Shadows seemed to dance around them as Jimmy edged passed him and thrust the flame toward bands of white quartz embedded in the dull gray granite. The sight of pure gold brought a reverent curse from his lips.

"I don't know how deep into the mountain this vein runs," Riley said casually, "but it looks like a big one."

Jimmy moved closer, squinting. He reached out and touched the gold. He sniffed his fingertips and swore again, this time expressing disgust.

"What's wrong?" Riley asked.

"Gunpowder," Jimmy replied. With his free hand, he drew a folding knife from his trouser pocket and flipped the blade open. He leaned close, scraping away gold with the flat edge of the blade.

"Salted," he said, straightening up. "This mine's been salted."

"What?" Riley asked.

Jimmy turned to him. "You've got nothing here but one big deposit of leaverite." He folded the knife and dropped it into his trouser pocket.

"Leaverite," Riley repeated. "What're you talking about?"

"It's country rock," Jimmy answered. "Sandstone, granite, cow manure, it's all the same. Miners call it leaverite because you might as well leave-her-right there. This mine is worthless."

"But you can see the gold for yourself," Riley said.

"An ignorant fool might be dazzled by it," Jimmy allowed.

Riley eyed him.

"Hell, no one likes to admit to being snookered," Jimmy said. "How I see this, either you and your trigger-happy brother killed two miners for a worthless hole in the ground, or you bought it from someone who did. Which is it?"

Riley thought about that. Hoyt's words came into his mind as though the gambler spoke from the grave: *Make your opponent think you're a sucker before you clean his damned clock.*

"Won it in a poker game," he said at last.

"Well, sometimes the winner loses," Jimmy said. "You got cheated." He turned and headed for daylight.

Riley followed. Outside the tunnel, just as he blew out the candle, he was startled by a shout. While his vision adjusted to the bright sunshine after the darkness of the mine, Riley heard a string of curses. Foul threats were slowly uttered in a deep voice. Blinking against the glare of the morning sun, Riley made out a pair of horsebackers. A man and a boy sat their saddles at the far edge of the meadow.

"I've been watchin' the road, ye murderin' bastard. Figured we'd cross trails, sooner or later."

Riley saw him now. Gray-haired, the man slouched with one arm suspended in a bandanna sling. His good hand clutched an old Navy pistol.

Riley recognized the leader of the outlaws who had attacked the coach. According to information Greta had acquired from the Valmont City marshal, this was Dad Anders. That would make the pimple-faced kid his surviving son. The kid held a small pistol, aimed at no one. Neither was well mounted.

Jimmy demanded: "Who the hell are you?"

"Git outen the way!" Anders ordered. He cocked the big

151

revolver and squeezed an eye shut as he took aim at Riley. "My fight's with this here murderin' bastard. He done kilt two of my boys, and he done put a bullet in me." He pulled the trigger.

The handgun roared and bucked with a great plume of smoke, sending Jimmy running to his left. He tripped over the exposed arm of the corpse and fell, landing face down on the body in the shallow grave.

Riley heard Jimmy retching in the dry heaves. Looking down at himself, Riley was surprised to find the bullet had gone wide. He heard a click as the old single-action handgun was cocked again. Riley raised his hands. "I'm not armed."

"I ain't fallin' fer none of yer tricks," Anders said. "Yer gonna die. Right now, right here, alongside of my two boys, yer gonna die. . . ."

"No tricks," Riley interrupted. "My brother's got you in his rifle sights. One word from me, and he'll knock you out of that saddle."

Anders glanced around. "Can't you do better'n that?"

"You and your boy ride," Riley said. "This is your last chance. Ride out now, and you won't get yourselves shot up again."

Anders cursed him. He raised the heavy pistol, squeezing an eye shut. The thick barrel wavering, he fired again. The gun roared, sending black powder smoke billowing in front of him. The bullet struck granite near the tunnel.

"Matt!" Riley shouted. "Matt, shoot him!"

Anders winced. When nothing happened, he bared yellowed teeth in a grin. Refining his squint-eyed aim, his finger tightened on the trigger. "Reckon I done got the range now."

The first rifle shot took the hat off Anders's head and sent it sailing in a lazy arc high into the morning sky. With smoke drifting out of a deadfall to Riley's right, the second shot plowed the ground inches from the Anders's horse's front hoofs, spraying dirt and pebbles. The nag snorted and tried to rear up. Front hoofs lifting a few inches, the animal came down heavily, listed to one side, and peed.

Dad Anders dropped his gun. Using his good hand, he grabbed the saddle horn and managed to stay aboard the leaning horse. His son, eyes wide with fear, yanked a rein while administering a severe kicking to his sway-backed plug. The horse turned and walked out of the clearing in slow retreat.

"The stink of death!" Jimmy yelled. "I've got the stink of death on me!"

Riley turned his attention from Dad Anders to Jimmy. The red-haired man came to his knees over the ashen corpse, his face sheet-white, hands frantically brushing fouled dirt and pine needles from his clothing. Beyond him Matt materialized out of a deadfall as soundlessly as a ghost from the nether regions of the forest. This spirit was armed with a repeating rifle.

Anders stared in disbelief. The ghostly figure coming out of the trees was a dead ringer for the man he had meant to kill.

"Next time," Riley shouted angrily, "don't wait so long to shoot! Hear me?"

"I hear you." Matt jacked a fresh round into the breech and strode out of the morning shadows into the sunny meadow. He brought his Winchester to bear on Dad Anders.

Riley turned to the outlaw, a man clearly baffled by the sight of twins. Riley ordered him to leave under threat of death.

"I'll ride," Anders conceded, "but, damn it, one of ye done wronged me . . . kilt my boys, and hurt me bad. I had to swap my good horses to pay a doctor, an' after the sawbones cut a little bullet outen me, I hurt worser." He drew a ragged breath. "How am I gonna make a living now? Answer me that, ye murdering bastard."

"Don't you sound pitiful," Riley said. "Want us to take up a collection?"

Anders roundly cursed him.

From the trees behind him came a boy's shouted plea: "Pa! Pa!"

Amid another round of dry retching from Jimmy, the outlaw's aged horse slowly righted itself. Dad Anders turned the animal. He made his way out of the meadow, leaving his pistol in a pool of horse urine. He did not retrieve his hat, either, as he followed the plodding, sway-backed plug ridden by his son.

Jimmy got to his feet. He staggered away from the grave, cursing Riley for breaking his word. "You lied. You brought your trigger-happy brother."

Riley gazed at him. "Good thing I did."

"The hell," Jimmy said angrily. "I trusted you, you lying son-of-a-buck. . . ."

"Don't underrate Dad Anders," Riley broke in. "If Matt hadn't been here, we'd both be dead."

"That was Dad Anders?"

Riley nodded. "Anders would have gunned me down out of revenge, and he'd have shot you to silence a witness."

Jimmy offered no argument. His chest heaved. He surveyed his clothes, as though expecting to see caked blood from the corpse. "God, this stink is awful. I'm going to have to burn these clothes."

On the ride back to town, Jimmy continued to complain about the smell. He could not escape it, and feared the stink of rotting flesh had permeated his skin, a stench to plague him forever.

154

"Where are Anne Marie and Sarah?" Matt asked.

"I'm not telling you anything," Jimmy said dully.

"They're either in the sporting house or Collier's place, aren't they?" Matt asked. When Jimmy did not reply, he added: "If I have to kick in doors to find them, I will."

Jimmy turned to Riley. "See why I don't like this ugly brother of yours?"

"Ugly," Matt repeated with a scowl.

In Valmont City, Jimmy headed for Collier's mansion, his face pale as he hunched over the saddle. Matt and Riley followed the main route through town. The brick-paved street was congested with heavy freight outfits, ore wagons, tankers, and numerous passenger coaches from Denver. The twins got separated by a line of bull trains.

In the saloon district at the far end of town, Matt drew rein. He turned in the saddle and looked back. He saw Riley gazing over his shoulder, his eyes fixed on something. Or someone.

Matt stood in the stirrups to see past a loaded freight wagon drawn by eight oxen. Leaning against a post in front of the Bulldog Saloon was a stout gent, short arms and bandy legs, one who might have passed for a bulldog himself. He wore a five-pointed star on his vest.

"Know him?" Matt asked when Riley caught up.

He nodded. "Tug Larkin."

After riding a distance down the street, Riley said: "Ochs sent his hound to sniff out the rabbit."

Matt asked: "Think he spotted us?"

"He couldn't see you for the traffic," Riley answered. "I'm the one he was looking at."

"How do you know Ochs sent him?"

"My description," Riley began, and corrected himself, "*our* description is posted all over Denver on flyers. Plenty of people saw me buy a coach ticket for this burg. Or maybe

155

Ochs made a lucky guess. Doesn't matter. Larkin's here. And now he knows I'm here."

Matt looked back. "He hasn't moved."

"Larkin will pick his time," Riley assured Matt. "He'll partner up with the local marshal, and they'll come after me." He asked: "You're staying?"

Matt nodded. "I gave my word."

"The noose sized for my neck," Riley reminded him, "fits yours, too."

"I'm not leaving Valmont City," Matt insisted. "Not without Anne Marie and Sarah."

Riley studied him. "How do you aim to do that?"

"Your scheme didn't work," Matt said. "So I reckon I'll take the straight route."

"That means kicking in doors," Riley asked, "and poking your gun into people's faces?"

"If that's what it takes," he replied.

"Sweet on Anne Marie, aren't you?"

Matt shook his head.

"Lying to your twin," Riley said, "brings bad luck."

"A proverb from Hoyt Wilcox?"

"No, I made that one up myself," he said. "Here's another one . . . 'Love blinds a man, blinds him and cripples up his brain.' "

"Is that what happened to you with Nell Bloom?"

Riley abruptly drew rein, face set in anger. "I won't have you speaking her name, brother. You never knew her. You don't know what you're talking about."

"Then finish your story," Matt said, "so I will know. Or do you aim to run before dawn?"

"I ought to knock you down, brother."

"You ought to try," Matt said. He paused. "Haven't we had this talk before?"

"This time I won't drop my shoulder."

"You aim to trade punches here in the street," Matt asked, "or go somewhere private?"

Their staring contest ended when Matt lifted the reins and signaled Riley to come with him. He rode on, wondering if Riley would follow. He did not look back. He did not have to. Over the rumble of wagons and the rough shouts of the teamsters crowding Valmont City at midday, he heard clip-clopping hoofs. The speckled gray gelding bearing the Two-Bar brand came along behind him.

For once Riley made no complaint about the choice of a campsite, which Matt noted. And he noted his twin had not cut and run, not yet, but had followed without objection as they returned to the aspen grove downrange from Valmont City.

"Hell, I'm not going to fight you, brother," he announced, dismounting. "Not now."

"When?" Matt asked.

He shook his head slowly. "Just let it go, will you?"

"No, I won't let it go," Matt said. "Are you going to tell me about that woman, or do I have to knock the words out of you?"

Riley was agitated, but his anger slowly gave way to a grin. "When I'm ready, I'll tell you."

"Before sunrise?"

"Yeah, before sunrise."

They spread their blankets in a small clearing by the creek. Matt backtracked on foot, and took up a position at the edge of the aspen grove. He returned to camp when he was satisfied they had not been followed by Jimmy or Tug Larkin, or anyone else. As a further precaution, though, he insisted on a cold camp. After tending their horses, they drank from the creek and opened tins for their supper. Afterward, they stretched out on the bedding, boots off, mirror images of one another as they listened idly to the gurgling creek.

Matt sat up and took out the makings. He methodically built a smoke, fired it, and waited. He knew better than to prod Riley further, believing he would speak when he was ready. Patience was rewarded. At last the words, never before spoken, came haltingly. Riley had described the moment he had first seen Nell Bloom strolling through a cemetery. Now he recounted her final resting place.

The cemetery overlooked the town, and from it Riley observed the teeming life below—men, women, and children going about the routines of their lives. From here they seemed to him to move in silence like ants on a mound, slow or fast, coming or going, all of them busy and filled with great purpose. Yet individuals were insignificant to one who watched from a distance.

The first time Riley found Nell stupefied by opium, he believed she was dying. Her nude body limp, her eyes closed, she lay sprawled on the bed, breathing shallowly. From that upstairs room of a "boarding house for ladies," Riley stepped into the hall and called to the madam.

Broad in the beam, she came huffing up the staircase and rushed down the narrow hallway, bumping into walls like a boat in a canal. Once in the room she leaned over Nell and covered her with a blanket. She assured Riley this girl would survive, that he should select another chippie in the parlor downstairs, or, if Nell was solely to his liking, he could come back another time with no additional charge for services rendered.

Riley did not believe in the existence of Cupid, the archer deity of ancient Rome said to be the son of Venus. But that night he learned love descends upon a mortal man like a supernatural force, and is not meant to be shed by any power short of death.

Worried, he called on Nell the next day in the parlor of the house. She was lethargic and heavy-eyed, but very much alive and glad to see him, as though nothing out of the ordinary had happened. Two days later, they picnicked on the grassy shoreline of an irrigation pond, ducking for cover during a rain squall that dropped hailstones like pearls from above. They collected half a dozen perfectly round ice balls the size of peas, only to watch them turn to water in the palms of their hands.

Nell had brought a silver flask. A gift from a client, it was engraved with her initials in swirls of elaborate script, and contained a pint of her favorite sour mash. While lightning flashed and thunder crashed, they drank whisky, laughed easily, and talked endlessly.

About what? Together often in the following weeks, they talked about everything and nothing, communicating even in long silences. For Riley, the warmth of her presence held more meaning than words. He remembered fragments—private jokes about pearls from heaven, comic observations that were meaningless to anyone else. What he recalled vividly was her laughter. It burst musically from her lips with a full smile and a toss of her head. Her gaze stirred him, tugged at him as one magnet pulls at another with invisible power. Never forgotten was his dizzying love for her, his certainty that she would leave the brothel for good, and ever after they would walk side by side, hand in hand.

Riley had first met her in the quiet place where she sought solitude. Three months later he stood by a gravesite on this grassy hill overlooking the town. He knelt and touched the granite marker bearing the name of his beloved, a polished, gray stone surface inscribed according to his instructions:

**So here we are,
Pondering life's ironies
As we wander among the dead,
You and I, the living.**

Matt broke a long silence. "She killed herself, didn't she?"
Riley did not answer.

At dawn they broke out of the aspen grove and headed for
town at a high lope. Dim light seeped into the horizon due
east. At an elevation of 10,120 feet above the sea, summer
days dawned swiftly, the fiery sun chasing cold shadows.

For once the twins had agreed on a course of action—they
would confront Maude Riley. If the Painter sisters were in her
sporting house, Matt and Riley would free them, at gunpoint
if necessary, and ride out, Denver-bound. If Anne Marie and
Sarah were not in the house. . . .

In truth, their plan was incomplete. Neither Matt nor
Riley relished the prospect of a gunfight with Eldon Collier's
hired men. Kicking in the front door of the clapboard house
in Valmont City's red-light district was the only logical next
step, and it was readily accomplished when Matt crossed the
porch, raised his right boot, and let go. One kick, and the
wood splintered in the doorframe. A second kick, and the
latch gave way. After his third kick, the door swung open,
banging against the papered wall of the entryway. Matt drew
his Colt and stepped inside. Riley came after him, Greener in
his hands.

The door to the first room on the left opened. Philip
lunged out, fists up. He was quickly followed by Maude
Riley, their faces registering alarm from the rude awakening.
The madam looked past Matt and Riley, her flinty gaze sur-
veying the broken doorjamb. She swore.

"That door wasn't locked, you ignorant cowboy," she
said, disgusted. "You coulda tried the handle . . . unless
you've never seen anything on a door but a latch string."

Matt regarded her. He turned to Philip. Bare-footed, the
bouncer wore a white satin nightgown with lace trim and red

ribbon drawstrings. Philip's enraged charge from the bedroom had abruptly halted when he saw the guns.

Fists opening, he raised both hands shoulder high. "You gonna rob us?"

Matt moved a pace closer to the big, bald man. "What kinda get-up are you wearing this fine morning, Philip?"

"What I wear is none of your damned business," he replied, adding: "You broke my nose."

"You came after me," Matt reminded him. "All I wanted was a couple questions answered." He eyed him again from the hairy toes of his bare feet to his cue ball head. "If you're gonna wear ladies' nightgowns, you probably ought to expect a question or two."

"You can go to hell," Philip said. "Put that gun down, and I'll fight you."

"You don't learn real good, do you, Philip?" Matt said, and holstered the revolver.

Maude Riley pushed past him. "Get out! Both of you drunken cowboys, get out . . . !" Her voice trailed off as her eyes darted from one uninvited guest to the other. "Good Lord, you're . . . you're . . . twins."

"Good guess," Riley said.

"One of you. . . ." Again her voice trailed off.

"One of us what?" Matt asked.

"Dunno who is who here," she said, "but one of you asked, did I ever give birth to twins. What's that all about?"

"Just a simple question," Matt answered. "What's the answer?"

"No!" she replied. "That's your answer. I never borned a child, not one, and sure as hell not twins." She paused and repeated an earlier statement. "Don't you start rumors about me killing babies."

"We're not here to start rumors," Matt said.

"Then why are you here, busting up my place?"

Matt looked past her. Down the hall, doors had eased open. The sleepy faces of young women peered out.

"Take us to Anne Marie and Sarah," Matt said. "We'll leave as soon as they pack their bags."

"Them two aren't here," Maude Riley said.

Matt cast a doubting look at her.

"You can bust down every door in this place," she said. "You won't find them here. I won't allow neither one on the premises. One whimpering, the other threatening me. . . . Eldon sent a couple men to take those crying bitches away in his Concord. He can have them."

Riley stepped forward a pace. "Collier made a cash loan to Sarah, and then you stole it from her after she drank loaded tea. Did you return the money to him?"

Maude Riley vigorously shook her head. "I had nothing to do with it. That's the truth. Talk to Eldon, not me."

Hats off, Matt and Riley lay prone in the empty haymow. They peered out of the access doorway, looking past the pulleys and ropes of the block and tackle to Eldon Collier's mansion and carriage house. After leaving Maude Riley's Sporting House, Matt had led the way to the empty barn. They had slipped in from the alley, tied their horses, and climbed the ladder to the mow.

Now, shaded from the rising sun, Matt and Riley observed the great mansion like a pair of birds perched in a treetop. Surveillance had been Riley's suggestion. He wanted to watch the goings-on at the mansion and carriage house before making a move.

Matt went along even though the plan was not to his liking. He figured Maude Riley would send a runner to warn Collier, giving the gunmen time to prepare. The hour was early, though, and so far no one had come in or out of the mansion. Not the carriage house, either. The sliding door was partially closed. If the black coach and horses were in there, he could not see them. From here he detected no movement in the interior shadows. Collier's men had not shown themselves yet.

The morning air grew fragrant with the pungent odors of coal and woodsmoke as cook fires were stoked throughout the neighborhood. The rhythmic sounds of an axe biting into wood reached them. After another long half hour, Matt turned to Riley and again argued the direct approach was the best one.

"Charge the carriage house," he said, "and disarm the gunmen. Then we'll bust into the mansion, knock Jimmy on his butt, and take Anne Marie and Sarah away from Collier."

Riley listened, shaking his head. "Brother, a plan like that will get us shot to pieces."

"Not if we surprise them."

"We're outnumbered and outgunned," Riley countered. He paused. "If we can't figure out a way to slant the odds in our favor, those jokers will cut us down."

"Odds and jokers," Matt repeated. "You see everything through a gambler's eyes."

"Life's a gamble," Riley replied.

"Is that what Hoyt Wilcox used to tell you?"

"Matter of fact, he did."

Matt raised up on his elbows. "This gamble's worth taking."

"Those gunmen are armed to the teeth. . . ."

Matt cut him off when he pointed to the four chimneys of the mansion. "Look."

"I don't see anything."

"That's what I mean," Matt said. "No smoke."

Riley looked out there. "Maybe they're sleeping late." He thought about that. "Or they've been warned, and they're laying for us."

"More likely," Matt said, "the place is empty. Can you see the Concord coach in the carriage house?"

"No."

"Horses?"

"No."

Matt edged back. "Me, neither."

"Where're you going?"

"To find out if Mister Eldon Collier is home this fine morning."

Riley briefly protested. Then, drawing a deep breath, he followed his twin to the ladder and descended it. After checking his weapon, he followed Matt out of barn shadows into the morning sunlight.

They hurried down the alley to the next cross street where Collier's mansion dominated the other residences. In a one-story house across the street, Matt caught a glimpse of the nosy neighbor woman. Curtain pulled aside, she peered at them through her front window as they angled across the street. She ducked away when she knew she had been spotted.

Matt found the carriage house empty. The black Concord coach was not there, and the horse stalls stood vacant. No sign of the hired men, either. He turned and jogged across the yard to the mansion's columned porch. Riley came behind him. They mounted the steps and strode to the front door. Recalling Maude Riley's admonition an hour ago, Matt reached out and grasped the handle. He turned it. The door opened silently on machined steel hinges.

Matt glanced back at Riley. They entered, guns drawn.

No one was in the foyer. Matt caught Riley's eye and

touched a finger to his lips. They stood still for several moments among the framed paintings, polished wood furnishings, and an oak newel at the bottom of the staircase. Both men were alert for the creak of an upstairs floorboard, the click of a door latch, hushed voices—any sound in this cavernous place.

Silent as a tomb, Matt thought.

With Riley following, he moved to the door of the library, his footfalls cushioned by the thick carpeting. The door was closed. Matt reached for the handle and turned it. He pushed the door open. The dry odor of dust filled his nostrils.

Believing the room to be empty, he stepped in. His gaze was drawn to the floor safe beyond a leather armchair and ottoman in the far corner. The corvette had sailed. The thick steel door bearing a painted image of a sailing vessel bucking rough seas stood open. The safe was empty.

Matt eased into the room ahead of Riley. He saw a man's arm on the floor, his lifeless hand upturned. The sleeve of a blood-splattered white shirt was neatly held by a gold cufflink bearing engraved initials—**EC**.

Matt moved beside the corpse and dropped to one knee. The arm belonged to Eldon Collier. The carpet was blood-soaked where the big man lay sprawled on the floor near the safe, eyes wide open as though horrified even in death.

"Shotgunned," Riley said, his voice hollow. "Close range. Just like Miss Augusta Benning."

Chapter Eleven

"Whoever killed him, robbed him, too."

Matt nodded agreement. Shifting his gaze from the fatal wound where a load of buckshot had shredded fabric and peppered flesh in Collier's chest, he looked at the empty shelves in the safe. A small strongbox was in there, open and empty, too.

"We'd better get out of here," Riley said. He turned and headed toward the door.

Matt stood. "Run before dawn?"

Riley halted. "What's your half-assed plan this time, brother . . . wait around so Tug Larkin can lynch you?"

"I remember hearing you talk about settling the score," Matt said. "Something about honoring the memory of a woman named Nell Bloom."

"And I recollect telling you," he countered, "that I aim to live a long life."

"I'm not leaving," Matt repeated. "Not until I find Anne Marie and Sarah."

"What if they're not . . . ?" His voice trailed off.

Matt filled in the missing word: "Alive?"

Riley nodded. "Maybe the killer of Miss Augusta Benning came here."

Matt eyed him. "What's the connection?"

"Don't know how it adds up," he said. "But I've seen two people shotgunned, and, it turns out, they were once married. All I know is, we'd better get out of here. . . ."

Matt moved past him. "Alive or dead, I aim to find Anne Marie and Sarah."

He left the library and headed across the foyer to the staircase. Grasping the handrail, he took the carpeted stairs two at a time. At the landing, the image of Augusta Benning regarded him in her fixed stare. As he turned and headed down the hall, he glimpsed Riley coming behind him.

The door to the first bedroom was locked. When Matt rattled the handle, he heard a woman's gasp, then hushed voices.

"Anne Marie? Is that you?"

"Matt?" she asked, and then shouted: "Matt! Sarah and I are in here! The door's locked!"

"I'll get you out," he said. He gauged the distance, raised his boot, and kicked the door—once, twice, three times. Instead of giving way, it withstood repeated kicks.

Riley watched, grinning. "Looks like I was right."

"Right about what?"

"From the day we first met," he replied, "I figured you must be part mule."

Matt cast an annoyed glance at him, and kicked the door again to no avail.

"Half mule," Riley went on, "and two-thirds ignorant cowboy."

Matt turned to him in sharp anger. "I thought you were leaving this hayseed territory."

"A bumpkin like you," he answered, "needs to be told to unlock that door."

"How the hell can I unlock it . . . ?" Matt stopped. He remembered the ring of keys Collier had pulled from his pocket. The last time they stood here, the man had unlocked this door.

"Are we recollecting the same thing?"

Matt nodded. "Keys."

"Keys," Riley confirmed.

"Wait here," Matt said. He gestured to the Greener in Riley's hands. "Keep an eye out. There's plenty of room to hide in this place, if that's Jimmy's game."

With a last word to Anne Marie through the door, Matt turned and strode down the hallway to the staircase. He bounded down the stairs and crossed the foyer, noticing now that he and Riley had left the front door standing open.

In the library he knelt beside the body of Eldon Collier. His gaze moved from the awful wound to the dead man's open-eyed countenance. Even though he knew what must be done, rifling the pockets of a dead man ran contrary to his instincts. As a scout for the Army, he had seen corpses, some mutilated by man or beast, but he had never been ordered to search one.

Matt looked at the stilled face with a graying spade beard, recalling a loud and bombastic man, aggressive and overbearing. While serving under the flag, he had known cavalry officers of Collier's ilk, prideful men roundly hated by soldiers in their command, yet obeyed without question. Then he realized the tic was gone. Reaching out, he closed the staring eyes with his fingertips. For this old soldier, the war was over, the suffering ended.

In Collier's pockets he found a folding wallet of red Moroccan leather, a sterling silver cigar holder, an ivory-handled penknife of Sheffield steel, a Waltham pocket watch, and a plain brass ring of keys. Key ring in hand, he got to his feet. After a last look at the corpse, he left the library.

In the foyer the morning sunlight streamed in through the front doorway. A single beam shone on Collier's portrait, a rich glow illuminating the stern face. Matt glanced at it as he crossed the foyer, and hurried up the stairs. At the landing he came under the stony gaze of Augusta Benning again. He wondered if there was a connection between the murders, or even if there was any way to find out now that both were dead. Pushing the thought away, he strode down the hallway to the door where Riley waited.

The fourth key released the latch. Turning the handle, Matt shoved the door open. He entered a high-ceilinged room furnished with a settee and ladderback chair, maple washstand and bureau. Anne Marie and Sarah sat close together, huddled on a brass bed near the wall to his right.

Matt saw bruised faces. Terror lingered in their eyes. The sisters gazed at him as though all hope had been lost and this rescue was too good to be true. The moment passed, and fear gave way to tentative smiles of relief.

Anne Marie stood. She crossed the room. Holding her arms out, she stepped into Matt's embrace, and held him tightly.

"I'm taking you out of here," he whispered.

The urgency of the moment was unspoken, but clearly understood. With no words uttered, the sisters rushed to pack clothing, toiletries, combs and hairpins, and spare high-button shoes. Within minutes they headed down the wide staircase, following Matt and Riley to the foyer.

Anne Marie paused, her gaze moving to the library door. Matt halted. When she turned to him, he shook his head.

"Something terrible happened, didn't it?" she said.

Matt nodded.

"We heard a gunshot last night. . . ." Anne Marie did not finish.

"Collier's dead," Matt said. "Come on," he added, and knew immediately he was too late. A drumbeat of footfalls on the porch reached him as he spoke.

Maude Riley trooped in through the open door. She was followed by Philip. The bouncer of the sporting house wore a narrow-brimmed felt hat and a tailored suit. His pin-striped vest over a white shirt and starched collar showed a gold watch chain. A black tie was held in place by a diamond stickpin, and his black boots were polished to a gleam.

"Nice duds," Matt said.

Philip cursed, his fists clenching.

Maude Riley waved him away like a pesky housefly. She eyed the luggage. "Appears you folks are leaving the district."

The madam was dressed in her finery. She wore a plumed hat and a long, dark brown dress decorated with gold sequins. Styled with wildly puffed sleeves, the outfit seemed to require only a flapping of her arms to take flight like some great, gaudy bird of prey. Through the doorway behind her, Matt saw a high-wheeled, one-horse carriage standing at the mansion gate.

Maude Riley gave the sisters a second look, and glanced around. "Where is everybody?"

"You're right," Matt said. "We're leaving."

"Hold on, cowboy," she said, lifting a hand as she faced him. "I've been thinking about what you said."

"Said about what?" he asked.

"Twins," she said. "I finally put it all together. At first, I thought you were accusing me of burying smothered babies in the flowerbeds of my establishment. You wouldn't be the first to start rumors about the reason for my pansies blooming so bright and velvety." She drew a breath. "But now I've got this thing figured out. You two are on a search. Hunting your ma, aren't you? And somehow you think I'm the one."

Riley muttered: "God, I hope not."

Maude Riley whirled to face him, and loosed a string of curses. "One of you is a sight worse than the other, but right now I can't keep it straight who's who."

Matt was struck speechless, not by her soft, growling curses, but by the sensation that everything that had happened from the time he first laid eyes on his twin had led to this moment. With Anne Marie and Sarah looking on in watchful silence, Matt found his voice. He repeated his question.

"Did you . . . did you ever give birth to twins?"

"I told you the truth," Maude Riley replied, "and Philip drove me here so I can tell you again. I never borned twins . . . not twins nor no other babies. So help me, cowboy, that's the truth." She looked past him. "Now, where's Eldon?"

Matt did not answer.

"Well?" Maude Riley demanded.

Riley said: "We found him in the library."

"Found him," she repeated, turning to him.

"Someone shot him," Riley went on. "He's dead."

Philip made a guttural sound. Maude Riley stood as still as a statue for a tortured moment. "Dead," she whispered, tears welling in her eyes. "Dead."

Philip charged past them and strode into the library. Almost immediately, he came back, face pale. "Stay out of there, Maudie. Stay out."

Maude Riley faced the twins, rivulets of tears coursing down the deep wrinkles in her powdered cheeks. "What'd you kill him for?" Her gaze darted from one to the other. "Where's Jimmy? Did you gun him down, too?"

Before either Matt or Riley could answer, Anne Marie spoke up. "They didn't kill anyone," she said. "They weren't even here when Mister Collier was shot. Sarah and I heard it last night, late. One loud shot. That's what we heard."

Maude Riley wiped her tears. She regarded Anne Marie and Sarah. "Did you see who pulled the trigger?"

"No," Anne Marie replied. "Mister Collier locked us in a bedroom upstairs. Jimmy came in and beat us with his fists. He threatened to kill us if . . . if we didn't do what he wanted.

Then, later in the night, we heard the shot." She repeated: "One loud shot."

Maude Riley's eyebrow lifted. "Truth is, you don't know who killed him."

"But Matt and Riley couldn't have," Anne Marie protested. "They didn't get here until this morning. . . ."

"You didn't see them until this morning," she corrected her.

Philip eyed the Greener in Riley's hands. "Whoever done this killing used a shotgun."

Riley turned to him. "Two of Collier's men carry cut-down shotguns."

"Before you start accusing anyone," Matt said, "we need to know where Jimmy ran off to."

Matt saw Philip edge to the door. The big man tilted his head toward the doorway in a silent signal to Maude Riley.

She stiffened. "Fetch the marshal, Philip."

"Don't have to," he replied.

Maude Riley cast a hard look at him, as if he had dared to disobey.

"Marshal's standing right out there by the gate," Philip went on, pointing to the doorway. "Him and another man."

Matt moved to his left and looked outside. So did Riley. The town marshal was there. Tug Larkin stood at his side. Both men held lever-action repeating rifles.

Matt was aware of sudden movement. Maude Riley rushed past him. She cleared the doorway. A step behind, Philip ran for his life, too, quickly overtaking the madam on the porch. He jumped the steps and sprinted ahead of her to the gate, one hand holding his hat in place on his bald head. With her long dress hiked above her bony white knees, Maude Riley leaped awkwardly down the steps like a flushed turkey. She ran the length of the stone walk through the front gate, passing the marshal and Larkin. She circled the one-horse carriage and ducked behind the vehicle with Philip, both of them cowering there as though expecting to be shot.

"Brother," Riley said, "this could be trouble."

Matt nodded.

"Who sent for the law?" Riley asked.

"Neighbor lady across the street, most likely," he replied, and told him about the woman he had seen in the house. She'd had time for a quick hike to alert the marshal of armed men skulking about.

"What's your plan for busting out of this place?" Riley asked. "You aim to set off bombs and burn it down?"

Matt shook his head. "As the horse soldiers say . . . 'When in doubt, charge.' "

"The hell," Riley said. He looked at him in alarm. "We can't charge them. . . ."

"We don't have much choice," Matt interrupted. "Or time, either."

Anne Marie exclaimed, "But you're innocent . . . !"

Riley broke in: "See that deputy out there? Guilty or innocent, he has a noose waiting for me."

"Come out!" the marshal shouted. "Come out so we can talk this over! You men ain't been accused of a crime! Lay your firearms down and come out!"

Riley turned to Matt. "Jimmy did it, didn't he?"

"I figure Jimmy and those hired gunmen planned to rob Collier all along," Matt said. "They were just waiting for the right time."

Matt drew a deep breath. A strange sensation swept over him as he faced the probability of a deadly confrontation with those two lawmen by the gate. He could hear Maude Riley's voice. No doubt she was accusing him and Riley of killing Eldon Collier. He had no doubt, either, that by now Tug

Larkin had told the marshal of the murder of Miss Augusta Benning in Denver.

More than mere disbelief, a sense of complete estrangement from reality washed over him like a hot wave. Three weeks ago he would never have believed he'd be on the wrong side of the law, a hunted man accused of murder. Now his only chance for survival was to escape arrest—and if he succeeded, he'd have to flee the territory like a common criminal.

"Jimmy killed Collier?" Anne Marie asked in a low voice.

"No other reason for him to fly the coop," Riley answered, "along with the three jokers Collier hired for protection. They must have forced him to open his safe, or spied on him until he spun the combination. Either way, they cleaned him out before he had a chance to leave Valmont City." He paused. "Collier wasn't a man to fold. Jimmy or one of those toughs must have gunned him down. Then they loaded up the coach and rolled out of here in the night." Riley looked at Matt. "Is that how you see it, brother?"

Matt nodded. He heard, but as in a waking dream; the image of black horses filled his mind, a team of six pulling a black Concord coach into the night. At once Matt recalled the tale of the phantom stallion, and he visualized a white horse galloping across the snowy plain, forever free of man's cruelty.

The marshal shouted again. This time he ordered the two women to come out. Anne Marie glanced at Sarah, and turned to the twins. "We'll tell that marshal the truth," Anne Marie said. "Then he'll go after Jimmy."

"A hundred to one says he won't," Riley said. "Make that a thousand to one."

"What makes you think that?" she asked.

"It's a safe bet Larkin aims to collect the reward on me,"

Riley said. "Here's a side bet for you . . . a miner's court in Valmont City will take five minutes to find Matt and me guilty of killing Collier. They won't try to sort out which one of us pulled the trigger. Local gents will vote, and they'll hang us from the nearest head frame. After we've kicked our last kick, they'll celebrate justice in a saloon."

The marshal called out: "I'm a patient man, but you're trying me! Come outta there! Send the women out first. Then you all come out so we can talk this over, peaceable."

Matt shook off the lingering images of the charging black horses and a galloping white stallion, all of them crossing an endless snowfield in the geography of his imagination. He brought himself back to reality and turned to the sisters. "As soon as you get past that gate," he said, "walk as far as you can, as fast as you can. You'll be safe if you. . . ."

"No!" Sarah exclaimed.

Matt looked at her. He was surprised by the tone of the voice from the woman who had barely ever spoken.

"You helped us," Sarah went on with a glance at her sister. "Now we'll help you. Won't we, Annie?"

Anne Marie nodded agreement, but gazed at her in silence, clearly wondering what they could possibly do now.

"Help yourselves by getting out of here," Matt insisted, "before bullets and buckshot start flying." When neither sister moved, he stepped closer and shouted: "Get out! Get out of here, or I'll lock you in that bedroom upstairs!"

Sarah drew back, clearly offended by his threat and shocked by his harsh tone.

Anne Marie watched soberly. "Come on, Sarah," she said in a low voice, and picked up her carpetbag. She moved into the doorway. With a last troubled look at Matt, Sarah grasped the handle of her valise and followed her sister outside.

Matt watched them stride to the gate, side by side, shoulders squared. Anne Marie leaned close to her sister and spoke to her, too far away for him to hear her words.

Riley asked: "You all right, brother?"

Matt nodded.

"You look a little pale around the gills."

Matt faced him. "I know what we have to do."

"You still figure on charging those jokers?"

"Our only chance is to rout them," Matt said, "before that marshal sends for help. If we wait until we're surrounded, we're dead."

"Charging into the guns of lawmen doesn't seem like a plan for a long and happy life, either."

Matt conceded the point. "Reckon you're right."

"Why is it?" Riley demanded suddenly.

"Why is what?"

"Every time you agree with me," Riley said, "it's bad news. Every damned time. Why is that?"

Matt turned at the sound of raised voices. "Look."

A fierce argument had erupted between Anne Marie and Maude Riley. Matt saw them standing, nose to nose, bent at the waist as they shrieked at one another. The madam suddenly lashed out, clawing at Anne Marie's face. Anne Marie did not retreat. She straightened, dodged the slashing fingernails, and batted her opponent's hands away. Then she knocked the plumed hat off Maude Riley's head. Grabbing a handful of gray hair, she yanked with both hands as she raised a foot and kicked at her shins.

Matt and Riley stared. They watched the two women tussle, rocking violently back and forth in a push-and-pull struggle until both went down. With one on top and then the other, slapping and kicking, they rolled into the brick gutter. The two lawmen stood by, watching, their expressions showing a mixture of helplessness and keen interest.

Philip moved in and tried to pull them apart. Sarah darted behind him, unseen. As he bent over, she hiked her skirt, drew her foot back, and kicked him between the legs. The point of her shoe found the target. He gasped, color draining from his face. Sarah pushed him down, or tried to. Philip stumbled, but caught his balance. He came upright and wheeled, scowling at her. His hand shot out, grabbing her forearm. Nearly pulled off her feet, Sarah lowered her head and bit him. Howling, the big man released her and danced away, clutching his bleeding wrist.

Maude Riley's carriage rocked as the tethered horse tried to rear up and kick over the traces. Tied at the hitching post, the animal could not escape the frightening disturbance behind him. A rear hoof shot out, striking the marshal's lower leg. Dropping the rifle, he hopped twice and fell to the street, writhing as he grasped his leg.

Tug Larkin gave the panicked horse a wide berth and tried to break up the fight. Sarah bent down and picked up the marshal's rifle. Holding it by the barrel in both hands, she raised it skyward, paused, and brought it down in a chopping motion. The butt struck Larkin at the base of his thick neck. Staggered, he took a step back and slowly sank to his knees. Sarah backed away with a look of amazement. She turned the rifle, grabbing at the stock while she reached for the trigger. Swinging the barrel in a wide arc from left to right, she brought it to bear on the men.

From this distance Matt could not hear her words, but clearly she was taking command of the situation. Philip and the marshal raised their hands shoulder high. Larkin was still down, dazed. Matt saw Anne Marie stand, brushing dirt and débris from her dress. Puffed sleeves torn, the madam tried to get to her feet. Anne Marie moved closer and planted a foot in the middle of her back, pushing her into the gutter, face down.

Matt and Riley exchanged a glance. Without a word, they ran outside, crossed the porch, and leaped down the steps. Guns up, they sprinted along the stone walk to the gate, needlessly covering Philip and the marshal. The lawman was up and limping now.

Sarah edged close to Matt. Turning her back to the others, she whispered: "How do you shoot this big gun?"

Matt grinned. "Doesn't look like you'll need to."

She looked down at her shaking hands. "I've never been so scared in my life."

"I'm proud of you, sis," Anne Marie said, backing away from Maude Riley.

Matt turned to Philip. "Give your lady a hand. We're going into the mansion." He turned to the lawman. "Marshal, looks like Larkin needs a little help, too."

The marshal glowered, but offered no argument.

Matt and Riley stood by while the marshal hefted a dazed Tug Larkin to his feet. Philip helped Maude Riley out of the gutter. The side of her cheek was scraped raw in a bleeding abrasion. She roundly cursed Anne Marie and lunged at her. Philip restrained her, eyeing the guns trained on them.

Matt waved his Colt toward the open door of Collier's mansion. "Get a move on. All of you."

Chapter Twelve

With Anne Marie and Sarah riding behind their saddles, Matt and Riley made their way out of Valmont City. On the outskirts of the business district, they joined the congested freight road where it descended a long hill stubbled by pine stumps. The road curved past the steam-powered sawmill and angled around heaps of sawdust into the first of a maze of cañons between this mining district and the territorial capital of Denver.

The horses were well rested, and the twins held a pace as fast as they dared without jostling their passengers. Even so, the ride was uncomfortable for both women, and rest stops were frequent. At every stop, Matt and Riley reined their mounts into the trees beside the road and watched their back trail, guns drawn. In the lengthening shadows of afternoon they breathed easier—the usual traffic, but no sign of mounted riders. Matt recalled that Greta Schumann had quoted the marshal's complaint that he had been unable to raise a posse to pursue and capture Dad Anders. Maybe the same absence of civic duty in the Valmont mining district precluded a chase now.

At Collier's mansion, Matt and Riley had marched the limping marshal, Tug Larkin, Philip, and Maude Riley into the library, leaving them locked inside with the corpse. Matt had little doubt the three men would be able to force the door, but the task would not be easy or accomplished quickly. Meanwhile, he and Riley would put some distance between themselves and Valmont City. Without a posse nipping at their heels, they would be safe.

Riley conceded no posse was in close pursuit, but he held to his theory. "Larkin figures we'll head for Denver. He'll put his nose to the ground and take up our trail." Riley paused. "That's why I'm leaving town. Hell, I'm leaving the whole territory in a cloud of dust before the next lynch mob comes for me."

"But you're innocent!" Anne Marie said. "Isn't there any justice?"

"Justice," Riley scoffed. "I haven't seen *any* justice in this territory. Right now, Jimmy and those hired guns are rich. They got away with murder. There's your justice."

Matt turned to Sarah. "Speaking of money," he said, "you won't have to worry about the trumped-up debt of eight hundred dollars. That whole scheme died with Collier."

"Now I'm back where I started," she said.

"How's that for justice?" Riley asked ironically.

When they reached a familiar turn-off, Matt suddenly reined up. Seeing the abrupt movement, Riley turned his horse and reached for his shotgun until he saw Matt studying the ground. Wheel tracks and the imprints of shod hoofs were visible here—a dim trail leading upslope into the trees. This was the little-used wagon road that led to the abandoned mine Riley had salted. Not so much a road as a winding track through the forest, it was wide enough, barely, for an ore wagon's passage.

The twins exchanged a glance, but held their silence while a line of bull trains passed. The outfits rumbled by, each with a bearded, gun-toting teamster walking alongside his team of oxen, whip in hand.

"You thinking what I'm thinking, brother?"

Matt nodded. "Reckon so."

Anne Marie smiled. "You two are starting to think alike now?"

"No," Matt answered immediately.

"Yes," Riley said with a grin.

Anne Marie asked: "Well, what are you two thinking?"

"Matt and I happen to know that set of wheel ruts leads to an abandoned mine," Riley said, pointing to the trail winding through the forest. "If Jimmy's looking for a place to hole up, that one fills the bill."

Over his shoulder Matt said to Anne Marie and Sarah: "Wait here, while we look into it. . . ."

"Sarah and I have come this far," Anne Marie interrupted. "We'll stay with you."

Matt turned in the saddle. He gazed at her, ready to argue until he saw the determined look in her eye, an attitude he had come to recognize—and respect. Matt drew his Colt. He urged his mare off the road.

Five hundred yards upslope, the trail led into the clearing where Cornish miners had opened the tunnel to follow a vein of gold into the massive granite formation. Anne Marie gasped, surprised by the sight of a black coach, and at once repelled by a mighty stench. Hand covering her nose and mouth, she moaned. Sarah did the same.

When Riley entered the clearing behind Matt, he commented—"I'll be damned."—reining up.

The black Concord stood before them, in the middle of the clearing, tongue down, doors open. No horses in sight. No living men, either. A horrible stench of death wafted into the air, and beyond the empty coach Matt saw the two corpses on the rocky ground. Both had been dragged from their shallow graves by animals, the fabric of their clothing chewed and torn, rotting flesh gnawed, exposed innards pecked by birds. Anne Marie averted her eyes as Matt rode in a wide circle around the coach, passing the remains of Dad Anders' two sons. He drew rein suddenly, and dismounted.

"What're you doing?" Riley demanded.

Matt bent down. He picked up two gold coins on the ground. He briefly examined the half eagles, and handed one to Anne Marie and the other to Sarah.

"Jimmy and those gents must have been in a hurry," Matt said. He turned, thrust a boot in the stirrup, and mounted. "Looks like they divvied up the loot and rode out."

"That explains why we saw Collier's hired men breaking draft horses to saddle," Riley said. "They planned to use the coach to get out of Valmont City without raising suspicion. From here, they were on horseback."

Matt agreed, or started to. He was interrupted by Anne Marie and Sarah speaking in unison.

"Can we talk somewhere else?" the sisters said, speaking through their fingers.

On the second day the rump-bruising misery of riding double ended when a half empty coach came along. Riley flagged the vehicle. Agreeing to prorate the fare to be paid on arrival at the Denver station, Anne Marie and Sarah rode in the comfort of the coach while Matt and Riley followed on horseback. Still, the twins were cautious, looking back frequently to be sure they were not followed.

In Denver, Riley pointed out Wanted dodgers bearing their description. The flyers were posted on buildings and lampposts throughout the town. The reward had been raised to $500.

The two sisters spent the last of their money when they settled up with the ticket agent. Then they rode behind Matt and Riley, completing the three-mile distance to the Painter homestead on horseback.

Evening brought a prairie breeze. Gusts spiraled dust devils out of the ground like spirits. When the farm came in sight, the riders were greeted with shouts of joy. Micah and Samuel came running.

Dismounting in front of the log cabin, Matt handed down Anne Marie, briefly drawing her close. She gazed into his eyes and did not pull away, but when Riley swung down and helped Sarah to the ground, the boys leaped into the arms of their half-sisters. They hugged them while demanding to know all that had happened in Valmont City. Anne Marie and Sarah promised to tell them later, and inquired about the state of their father's health.

"Papa's bad sick," Samuel replied immediately.

Micah added: "He won't get out of bed."

Exchanging a swift glance, Anne Marie and Sarah told the boys to wait outside. Arm in arm, they turned away and hurried to the flat-roofed cabin, closing the door behind them.

Matt figured the sisters had talked it out by now, rehearsing what they would say to their father. He noted Sarah held on to Anne Marie as though braced for a storm. From their resolute manner, it was clear they had agreed to support one another in Paul Painter's presence.

Finding a patch of afternoon shade, Matt knelt and rolled a smoke, or tried to. A sudden breeze blew the shredded tobacco out of the paper. Turning his back to the gusting prairie wind, Matt shook tobacco from the sack again, rolled it, and sealed the paper with a quick lick. Another breeze kicked up just as he struck a match.

Riley sat nearby, hat pulled low on his forehead. Neither one of them had a tangible reason to tarry, but one sensed the other's intent. After all they had been through with the Painter sisters, the trek from the high mountains to the prairie was incomplete without a last good bye. The fight initiated in Valmont City by Anne Marie and backed up by Sarah had distracted the marshal long enough for Matt and Riley to make their move. They had thanked the sisters as they rode out of town, but both knew more than a few words of gratitude were due to repay the debt.

The flame danced and went out. Matt flung the cigarette away. He heard Riley ask: "What's the matter?"

"Not a thing."

"Bad luck to lie to your twin, remember?"

Matt did not answer.

"Something's caught in your craw," Riley said, pushing his hat up on his forehead. "What is it?" When Matt did not reply, Riley raised a fist. "Looks like I'll have to knock the words out of you."

Matt did not acknowledge the ribbing.

"This has something to do with Anne Marie Painter, doesn't it?" Riley said.

Matt exhaled. "More than that."

"More than what?"

Without explanation, Matt said: "You're right."

"I'm right . . . again?" He looked upward in a theatrical gesture, wincing as though expecting the sky to fall. "Must be something bad about to happen. I'm scared to ask, but . . . what am I right about?"

"Leaving the territory," Matt replied, ignoring his sarcasm. "I've come around in my thinking to agree with you. We can't stay here. We have to turn tail and run. Run before dawn."

Riley shrugged. "Could be worse, brother. The West is a big place. We'll make a fresh start somewhere. . . ."

"That's the difference between you and me," Matt broke in.

"What do you mean?"

"Look at you."

Riley looked down at himself. He brushed imaginary dirt from his clothing. "I don't look any worse than you do."

"That's not what I mean," Matt said. He lifted his gaze toward a darkening horizon. "You've been on the run all of your life. I've been settled, or looking for a place to settle. Ever since I went to work for Old John, I've been saving money and looking for a piece of ground that's right for me. Now we've got two murder charges hanging over our heads. No choice but to leave the territory." He paused. "You'll go your way, and I'll go mine. . . ." Matt looked at the cabin. Fashioned from cottonwoods, the flat-roofed structure was made of logs soon to rot and a roof bound to leak, an impractical design from top to bottom.

Riley eyed him. "Anne Marie was starting to fit into your plans, wasn't she?"

Matt turned away, jaw clenched. That was true, but he was even more troubled by the fact that he was a wanted man. Worse than a common outlaw, he had been branded in the territory as a murderer, and the pain of disgrace and dishonor was keenly felt.

The tow-headed boys, who had been watching from a distance, now edged closer. Both were silent, as wary as half-wild creatures testing the scent and mood of strange animals in their territory. They eyed the Colt revolver holstered on Matt's cartridge belt.

"Are you gunmen?" Micah asked suddenly.

Riley turned to him and grinned. He jerked a thumb at his twin. "He's the gunman."

"Don't listen to him," Matt said softly.

"My sister, Annie, says you're gunmen," Micah said. "Both of you."

"Just him," Riley insisted, dead pan.

Samuel asked: "Is that how folks tell you apart?"

"Yeah, that's it," Riley said with a laugh. "Matt's the shooter. I'm the talker."

Before Matt could set this matter straight, the cabin door swung open. His head snapped around when the door banged against the log wall. Anne Marie came out on the run. Matt saw tears streaming down her cheeks.

"We need a doctor!"

In the gathering darkness Matt made a hard ride to Denver. Guided by oil street lamps in town, he found Dr. Jefferson Drumm's office above the **Denver Dry Goods & Company** on Thirteenth Street. Blood speckled the floor where Drumm treated a patient knifed in a saloon fight. To save time, he sent Matt to the Wild Horse Livery for his buggy and horse. When Matt returned with the vehicle, Drumm had finished his bandaging job, casually noting this was the third time he had treated the man this month. Paid with a silver dollar, Drumm advised his patient to select his opponents with greater care.

"Find one you can defeat. . . ."

"Now, Doc," the man interrupted, "don't downgrade my reputation. All I got was a cut or two . . . not bad, just enough to raise my temper. You oughta see how bad off the bastard is. He called me out, but I whupped up on him worser than he done me. He's danged lucky to be alive, and ever'body in this town knows it."

"Yes, yes," Drumm said, and sent him on his way. With an exasperated shake of his head, he snatched up his black bag and followed Matt down the staircase. From town, they rushed to the Painter homestead.

"A younger man might have weathered the wintry chills and blazing fevers of this consumptive sickness. But your father . . . well, I am sorry he did not. Deeply sorry."

Matt overheard the heartfelt condolences from Drumm.

He had noticed the voice did not match the man. Short in stature, he stood barely five feet, but spoke in the deep, compassionate voice of a gentle giant. When Drumm emerged from the Painter cabin, Matt watched him close his doctor's bag and toss it into his buggy. Climbing in, he sat on the tufted seat and took up the reins.

Before driving away, he turned to Anne Marie and Sarah in the doorway. The boys peered around their sisters.

"The Reverend Wilbur Henry Knowles is a good man," Drumm said. "He can help you with burial arrangements and a funeral service." He added: "If you wish, I shall notify him of your loss."

With the boys clinging to their sisters' dresses, Anne Marie and Sarah gazed at one another, their expressions empty. That Paul Painter's death was not entirely unexpected did little to relieve the shock of it. He had been conscious when his daughters arrived, but then his eyes closed. Until moments ago Anne Marie and Sarah had hoped the doctor would somehow revive their father, that a fine medical procedure would awaken him from a deep sleep. Instead, Drumm had spread a blanket over the corpse, and stepped back, head bowed as he offered condolences.

"Yes," Anne Marie murmured now. "Yes, thank you very much."

"We have no money to pay you, sir," Sarah added. "We can send eggs with the boys in a day or two. . . ."

Clearly not surprised by an offer of barter for medical services, Drumm declined it without mention of obvious charity. "I have done nothing to warrant payment of any kind," he said, and with a last look at the distraught family, the doctor lifted a gloved hand in parting and drove away.

Perhaps it was the sight of a lynch rope meant for him, but, for whatever reason, Riley had come to believe his existence was defined by cemeteries—"Terrain six feet closer to hell," as Hoyt liked to say—and that fatalistic notion swept over him again during the funeral service for Paul Painter. Memories of Hoyt Wilcox and Nell Bloom tumbled through his mind like boulders while he listened to the words intoned by a preacher unacquainted with the deceased, the text giving Painter the benefit of the doubt for, after all, his God-fearing daughters had summoned a man of the cloth to this cemetery for a proper burial. Surely there was hope for saving a soul from eternal damnation in the hereafter, and, as Knowles held his Bible before him, his voice rose in a spirited crescendo while he quoted the Holy Word and addressed the possibility of redemption.

Riley avoided the preacher's gaze. So far, he alone knew this sun-washed day was not the first time they had stood eye to eye. Knowles had been summoned by Hiram Ochs to the cell-block at a time when Riley was about as close to the business end of a gallows as a convicted man could get without paying the price. Even though Riley saw no sign of recognition in Knowles's double-chinned face, he held back, hat brim down, thinking again—*Can't seem to get away from folks who have laid eyes on me in this hayseed town.*

A chill ran through him when he realized Matt was unaware of this fact. His twin took the preacher aside and paid for the hearse rental and the funeral service. This was done surreptitiously while the Painter sisters' attention was fixed on the coffin. A commendable act, Riley thought, but noble as it was, he wished Matt would avoid looking the man straight in the eye while doing it.

Hoyt Wilcox had taught him to observe players across a gaming table, a practiced search for some flicker of recognition or an inclination for violence, and with this in mind Riley watched the minister's eyes. During the service Knowles was stone-faced, a pose giving Riley a measure of hope. As an inmate in the jail he had been clean-shaven, hatless. Now he and Matt sported mustaches, dark beard stubble of four days, and they wore full-brimmed stockman's hats. Occupied with his mission here, Knowles did not give either of them a second look.

Anne Marie held Micah's hand while Samuel clung to Sarah, both boys staring at the pine coffin lowered into the grave. Matt and Riley took turns shoveling dirt into the rectangular hole they had dug with a spade and pick brought from the Painter homestead. Dry clods of prairie soil burst into dark powder upon impact with the coffin, and stones struck it with hollow reports, unexpectedly loud sounds in a quiet place. The boys flinched while their sisters wept. When the burial was finished, they departed, all of the family members glancing back at a grave marked by a mound of freshly turned earth, nothing more.

Nightfall on the Painter homestead brought Anne Marie and her half-brothers outside. Matt heard sobbing when the cabin door opened and closed. Anne Marie held a lamp as she crossed the yard and climbed into the Conestoga wagon behind the boys. Light from within sent dim shapes moving across the sun-bleached canvas.

Matt heard them talking for several minutes while the sounds of weeping continued from the cabin. When the canvas wagon cover went dark, Anne Marie came out. She pulled down the flap after her and sought him out among the starlit shadows.

"Matt."

"Over here."

She reached out and found him, clasping his hand in both of hers.

"I hear Sarah crying," Matt said to her.

"She knelt at Father's bed," Anne Marie whispered. "I know she wanted to forgive him . . . and she wanted to be forgiven by him. But he passed away without a word to her." Anne Marie paused. "The boys don't quite understand Father's gone . . . gone from our lives forever. I told them he is with Mother in heaven, but they don't remember her. It all seems . . . fanciful to young minds. Fanciful and frightening." She added: "Even to me."

Matt drew her into his arms and held her. He felt her warmth and her soft breathing against him.

Anne Marie whispered: "You'll soon be gone, too."

"That's what I figured," Matt said, "until a while ago. I looked at you, and. . . ." He left the sentence unfinished.

She tipped her head back and gazed at him by the starlight.

"I love you," he whispered.

"Matt. . . ."

"Anne Marie, I love you," he said again louder. He wanted to shout the words, this truth the world must know, but he only held her close, as though pressing his feelings into her body.

"Oh, Matt, I love you, too," she whispered. "I have always believed fate sent you to me . . . but you have to leave. You have to. Tonight."

"Can't do that," he said with a smile.

"Matt, listen to me," she said, hands grasping his forearms with sudden urgency. "I know what kind of man you are. You're loyal and you're brave. But we both know Tug Larkin will come here."

"He'll bring Sheriff Ochs and a posse of townsmen with a lynch rope. Don't forget that," said a voice out of the darkness.

Matt swiftly turned at the sound of Riley's voice. "Snooping on us?"

"I couldn't help but overhear two lovebirds flapping their wings," Riley explained as he moved closer. He added with a chuckle: "Brother, I knew you had feelings for her before you did. Isn't that a fact?"

Matt said: "Reckon so."

"Anne Marie's giving you good advice," Riley went on. "Mount up, and we'll ride." When Matt did not reply or make a move to leave, Riley went on: "Think it through, brother. If Larkin catches up with you here, there'll be a gunfight with innocent women and children ducking bullets."

Matt did not concede the point.

Anne Marie said: "Remember when you shouted at Sarah and me?"

"Shouted," Matt repeated. "What're you talking about?"

"We were in the foyer of Collier's mansion," she said, "and you threatened to lock us in that bedroom where Jimmy left us."

"For your own good," Matt said.

"I know," she murmured. "Now I'm asking you to leave. For your own good."

He gazed at her.

"Sarah and the boys and I can fend for ourselves," she said, "just as we have ever since Father got sick." She paused. "I believe the time will come when you can return . . . after statehood, perhaps."

Matt gazed at her in the near-darkness. She seemed older than she was, he thought, as though the crucible of life experiences had given her strength and propelled her into adulthood. He did not argue, but he knew the fallacy of her first statement. Even though weakened and ill, the mere presence of Paul Painter had kept certain men from approaching his young daughters. Now Painter was gone. Word of his death would soon get around Denver.

Matt did not voice his opinion. Nor did he protest when Riley handed him the reins to his mare, saddled and ready to ride. Anne Marie came to him.

Matt held her again, whispered to her, and they kissed one last time. Her lips were soft and warm, her body taut in his arms. His emotions surged, and for some unknown reason the image of the corvette filled his mind, a sailing vessel bucking the high seas, alone in the storm. He was torn by a dilemma unlike any he had ever faced. Guided by instinct, he was determined to stay, determined to be with the woman he loved, now and forever. Yet at once he knew they were right. He knew it, but could not say the words out loud.

Anne Marie pulled away. She turned and walked to the cabin, a structure twelve feet square, with no windows, a plank door held in place by rawhide straps for hinges. Now bathed in the light of the stars, the cabin with its rusted stovepipe, the cockeyed barn, the broken-down Conestoga wagon—these represented the worldly possessions Paul Painter had bequeathed to his children.

Matt heard the creak of saddle leather behind him as Riley swung up. His twin offered no more persuasion. Turning the gelding, Riley rode away, a night shadow fading from his view.

Matt did not move for a long moment. The *clip-clop* of hoofs died out. He caught a last glimpse of Anne Marie as she entered the cabin and closed the door. Sarah had stopped sobbing. The night was suddenly still. Even the crickets were silent, as though somehow aware of Matt's inner turmoil. He drew a deep breath, and moved to the left side of his horse. Thrusting a boot in the stirrup, he grasped the horn, and mounted. He reined the mare around, and lightly spurred her into a canter to catch up with the gelding.

Chapter Thirteen

"You know I can't do this, don't you?"

Riley turned in the saddle and looked at his twin by starlight. "Can't do what?"

"I thought you were a mind reader."

"Not in the dark," Riley said as though stating an obvious fact. He asked again: "What is it you can't do?"

"Ride off and leave Anne Marie," Matt answered. "Who's going to look out for her and Sarah and those two boys?"

"Sounds like you are," Riley said. He drew rein. "What's your plan?"

Matt halted beside him. "Circle back."

"Where to?"

"I'll camp just over the crest of that rise north of their cabin," Matt replied. "If Ochs and Larkin bring a posse from Denver, I'll see them coming."

"Then what?"

"I figure by now Ochs knows we're twins," he replied. "He won't find us on the Painter place, and he'll hear the truth when Anne Marie tells him we left for parts unknown."

"So you figure he'll give up the chase and leave," Riley said.

"For now," Matt said.

"What about later?"

"All I know is," Matt said, "if anyone makes trouble for the Painter family, I'll be close enough to lend a hand."

Riley thought about that for a long moment. "You can't leave," he said, "and I can't stay."

"Looks that way."

Riley fell silent. "The time has come, hasn't it?"

"I didn't aim to part company like this," Matt said. "Not in the middle of the prairie on a dark night."

"Had to happen somewhere, sometime," Riley said. Saddle leather creaked when he leaned closer and held out his hand to shake.

Matt clasped his hand. For a long moment neither spoke.

"I reckon you know I'm grateful to you, brother," Riley said, his voice thick with emotion.

"Yeah," Matt replied. "I know."

Riley cleared his throat. "Tell you what. I'll leave your gelding at the Sixteenth Street Livery Barn, one week paid in advance. You can come for the plug when you're ready."

"All right."

"I saw you pay off that preacher at the cemetery," Riley said. "You must be rock-bottom busted by now."

"I've got enough."

"How much?" he persisted.

"About three dollars."

Riley scoffed. Coins clinked when he reached into his pocket. "Here's a few eagles to tide you over."

"I can't take your money. . . ."

"Sure, you can," Riley interrupted.

"But. . . ."

"Don't worry about me," Riley said. "I'll sit in on a few hands of poker tonight, and in the morning I'll be a passenger in the first coach out of this hayseed territory. Go on, take the money. Call it back rent, my payment for riding this big old castrated cow horse of yours."

After a moment Matt reached out and took the money from his hand.

Riley added: "Maybe we'll hook up again sometime."

"Yeah. Maybe so."

"Well, so long, brother."

"So long. Brother."

When Riley rode into Denver that night, he passed the sheriff's office and jailhouse. In the open field next to the building, the charred gallows in the starlight looked like the black skeleton of a creature from mythology. The sight of it sent his thoughts drifting to his twin, his mind reviewing all that had happened since Matt had freed him from a death sentence. Tonight, parting with him had been harder than he had imagined, much harder. But he had no other choice, really. Difficult as it was, this was the time to move on.

Five blocks farther he turned onto Sixteenth Street, swung down, and led the gelding into the livery barn. He boarded the animal, left his valise, and from there he went on foot, walking toward the saloon district and gambling halls beyond the Inter-Ocean Hotel.

To hell with playing it safe. He had decided to sit in on games of blackjack in Denver's largest gambling halls, moving from one establishment to another in the course of the night. That had been Hoyt's strategy when he was new in town—lose a few hands, win a big one, walk out—quick hits to avoid raising suspicions among dealers watchful for professional gamblers trying to blend in with the novices. The last time Riley had gambled in Denver he had played it safe. In the back room of the Longs Peak Saloon, he had sweated out a few measly dollars over a period of several hours—and barely averted a gunfight for his trouble. Low stakes meant low pay-offs. Looking back, he realized he had proven one of Hoyt's axioms: Wager small, win small.

All things considered, the risk of discovery by a lawman in one of the big gaming halls was minimal. The description on Wanted fliers posted around town made no mention of a mustache and scrubby growth of beard. As long as neither Ochs nor Larkin got a good look at him, close up, he could run high, wide, and handsome, and depart with a sizeable stake fattening his wallet.

Riley tensed as he walked along the boardwalk across the street from the Inter-Ocean Hotel. His troubles had begun there. With its decorative banners over a wide portico and flags at the corners on every floor, the four-story hotel loomed out of the night just as he remembered it. The polished lamp reflectors cast bright light across the portico and spilled onto the street, a summer's night gathering place where gents lit up pipes and puffed on cigars to discuss serious topics—money, women, horses.

Riley slowed his pace. He paused at the window of the Rocky Mountain House, wondering if Anne Marie would return to work in the café. Inside, he spotted the gaunt waiter Matt had identified as a "strange bird," the narrow-shouldered man in tails, beak-like nose, oiled hair combed back from a high, shiny forehead.

The plate glass window caught a flash of reflected light when the hotel door opened and closed across the street. Riley turned. Men regularly came and went from there. Some headed for the saloon district, others pitched the stub of a last cigar into the street, and retired to their rooms. Now his eye went to the stout man who had opened the door and stepped outside. It was Tug Larkin.

Riley stared. The door closed behind Larkin as he moved across the portico. The man stood in just about the same spot he had occupied when Riley and Matt had first ridden past on horseback.

Now Riley retreated, easing into the night shadows under the roof overhang of the shoe and boot repair shop next door to the Rocky Mountain House. Something was different about Tug Larkin. For one thing, a new, low-crowned hat with a shiny silk band topped his head. For another, he wore a fitted suit over a silver-buttoned vest, and a silver watch chain glittered as it caught the light. Riley noticed Larkin was not showing the five-pointed star of a deputy sheriff.

The hotel door opened again. Another well-dressed gent stepped out. He joined Larkin. Firing a cigar, he drew on it and tilted his head skyward as he blew a cloud of smoke into the still night air.

Riley drew back. That lanky man over there was Jimmy.

The flaw in Matt's plan was soon apparent to him—no man could stay awake day and night. Well after sunrise, he lay drowsing on the warming earth, partially concealed behind a clump of sagebrush with his Winchester and canteen at his side. He remembered looking down at the homestead where woodsmoke plumed from the rusted stovepipe in the flat roof. He remembered idly watching over the place, spying unseen as the boys gathered eggs, milked, separated cream to be churned for butter, and performed other morning chores. He caught glimpses of Anne Marie and then Sarah when they hiked to the outhouse and returned to the cabin, and suddenly—or so it seemed—he was awakened by drumming hoof beats.

Eyes opening, Matt was aware the sun had climbed high in the sky, that he had slept for two or three hours, and now a trio of armed riders galloped up to the homestead. Each man was armed, each one mounted on a sleek black horse. Their charging black horses seemed at first to be a hazy image from a forgotten dream, but as the men drew their revolvers and fired into the air, the dust and powder smoke and noise were all too real.

Storming the poor excuse for a barn, they opened stalls

and sent the two milk cows lumbering away. Both animals headed for the pond while the gunmen kicked apart the chicken coop and sent fowl fleeing with wings madly flapping. They rode after the cows and shot them on the muddy bank of the pond. One dropped to her knees and slowly toppled over. The other bawled in agony, staggering as she tried to escape her tormentors. She fell with a great splash and rolled on her side, legs thrashing in death throes. She bellowed and churned, the water reddening until she lay still.

Matt was on his feet and running downslope as the riders wheeled and trampled through the garden. They halted in front of the cabin and leaped out of their saddles. From a distance Matt saw them force their way in, shouting and firing their handguns again.

By the time Matt closed the distance to the barn, a gunman emerged from the cabin. He carried Micah and Samuel outside, one howling, leg-kicking boy under each arm, and dropped them to the ground. They cried out. Micah struggled to his hands and knees until the outlaw kicked him in the buttocks, hard, and sent him sprawling. Turning to Samuel, he drew his leg back and kicked him. The toe of his riding boot caught the boy in the ribs.

"Get out! Go on! Get outta here!"

The gunman's attention was focused on the boys until their crying abruptly stopped. Suddenly silent, they looked past him, eyes opening wide.

Matt saw the man stiffen before he whirled around. His clean-shaven face briefly registered surprise, then his right hand swept to his holstered gun. Matt was a heartbeat ahead of him as he drew his Colt. Bringing it up, he thumbed back the hammer and pulled the trigger. Matt felt the revolver kick violently in his hand. The gunman was driven back by the .45 slug, revolver falling from his grasp. The man staggered. He stared at Matt in disbelief. Then his knees buckled. He went down, blood blossoming across his shirtfront.

Micah and Samuel stared at the man. He lay still in the dusty yard, barely a dozen feet away from them.

Matt rushed past the downed man, kicked the door in, and lunged into the cabin. He caught the two men unarmed and unaware, believing the single shot outside had come from the third gunman. Matt saw one man kneeling on the bed, pants off, with Sarah lying prone on the mattress, nude, her torn dress and underclothes draped off the side of the straw mattress. Eyes half-closed, her mouth bled as she was obviously dazed from a blow to the jaw. Matt shot her attacker as he scrambled for his gun belt hanging on the bedpost. The impact of the bullet propelled him off the bed to the dirt floor.

Matt swung the Colt around. The third gunman cowered against the far wall. He held Anne Marie in front of him, one forearm pressing against her throat. The front of her dress was ripped open.

"Shoot," the man said, looking past her, "and you'll hit her. . . ."

"The hell," Matt interrupted. He raised the Colt, drew aim swiftly, and squeezed the trigger.

The bullet struck the man dead center between the eyes, snapping his head back. He slid down the wall to the floor, leaving a smear of blood and brains on the white cottonwood logs. Anne Marie lunged away from the dead man's grasp. Pulling her dress, she gathered the fabric around her.

"Matt," she whispered as he rushed to her. "Oh, Matt."

He took her in his arms. "Did he hurt you?"

"No."

At the sound of a man's pained moans, she looked at the wounded gunman near Sarah. Her sister still lay on the bed, half conscious. Anne Marie pulled away and went to her. She covered her with a bed quilt.

Matt moved around the foot of the bed. He knelt beside the gunman. The man's chest wound pumped red bubbles. Lying on the dirt floor in his own pooling blood, his eyes slowly blinked.

"Can you talk?" Matt asked.

Jaw clenching, the man did not answer.

"Better talk while you can, mister," Matt said. "Who sent you?"

Staring at the log wall three feet away, his only reply was a soft sigh, almost child-like.

"Jimmy," Matt said. "Jimmy sent you. Didn't he?"

The man lay still, but spoke clearly: "No."

"Who?"

"Larkin."

"Tug Larkin?"

"Tug Larkin paid us. . . ."

"Paid you? For what?"

"Rough up these bitches. . . ."

Matt demanded: "Why?"

"Tug said one of them hit him . . . in Valmont City . . . hurt those two bitches, he said . . . hurt 'em bad."

Matt leaned closer. "Who killed Collier?"

With a deep sigh, his eyes closed as he breathed his last.

Matt got to his feet. Turning, his gaze moved from Anne Marie and Sarah on the bed to Micah and Samuel. Standing in the doorway, both brothers stared at him.

"You boys all right?" Matt asked.

They nodded in unison, still wide-eyed and struck silent in the aftermath of the deafening gunfire and at the sight of the felled men, three hardened outlaws dying in the space of half a minute. At last Micah spoke, calling out to his sisters. "Annie? Sarah?"

"We're all right," Anne Marie said to him. "Are you hurt?"

"You said. . . ."

She stood beside the bed, clutching her ruined dress around her. "Said what?"

Micah shyly pointed to Matt. "You said he's a gunman. He sure is a gunman. Isn't he a gunman, Sam?"

"Yeah," Samuel agreed. "He sure is."

Riley could not have been more surprised if the sun had risen at midnight. Jimmy and Tug Larkin had been transformed into a couple of fine dandies—bathed, shaved, and outfitted head to toe in new duds. Riley awoke in the morning thinking about it. Last night the sight of them paired on the portico of the Inter-Ocean Hotel, both reveling in newfound luxury, shot a realization into him like a lightning bolt. Eldon Collier and Miss Augusta Benning had been shotgunned at close range. Same killer? Riley had suspected it ever since he had gazed down at Collier on the floor of the mansion's library.

Now he knew. The only man present at the scene of both crimes, aside from Riley himself, had been Tug Larkin. It added up if the deputy had entered Room 304 the day Miss Augusta Benning was murdered. He had pulled the triggers. Dropping the Greener on the carpeted floor of the hotel room, he had gone out the window, and escaped down the fire ladder. Instead of trying to flee in blood-splattered clothing, he had hidden in the alley. He became a local hero when he arrested the man who had an appointment in 304. The jury heard Larkin's concocted story while eyeing the defendant, a stranger in town who refused to give a name, whose only testimony was to proclaim his innocence. Twelve men listened, watched, ate a free supper, and reached the obvious conclusion.

Larkin must have been acquainted with Augusta Benning. More than acquainted, Riley thought now. He must have known she had received a letter from a gambler, that she had brought cash to the hotel room to settle a debt. According to the trial testimony, no money had been found among her possessions. Now Riley knew why. Larkin had stolen it.

Taken in this light, the clue to Tug Larkin's motive was clear enough—his preference for rubbing elbows with wealthy patrons of the finest hotel in the territory. Money, a lot of money, would place him among the gentry as a high-rolling equal. First, Miss Augusta Benning. Then Eldon Collier. Killed and robbed, both of them. Now the question was, how did Jimmy fit in?

Last night, from a safe distance, Riley had trailed them. In half a dozen saloons and gaming halls the two men drank hard and gambled recklessly. Standing near an outside door, Riley had seen them buy drinks for the house in the Wagon Wheel Saloon, and then he had followed as they staggered arm in arm, like brothers, reeling in laughter on their way back to the Inter-Ocean Hotel.

"Oh, Matt, what are we going to do?"

He stood at Anne Marie's side as they looked at the trampled plants in the ruined garden. Between here and the dead cows in the pond, panicked chickens flapped their wings as though knowing they would become coyote suppers if the boys failed to build a shelter before nightfall.

"We don't want to stay here one more hour," Anne Marie went on with a pained glance at the cabin and shabby outbuildings. "This is a horrible place . . . but we have nowhere to go. . . ." She spoke dully, her voice bearing a sadness beyond tears.

He reached for her. In a matter of a few minutes the

gunmen had nearly reduced this homestead to ruin. Repairs could be made, but Matt knew it was too dangerous for them to stay.

Anne Marie stepped into his arms, eyes closing as if to shut out memories.

"I know a place where we can go," he said.

Matt had another reason for urging her to leave this place. He did not say so aloud, but he wondered how long it would take Tug Larkin to figure out his hired gunmen were not coming back to Denver. By nightfall, probably, Larkin would suspect his plan had gone awry. No doubt the deputy would convince Ochs to send a posse, as Riley had predicted. And no doubt Larkin would concoct a tale to implicate Anne Marie and Sarah in the murder of Eldon Collier in Valmont City.

Matt wasted no time. He dragged the three corpses over the rise and buried them, concealing their graves as best he could. No matter what happened from now on, whether Sheriff Ochs launched an investigation or not, Matt did not want to face a phony murder charge as the outcome of what had happened here.

"Pack your gear and belongings in that old wagon," Matt said, pointing to the Conestoga, "and we'll roll in the morning."

Poisoning water was a high crime in arid regions of the West, and, while in all likelihood no one would be held accountable for fouling this one, Matt could not ride away with two cows left to rot and spoil a clean water hole. Using the black horses in tandem, he roped and dragged out one cow, and then the other, pulling the carcasses far enough away from the cabin to become wolf bait.

After that, he examined the Conestoga wagon. It was in rough shape, but usable. He jacked it up. Using firewood for blocks under the axles, he loosened the wheel nuts, twisted them off, and removed all four wheels. At his instruction, Micah and Samuel rolled each wheel into the water, submerging them. Spokes were loose, and, overnight, water would swell the wood, tightening them long enough to hold the wheels together until he reached his destination.

Matt had already decided to use Collier's horses for draft animals. He needed them to pull the big Conestoga. Taking off the heavy ox yoke, he cobbled together a harness of sorts, fashioned from ropes. In the wagon box he stowed the captured saddles, guns, and gear. He had never stolen anything in his life, certainly never a horse, and now he was unsure if this act fit a legal definition of thievery—three horses taken from dead outlaws who had stolen them from the owner, a man now deceased, too. Furthering Matt's crime, the pockets of the three gunmen had yielded a handful of crumpled greenbacks and assorted coins. He counted enough cash to buy two milk cows and purchase a wagonload of supplies. Legal or not, he aimed to use the money to replace everything the gunmen had destroyed, and any cash left over would be divided between Anne Marie and Sarah.

After sunset the work was completed. Anne Marie stood with her sister and brothers. In the light of early evening they gazed at the homestead in prayerful silence. Not long ago, they had devoted their labors from sunup to sundown to "prove up," with a goal of making enough money on the sale of the property to return home. Now, after losing nearly everything, they ventured into the unknown once again, facing the challenge of survival in a new place.

"I thought I'd be sad to leave our homestead," Anne Marie murmured, "but I'm not."

"Me, neither," Micah said.

"Me, neither," Samuel echoed.

"When I look around," she went on, "all I see is failure." She softly repeated the word: "Failure."

"But is it any better," Sarah asked, "this place we're going to?"

Anne Marie turned to Matt for an answer.

He thought about that before replying. "When we get there, take a look. Then tell me what you think."

Hoyt Wilcox had spent a lifetime deceiving unsuspecting folks, but on those rare occasions when he was the one who got snookered, he flew into a rage. Riley remembered the salted mine incident in Montana and a few other times the cheater had been cheated—or believed he had been taken. Stomping and cursing as though someone had dumped hot coals down his pants, Hoyt had been a sore loser, a man who would not rest until he had exacted a fair measure of revenge against those who had wronged him, real or imagined.

As Riley considered ways to settle the score with Tug Larkin and Jimmy, he realized with a start that he shared Hoyt's vindictiveness. As eager as he was to put this territory behind him, to get out of this damnable place once and for all, now he was determined to stay until he had evened the score.

If it was true the idle rich "cheered the bright midnight moon and slept past dullard noon," as Riley had heard it said, then Tug Larkin and Jimmy had quickly taken to the style of the rich. Riley watched the Inter-Ocean from a distance all morning, lounging in the shade against a hot midday sun, when at last the two men emerged from the hotel.

Riley stepped back, edging into the shaded space between two buildings. While locals passed by him, he leaned a shoulder against the wall and watched, wondering where Tug Larkin and Jimmy would go. Whatever their destination, they took their time about it. Riley figured they were nursing hangovers while they lingered on the banner-draped portico, but later, when they angled across the street to the Sixteenth Street Livery, he noted purposeful strides. He also noted both men carried side arms. He moved with them, keeping his distance as he remained unseen a block away. They entered the livery barn. Riley found another patch of shade and waited.

Presently the pair came out of the barn leading matched black horses—saddle mounts easily recognized from Collier's string. Tug Larkin and Jimmy tightened cinches and swung up. Lifting the reins, they turned the horses and headed out.

Riley paused before following on foot. Neither man looked back as they rode at a leisurely walk to the north edge of town. Beyond the last boardwalk on the outskirts of Denver, he drew up. He saw the riders pass the Arapaho encampment. They crossed the South Platte River on the plank bridge he and Matt had used after breaking out of the jail cell.

Riley knew he could not keep up this pace on foot. Even if he tried, he figured he would be spotted. Beyond the pioneer camp encircled by cottonwoods lay a vast expanse of treeless prairie. If he tried to follow Tug Larkin and Jimmy out there, they would see him. He turned back, hurrying to town.

At the livery, Riley saddled the speckled gray gelding. He made a hard ride to the Painter homestead. To his amazement, he found the cabin empty. A heavy, hickory yoke for oxen had been left behind, but the Conestoga wagon was gone. The two milk cows lay bloating under the hot sun, both carcasses bearing bullet holes.

Riley looked around, trying to make sense of this bizarre scene. A profusion of tracks left by shod horses baffled him. He saw various marks in the dirt, and a wide scrape left by the cows apparently being dragged out of the pond. He found the barn to be empty. The coop was broken open, eggs had been gathered, but the family's chickens were nowhere in sight.

He could only speculate at what had happened here. Clearly recent events had been catastrophic, and he guessed his twin and the Painter family had escaped. He was no tracker, but noticed uneven wheel tracks left by the heavy Conestoga wagon. Even Riley could see that it had been pulled by shod horses.

Riley followed the trail. Half a mile away, the wheel tracks veered off the road. Tracks showed they had cut cross-country through the sage. Another mile, and he lost the trail on barren hardpan. He reined up. The general direction up to this point had been westward, leading toward the brown foothills bunched against the far mountains. Riley looked in that direction, thinking Matt would instinctively avoid leaving a trail for anyone to follow. He thought about where his twin would feel safe taking the Painter sisters and their young brothers. Spurring the gelding then, he headed for the Two-Bar Ranch.

Chapter Fourteen

Matt did not relate the bunkhouse tale of the phantom white stallion to Anne Marie, or to anyone else. It was not the sort of story folks craved to hear, and he did not want to cast this place in a bad light before the Painter family had seen it with their own eyes. Besides, Riley might have been right. The account of a mean-spirited rancher kicked to death by the horse he had abused might have been nothing but a yarn spun by cowhands with idle time on their hands, lonely men engaged in the time-honored tradition of trying to out-lie one another.

No matter. He would not repeat the story. He had long believed this shallow valley bearing cool, clear water and high grass would be a good place to run a few head of cattle and a string of horses, a small spread where a man could settle down for a fresh start in life. Now in the back of his mind, he wanted Anne Marie to recognize the possibilities, too, at once fearing this was too much to hope for.

He need not have worried. The moment they crested the grassy rise overlooking the sod house and corral, Anne Marie drew a sharp breath. "Oh, Matt," she whispered. "Matt, do you . . . do you own this land?"

He shook his head. "Riley and I cleared out the snakes and worked on the cabin some." He cast a quick glance at her. "Anyone willing to improve the place and pay back taxes to the territorial government can lay claim to it."

"The whole valley?" she asked, turning to him.

Matt nodded.

Anne Marie's eyes glistened with excitement. She did not speak. No words were needed as their gazes met and held.

Matt felt a dizzying sensation, an immediate recognition of shared thoughts, as if they had come home after a long absence.

The silence was broken by the quiet sobbing from Sarah. Anne Marie turned to her. "What's wrong?" she whispered.

Sarah wiped her eyes, apologizing for weeping. "Ever since we left home, I feel like I've descended into Dante's hell. Every level is worse than the one before. I know I made a mistake when I went to Valmont City. I should never have gone there. But as terrible as it was, I came back to our homestead to find Father dying. And then those men came with guns blazing. . . ."

Anne Marie went to her and hugged her.

"Anyone can see what's happening between you two," Sarah went on. "I'm happy for you. But what you want is not what I want."

"What do you mean?" Anne Marie asked.

"I want no part in building another homestead from scratch," she replied. "I don't want to stay here. I want to go back home. But that is an impossible wish. . . ."

Matt looked at her as her voice was given over to more shedding of tears. Her cheek was bruised where she had been punched. She had complained of a sore jaw and a cut inside her mouth, but insisted she was not seriously hurt.

"I am happy for you," Sarah repeated after several minutes. "Truly, I am. But. . . ." She did not finish her thought.

"Slow down," Matt said. "I don't have enough money to buy this spread. I brought you here to dodge Tug Larkin. As long as he doesn't know where to find you, you're safe. We can hunker down for a spell. . . ."

Micah interrupted: "Know what I want? I want a horse and saddle so I can ride all around here. I want to gallop from one end of this valley to the other."

"Me, too!" Samuel said. "I want to ride from one end to the other!"

"Reckon that can be arranged," Matt said. "But first, we've got some chores staring at us."

There was a great deal of work to be done to make this place livable, even if only for a short time. Warned of rattlesnakes, the sisters wielded home-made brooms. They swept the dirt floor of the sod house and cleared countless spider webs from its corners. For a time, Sarah was too preoccupied to pine for home. She and her sister even laughed with relief when they threw down their brooms and declared the place to be clean at last.

Outside, Matt helped the boys secure chicken wire to contain the laying hens and roosters. Then they dug out the thick grass that fringed the well. Under Matt's direction, Micah and Samuel made a border of stones. To draw water, Matt would have to buy rope and a bucket when he went to town. A windlass would be needed, too, he found himself thinking, for permanent residency here. He began digging a vault for a new outhouse, and shoveled dirt from the new hole into the old toilet.

With everyone pitching in through the course of that hot day, the Conestoga wagon was unloaded. The Painters' sheet-iron stove was set up in the cabin, along with their bedding and few furnishings. The rusted stovepipe brought from the homestead was installed. The boys gathered firewood. Famished from their day's labors, all of them ate a hot meal in the gathering darkness of the prairie night.

The women slept indoors while Matt camped outside with Micah and Samuel. He heard one of the boys crying softly. Leaving his bedding, he knelt beside Samuel's blankets, seeing the boy's dim shape by starlight.

"You miss your pa, don't you?" Matt said softly.

"He died, and he's never coming back."

"I know."

"Why did he die?"

"He got sick," Matt said.

"But why?" he persisted.

"I'm not smart enough to know the answer to that."

"Annie says Father went to heaven," Samuel said. "He's walking among the stars up there. He's smiling."

"Reckon that's so."

"Annie says he's looking down on us from heaven," Samuel went on, "to make sure we're all right."

"That's how I figure it, too," Matt said.

"You do?"

"My ma and pa are gone," Matt replied, "but no matter what kind of scrapes I get myself into, I always have a feeling they're looking out for me."

"Will . . . will you go off and leave us?"

"Not for long."

"What do you mean?"

"I'm going to town in the morning," Matt explained, "but I'll be back by sunset."

"Take me!"

"I will next time," he said. "I need you to look out for your brother and sisters. Can you do that?"

"Yeah."

"Good night."

"Good night."

Before dawn, Matt ate a cold breakfast, kissed Anne Marie good bye, and left for his trip to Denver with the empty wagon. Arriving well before noon, he bought supplies in the general mercantile where Old John traded. Later he followed a liveryman's recommendation and purchased a pair of milk cows from a farmer on the outskirts of town, two jerseys to replace the animals shot to death on the Painter homestead.

Matt kept an eye peeled. He wondered if Riley was still in Denver, but did not venture into any of the gaming halls and saloons to search for his twin. Reward dodgers were up, and he was concerned about encountering Sheriff Ochs, Tug Larkin, or an eagle-eyed townsman. With peppermint stick candy for the boys, and all of his other purchases completed, Matt departed in haste, watchful of his back trail.

Riley approached the Two-Bar with caution. He paused on the road and observed the ranch from a distance before riding slowly to the water trough. Midday, he had not expected to find cowhands lounging there, and he had been right. The horse corrals were empty. He saw smoke drifting out of the stovepipe of the cook house, and heard the *clang* of a stove lid inside. While the gelding drank at the trough, Riley looked around, figuring he and the ranch cook had the place to themselves until the front door of the main house swung open.

"By damn! That you, Matt?"

Bare-headed, Old John came out, striding stiff-legged toward him. The rancher's white hair stood on end, and his thin-lipped mouth twisted into a scowl. As he drew closer, Riley saw bushy eyebrows the size of a pair of white caterpillars. He sensed no anger in the man, and figured this fierce, go-to-hell expression was his usual countenance.

"That you, Matt?" he asked again, squinting.

"Name's Wilcox . . . Riley Wilcox."

"I'll be damned!" Old John exclaimed. He grabbed his red suspenders and drew up as though halting a runaway horse. "Matt said you was twins. Damned iffen you two ain't a matched set. Dead ringers, that's what you are."

"I'm looking for Matt," he said.

"Ain't seen him fer a good long spell," Old John said. He squinted against the bright sun. "How the hell did you two get to be twins, anyhow?"

It was a strange question, but Riley figured he knew what the old-timer meant. "We haven't found anyone who can answer that," he replied, adding: "I don't believe we ever will."

"Wouldn't be the first time, now would it?"

"Sir?"

"Hell, I never knowed my ma or pa, neither," Old John explained. "Afore my memory started, my ma had died, and my pa, he sailed outta Baltimore harbor on a whaler that was never seen again. I was raised by relatives, a bunch of mean bastards and shrill bitches who passed me around like a bad penny. The only good to come of it was I larnt to be my own man. That's what I done, too, starting at age fourteen, when I run off." Riley heard bravado in the man's voice until that last remark. Old John paused, beard-stubbled jaw quivering, as though shoving painful memories into a deep, dark recess of his mind, a place rarely visited. He shook himself. "Well, where in hell have you boys been all this time?" Old John demanded.

"We went to Valmont City," Riley said, "and then we came back and stayed at the Painter homestead outside of Denver."

"Valmont City," Old John repeated. "That mining district is a fair piece from here."

"A long way," Riley agreed, "and a long story."

Old John stared. "By damn, I can't get over it."

"Get over what?"

"Hell, I feel like I'm a-talking to Matt," he said, "but I ain't. I'm a-talking to a stranger wearing Matt's face." He paused again. "Matt saved your neck from a hangman's noose, didn't he?"

Riley nodded.

"So how did you get from them gallows," Old John asked, "to Valmont City?"

"Like I said," Riley repeated, "it's a long story."

The rancher thought about that. He jerked his head at the gelding. "Go ahead and take that plug into the barn and grain him. He used to belong to me, you know, before he got too old to work cattle." He added with half a grin: "Hell of a thing, getting old."

Riley reached for the reins.

"My cook, Luther, he's a-fixin' grub right now," Old John went on. "I take my big meal at noontime. If you're of a mind, sit at my table and spin that yarn for me. I'd flat like to hear it."

Riley was not a man to confide in anyone, much less a stranger, but this rancher impressed him. Old John was straightforward in his talk, no-nonsense in his manner. If there was ever an exact opposite to Hoyt Wilcox born into this world, Old John Souter was that man. After the meal of fried steak and eggs and potatoes, Riley recounted recent events over a two-cent cigar and a dented tin cup of rye-spiked coffee.

Old John listened intently. Then he pushed back from the table. "Well, your twin and them Painters, they ain't here."

"Looks like I guessed wrong," Riley conceded.

"What's your second guess?"

Riley had been thinking about that. "The old ranch property where we camped."

Old John grinned. "All along, that's what I figured."

"How do I get out there from the Two-Bar?"

"Give my dinner a chance to settle," the rancher answered

as he stood and headed for his bunk, "and I'll lead the way."

"Annie! Annie! Bad men are coming! Two of 'em!"

In the shadows of early evening, Matt was shoulder deep in the toilet vault when he heard Micah's shouts. He had resumed digging after his return from Denver, and now he scrambled out of the hole, sprinting for his cartridge belt and holstered gun draped over a corral pole. Then he pulled up. He recognized the two riders approaching—Riley on the gray and Old John riding the brown and white saddle mount he favored.

"Hello, the house!" Old John bellowed, adding with a laugh: "Don't shoot! We're peaceable!"

After introductions were made and the horses watered and corralled, they sat around a fire outside. Old John remembered "Missy," and muttered an apology for insisting Sheriff Ochs lock her up on a charge of rustling. She countered with an apology of her own, expressing regret she had ever listened to "Mister Smith."

Riley and Old John listened while Matt described the violent attack on the Painter homestead and its aftermath. Then Riley explained why he had not left the territory.

"Jimmy and Tug Larkin," Matt repeated, shaking his head. "So they were in on it together."

"Now I need a tracker," Riley said.

Matt eyed him across the flames of the fire. "You figure those two cached that money somewhere on the prairie?"

Riley nodded. "I don't know what else they could have done with a load of gold and silver coins too heavy for saddlebags. They must have loaded miners' panniers on Collier's black horses at that mine site where we found the Concord coach. But now they have a problem. If they waltz into a bank in Denver with all those eagles and silver dollars, somebody'll put two and two together. Or, if they set out on their own, they run the risk of a hold-up by road agents."

"So you figure they're biding their time in Denver?" Matt asked.

Riley nodded. "Living high on the hog while they figure out how to move that loot is my guess. They must have been counting on those three gunmen for protection."

"Ochs should know about this," Old John said.

Riley shook his head. "That lawman's first order of business is to hang me. He won't take our word over his deputy. By the time he figures out he lynched the wrong man, it'll be too late."

Old John nodded slowly. "You boys walked into neck-deep quicksand, that's what you done."

Until then Anne Marie and Sarah had listened in silence. Now Sarah spoke up: "What will you do if you find that money?"

"Spend it," Riley answered with a quick grin.

Matt cast a sidelong glance at him. "We're not pirates on the high seas. If we locate Collier's money, we'll find out who inherited his estate. Then we'll turn the money and those black horses over to the rightful owner. The Concord, too."

No one disputed him, but his words were met with silence until Old John stood, announcing his intention to make a night ride back to the Two-Bar. Soon after he rode out, the boys fell asleep in their blankets. Matt and Anne Marie went for a stroll under the stars, leaving Riley and Sarah to tend the fire.

In the deep shadows beyond the corral, Matt embraced and kissed Anne Marie. Holding one another, they were silent until he whispered to her.

"I've never known anyone who can say so much without speaking a single word."

216

She whispered his name and kissed him again.

"You'll get danged tired of hearing me say the same words," he said.

"What words?" she asked.

"I love you," he replied. "Every time we're alone, I want to tell you . . . Anne Marie, I love you. Reckon I'll wear those words out."

She pressed against him. "No, you won't. But keep trying."

"I love you, Anne Marie."

"I love hearing you say it, Matt," she said. "And I love you dearly."

Early in the morning Matt and Riley headed out on horseback. Angling toward Denver, the sun was high in the sky when they intercepted tracks. This was bare ground, close to the place where Riley had last seen Tug Larkin and Jimmy from the outskirts of Denver.

Matt dismounted. He walked for a time, eyes downcast as he made his way through tufts of buffalo grass and around thick clumps of rabbitbrush. With a glance at Riley, he pointed to sun-dried horse droppings on the ground. Matt moved to his horse. He thrust a boot in the stirrup and grasped the saddle horn as he swung up. Farther on, the land was dotted with sage and stunted grasses, a great, treeless plain inhabited by lizards, long-eared jack rabbits, and bands of white-rumped antelope.

Matt increased the pace, occasionally leaning over the mare's shoulder as he read sign invisible to Riley's eye. Then, under the hot blue sky, Matt abruptly stood in the stirrups. He looked ahead, pointing to a dry wash at the bottom of slope a hundred yards away.

"Good spot for an ambush," Matt said.

"That pair of yahoos are too busy living like kings in Denver," he said, "to be out here, suffering under this sun."

Matt nodded agreement and rode on slowly. He knew Riley was right, but his instincts as a cavalry scout were ingrained. Gun out, he approached the crease in the land at an angle so as to present a smaller target. Riley followed, his cutdown shotgun at the ready.

They found the wash to be an eroded cut running through the baked prairie. In its sandy bottom a trail of horse tracks was obvious. The twins dismounted. Leading their horses, they descended a soft bank. At the bottom, imprints of shod hoofs led them around a bend to a pile of brush. The leaves were shriveled.

Matt kicked the brush away. He discovered sagebrush and rabbitbrush had been yanked out by the roots and heaped over a canvas tarp. All four corners weighted by stones, the tarp was partially covered with sand and dry soil.

Riley yanked the canvas free of the stones. He exposed half a dozen miners' panniers, heavy leather packs used for hauling equipment on the backs of horses or mules.

The twins knelt. They glanced at one another. The panniers bore a familiar monogram—**EC**.

Riley unbuckled the nearest pannier and opened the flap. Both men were struck silent. A fortune in gold eagles and silver dollars lay before them, coins too numerous to estimate a total value. Clearly, though, if the contents of the other panniers equaled this one, the combined amount would not be in the thousands, but tens of thousands of dollars.

Riley drew a deep breath. He slowly let it out. "Just like we figured, brother."

Matt pulled off his hat. He wiped sweat from his brow.

"Now what?" Riley asked.

Matt looked at him. "Reckon it's my turn."

"Your turn for what?"

"Reading minds," he replied.

Riley cast a severe look at him.

"You're thinking a dead man's money belongs to the finder," Matt said.

"Something like that," Riley conceded. "Now I'll read your mind, and it won't take long, your brain being the size of a walnut." He closed his eyes and made a show of concentration as though consulting divine powers. "Ah, yes, it's coming to me now . . . you're thinking . . . you're thinking this buried treasure belongs to Collier's heirs."

"As I said last night," Matt reminded him.

Riley grew serious. "Eldon Collier was a bad man. He was murdered for his money by men even worse than he was. Now we have it. Look at these coins, brother. Look at them and think of dreams coming true."

"Dreams," Matt repeated. "What dreams?"

"That ranch property, for one," he replied.

"What about it?"

"Your dream will come true when you own that little valley free and clear," he said. He paused. "For me, no more card games, no more deceit. I'll buy a business and live on the straight and narrow, the ghost of Hoyt Wilcox haunting me no more."

Matt was surprised to hear so much passion in his voice.

"And Sarah," Riley went on, "she will pay her way back to Ohio. Hell, the whole family can ride in comfort from here to Ohio."

Matt gazed at him. "Sounds like you two have it all planned out."

"We talked some last night," he conceded. "I was a little rough on her in Valmont City, and I tried to make it up to her. Fact is we both want the same thing . . . to leave this hayseed territory. The sooner, the better. That's her dream. Mine, too, in case I haven't told you lately."

"Stolen money," Matt observed, "makes nightmares come true, not dreams."

"How would you know?"

He paused. "My upbringing was different from yours."

"What are you driving at, brother?" Riley asked, anger in his voice.

"I'm saying honesty means something," he replied. "Some things in life you take on faith, and that's one of them."

Matt saw Riley glare at him, fists clenching, and thought they would fight again. The moment passed. Hands opening, Riley shrugged. He posed another question. "Well, we found it," he said. "Now what do you aim to do with it?"

"Haul it," Matt said, "and hide it."

"How? Where?"

"We'll use the Conestoga wagon to haul those panniers," he replied. "Where we'll stash the money, I don't know yet. But as you say . . . the West is a big place."

Riley did not openly object. Matt was keenly aware that he had not agreed to the plan, either.

They rode back to the abandoned ranch in silence, and returned early the next day with the big, lumbering Conestoga. Loading six panniers was heavy work, requiring both of them to lift each one, carry it out of the wash, and heft it onto the tailgate before shoving it into the wagon box.

When that part of the job was done, Matt guided the team of black horses away from the wash. He followed a circuitous route to the abandoned ranch, stopping frequently to rub out the tracks carved by the wobbling wheels and stamped by the hoofs of straining horses. By the time they reached the sod house, Matt had decided to conceal the panniers in the one place where no one would look for it—the vault of the new toilet.

First, Riley laughed. Then he objected. Matt did not budge, and finally Riley gave up, agreeing the idea was novel, if nothing else.

With a loop knotted in the rope Matt had purchased in town, they lowered each pannier down into the hole. Matt covered them with the tarp Tug Larkin and Jimmie had used to conceal the treasure. Then he and Riley shoveled dirt in, covering the canvas.

"I have to admit I've learned a thing or two from you," Riley said when they finished. "Now I've learned something else."

"What?" Matt asked.

Riley looked down into the hole. "How it feels to be stinking rich."

Daybreak brought a visitor. Riley called out to Matt, pointing to a lone rider on a brown and white horse. Coming at a walk, the rider drew closer.

Matt recognized him. Not too many men sat a saddle as straight and square-shouldered as Old John did. The twins stood shoulder to shoulder to welcome him, but two hundred yards away the rancher reined up and halted his horse. Matt and Riley exchanged a glance, silently wondering why the old-timer did not come in.

In the next moment, too late, they knew why. Old John was a decoy. From behind them came a man's shout from the back corner of the sod house. It was a commanding voice they had not heard for a long time.

"Now I'm the one who's holding the scatter-gun, gents. Hands up. Be quick about it."

Riley raised his hands shoulder high. Matt did the same. Both of them slowly turned until they faced Sheriff Hiram Ochs.

The lawman stepped around the corner of the sod house and closed the distance. He trained a long-barreled .20 gauge shotgun on them, a weapon with a range and load powerful enough to knock a goose out of the sky or a man off his feet.

Riley wondered how Ochs had managed to drop out of the sky, but after a moment's reflection he understood all too well. Anne Marie and Sarah were in the sod house with the boys. With no windows on the back wall of the structure, the lawman was able to move in, unseen, while their attention was fixed in the opposite direction on Old John.

As though slipping into a bad dream, Riley found himself thinking of Nell Bloom. By opening his heart to her, he had made himself vulnerable to a pain stabbing so deep that it threatened to end life itself. Now he had given his trust to Old John, trusted the rancher enough to confide in him. *Look what that got me,* he thought, *a lawman set on marching me off to the gallows.*

Riley cast a hard look at his twin. The more he thought about it, the more he was convinced Matt had been handing out bad advice from the start. A man was better off trusting no one. Hoyt Wilcox had been right. He often said a man could only trust himself in this old world of cheaters and liars. Riley remembered the man's exact words on the subject. In Great Falls, Montana they had once again escaped an inflamed citizenry fleeced by Hoyt Wilcox. Hiding in a riverbottom choked with willows, Riley's feet were wet and cold when he had gathered his nerve and whispered a question: "Why don't you take up a real profession instead of telling lies all the time? Why don't you live the way other folks do?"

"Because they're bastards," Hoyt had replied. "All of them. Bastards."

Baffled, Riley had pressed him: "What do you mean?"

"Just what I said, pistol," Hoyt had answered in a low, hissing voice. "They're lying, cheating, conniving bastards. All of these church-going, law-abiding, proper ladies and squinty-eyed gentlemen are nothing but thieves in finery. They'll cheat you, rob you, or worse, unless you get to them first. That's the truth, pistol. When you get older, you'll see."

"Guns, gents," Sheriff Ochs said again. This time he waved the big shotgun at the twins. "Firearms on the ground. Now."

"Bastard," Riley said.

Chapter Fifteen

"Steady," Old John said in a voice low and gentle enough to coax a mustang into a stall. "Steady now."

Matt was aware of the rancher easing closer to them. Tension filled the hot summer air, a great dampening force like the heavy silence preceding a prairie storm. Matt turned and saw Old John take note of Anne Marie and Sarah standing in the doorway with the wide-eyed faces of their brothers peering around them.

"Do as Hiram says," Old John advised him and Riley. "This ain't the time or the place for a shoot-out."

At a loss for words, Matt stared in disbelief at Old John, this man he had long trusted. Then he heard Riley speak again. His voice was deep and seething with rage.

"Told you he'd turn on us. Didn't I tell you, brother? He sold us out for a reward . . . for money that came out of my own damned money belt. . . ." Riley was interrupted by the sheriff.

"I'm not going to say it again," Ochs said. "Lay your firearms on the ground. Put them down, and back off. Then we'll have us a talk."

"Talk," Riley scoffed. "What about? Hanging an innocent man?"

"Mister," Ochs said to Riley, "if you'll button your lip and do what you're told, maybe you'll live long enough to find out."

Matt knew Riley was mad enough and desperate enough to end it all right here. And he knew Old John was right. This was neither the time nor the place for a fight. He shook his head at Riley, and eased his Colt out of the well-worn holster. Bending down, he put the revolver in the grass at his feet. Then he straightened up and backed away three paces.

Riley hesitated. Matt eyed him. The image of the shotgunned corpse of Eldon Collier swept into his mind, and he knew in a hairbreadth Riley could be sprawled on the ground, dead from a shotgun blast, too. He feared Riley would rather die that way than dance at the end of a hangman's rope. Movement in the doorway of the sod house caught his eye. Sarah appeared there. She lifted her dress above her shoe tops and ran headlong toward them.

"Riley! Riley!"

"Stay away!" he shouted.

"I won't," Sarah said, halting at his side. "I won't let you die for a crime you didn't commit!"

While it was clear she could do nothing physically to stop Riley from confronting Ochs, her voice had an unexpected effect. He blinked, as though awakening. Then he bent down and pulled his trouser leg up. Yanking the Greener out of his boot, he set the weapon on the ground and backed away with Sarah clinging to his arm.

"Now we can all breathe easier," the sheriff said. His gaze shifted from Riley to Matt, with only a glance at Sarah. "You had me puzzled for a spell, but now I see it. You're twins, all right."

"Keen eye, Sheriff," Riley said.

Ochs turned his attention to Riley. "I can't tell you two apart, but you must be the big-mouth. From what I hear, one twin is the quiet type, but the other won't shut up."

"Heard that from Old John, did you?" Riley taunted. He cast another look of raw disgust at the rancher, and then faced Ochs. "I'll talk you to death while you're hanging me, lawman, and my ghost will torment you and that double-crossing old bastard over there till the day you draw your last breath."

Old John stiffened, but conceded: "Reckon you ketched me in one lie, all right. When I left here, I didn't ride to the home ranch like I told you I was a-gonna. I rode to town, checked into the Cattlemen's Club, and sent for Hiram first thing in the morning. Over breakfast, I done told him ever'thing you done told me. Riley, I trusted you was a-telling the truth when we talked over my dinner table."

Riley studied the ground at his feet.

Ochs said to him: "You convinced Mister Souter you didn't kill anyone. He figures I'll change my mind about arresting you after I hear you out. So I gave him my word . . . no posse, no gunfire. I'm here to listen to your tale."

Riley lifted his gaze. He cast a sheepish glance at Old John, and turned to Ochs. "Nobody believed me the first time around. How the hell can I prove it now?"

"For starters," the lawman replied, "you can tell me your name. Then you can give me a reason why I should believe you at all."

Riley glowered as though he was being drawn into a pointless exercise. But after a nudge from Sarah he gave his name. Then he recounted the events leading up to his discovery of the corpse of Miss Augusta Benning in Room 304 of the Inter-Ocean Hotel—this time he admitted having written a phony letter about the IOU and signing Hoyt Wilcox's name to it. How, in a return letter, she had suggested they meet privately in the hotel to settle up. How Riley kept the appointment, believing he had hit the jackpot.

Unlike his brief trial testimony, Riley now accused Tug Larkin of the murder. He described how the deputy could have pulled it off and still look like a hero in the end. Larkin must have known Miss Augusta Benning, Riley said, known her well enough to be aware of her intent to pay out over a thousand dollars in gambling debts that day. He schemed to steal the money, arriving at the hotel moments ahead of Riley, and there was only one sure way to silence a witness. . . .

Ochs did not interrupt or attempt to defend his deputy. Stone-faced, he listened in silence. Instead of debating the fine points of Riley's account or challenging his suppositions, the lawman asked a question that caught all of them by surprise.

"Do you know a woman in Valmont City by the name of Maude Riley?"

"We know her," Matt said.

Ochs eyed the twins. "Mister Souter says at one time you thought she might be related to you. Is she?"

"No," Matt replied.

"Hell, no," Riley added.

"Talking to you two reminds me of Echo Cañon," Ochs said. "One speaks, the other repeats."

"What about her?" Riley demanded.

"Well, back in my office," Ochs said, "I have a letter from the marshal of Valmont City. Seems like this Maude Riley filed a report of fraud. Seems like she bought an unpatented gold mine for eight hundred dollars. Seems like it was salted."

"Eight hundred dollars," Riley repeated with a glance at Matt.

"That's what I said, Mister Echo," Ochs said. He went on: "She's a mite upset. She believes the man who cheated her absconded to Denver, and she wants him jailed until he returns the money."

"What's the name of this joker?" Riley asked.

"She identified him as one James Quinn," Ochs replied.

227

"Lean, tall, red-haired, she said."

"Jimmy," Riley said, and Matt nodded.

"You two know him?" Ochs asked.

"Eldon Collier's manservant went by the name of Jimmy," Matt said. "He fits that description."

"Tug Larkin and Jimmy make a pair," Riley added. "One killed Collier, and the other robbed him."

"Mister Souter told me about your theory," Ochs said, studying Riley. "Word of the robbery and murder of Eldon Collier came from Valmont City, quick-like. Collier was a famous man, and down here folks knew Miss Augusta Benning was his former wife."

"Sheriff," Matt said, eyeing the lawman, "I get the feeling you know more about this than we do."

"All I know for sure," Ochs replied, "is that Tug resigned the day he came back from Valmont City. Turned in his badge and took up residence in the Inter-Ocean Hotel. Just like that. Before Mister Souter bought my breakfast in the Cattleman's Club, I had no notion of how my former deputy came into enough money to afford to take up residence in the Inter-Ocean. So I've been suspicious of him. Your theory accounts for his newfound wealth. But without evidence and testimony, I can't prove who committed those crimes."

"Would you mind pointing that cannon some other direction?" Riley asked.

While talking, Ochs was aiming the shotgun at the twins. Now he shifted it to the crook of his arm, barrel slanting toward the ground.

"Sorry about the misunderstanding," the sheriff said, "but I figured if I didn't get the drop on you, we'd have us a shoot-out with me on the short end. That's why I worked it that way . . . with Mister Souter coming in from the front, slow-like, to hold your eyes in that direction. It was his idea."

Old John turned to Riley. "Not bad for an old, double-crossing bastard, huh?"

Riley drew a deep breath and exhaled. "I admit I shot off my mouth, Mister Souter. I was edgy."

"You had cause," Old John said. "No hard feelings."

Sheriff Ochs said to Riley: "You were right about one thing, but you're dead wrong about another."

"What are you talking about?" Riley asked.

"Well, Tug wanted to collect that reward, like you figured," he replied. "He was always looking for more money. When he gave your description to the agent at the stage station, he figured out you were a passenger on a coach headed for Valmont City. He went after you, quick-like." He paused. "You're wrong about the reward. Your money belt is still in my office, locked up, safe and sound. Maybe you can collect it someday."

"Someday soon," Riley said.

Ochs eyed him, his jaw set. "Maybe not."

"I don't like the sound of that," Riley said.

"Well, I've heard you out like I promised Mister Souter I would," Ochs replied. "I have to admit, what you say makes some sense. You've answered a few questions I've had in my head. But it doesn't change the one legal fact I have to abide by."

"Fact?" Riley asked. "What fact?"

"A jury found you guilty of murder in a legal trial," Ochs replied. "Remanding you is my duty. I'm bound by it."

Riley stiffened.

"Whatever you think of me," Ochs went on, "I want you to know I have no appetite for seeing an innocent man hanged. But you have to understand . . . Miss Augusta Benning was well liked. Folks haven't forgotten about her murder. What with statehood coming next July, and public opinion being what it is, I have to abide by the letter of the law."

Ochs raised the shotgun. "So I'm taking you in, Mister Wilcox."

Old John started to protest. He was cut off by a shout from Riley.

"The hell you are!" Riley said. He shoved Sarah away, or tried to. She clung to his arm with both hands. "You might as well shoot me where I stand, Ochs."

"No!" Sarah exclaimed.

Hiram Ochs was not easily intimidated. He took in the scene before him. "In your saddle, Wilcox, or across it, either way I'm taking you in. Your choice."

Old John angrily renewed his protest, to no avail. Clearly the rancher had not been informed of this "legal fact" when he had suggested Ochs ride out here.

Anne Marie left the boys in the doorway. She hurriedly approached Ochs from behind. He heard her coming and cast a quick look back, no doubt wondering if she were armed. Then he gave her a second searching look as he tried to place where he had seen her before.

Anne Marie moved to Matt's side.

"Looks like we've got you surrounded, Sheriff," Matt said. "You aim to shoot all of us?"

For the first time, a look of doubt crossed the lawman's face. But he did not lower the gun. "Anyone interfering with a lawful arrest will see the inside of my jail," Ochs said evenly. "If I leave here without my prisoner, I'll come back with an armed posse. I'll hire an Arapaho tracker, in case you have some notion of running."

"Hold on, Sheriff," Matt said. "Hold on." He paused in thought. "Maybe there's some way out of this."

"The only way out," Ochs said, "is for Riley Wilcox to surrender."

"But he's innocent!" Sarah insisted.

Anne Marie added: "We'll prove it."

Ochs gazed at the sisters with skepticism. "Just how do you two girls aim to go about that job?"

"We'll start out by doing what you should have done in the first place," Anne Marie said.

"And what would that be?" he asked.

"Ask questions," Anne Marie replied. "All you did was throw a man in jail to satisfy public opinion."

Neck bowed, Ochs said: "You seem to forget a jury found him guilty." He paused. "Who's gonna be on the receiving end of your questions?"

When she did not answer immediately, Matt spoke one name: "Jimmy."

Ochs turned to him. "James Quinn? What about him?"

"You aim to arrest him, don't you?"

"I will," Ochs allowed, "if that woman, Maude Riley, testifies against him. What does that have to do with the price of tea in China?"

"Lock Jimmy up," Matt replied, "and send word to Maude Riley. While Jimmy's cooling his heels in a jail cell, keep an eye on Tug Larkin. Sooner or later, he'll take you to the money. That's your proof, isn't it?"

"I suppose so," Ochs said slowly. His gaze moved to Riley. "But it doesn't change anything. This man is my prisoner. He's headed for Denver."

Riley taunted him. "You'll lock me up and rebuild the gallows just to satisfy your local lynch mob?"

"I've got a crew working on it right now," the sheriff assured him.

Riley looked at him in surprise.

"Folks demanded the gallows stand ready for the murderer of Miss Augusta Benning," Ochs went on. "I'm making sure it will be."

"Like I said, Sheriff," Riley repeated, "you might as well shoot me where I stand. I'm not moving from this spot."

"The hell you aren't," Ochs said.

Amid another eruption of protests from Old John, Anne Marie, and Sarah, Matt lifted his hand to quiet them.

"I'll go."

Ochs turned to Matt. "What?"

"I said, I'll go," Matt broke in.

"Just what in the hell are you talking about?" Ochs demanded.

Anne Marie understood immediately. "Matt, no."

"I'm your prisoner," Matt said to the lawman. He unbuckled his cartridge belt and let it drop to the ground near his revolver. "As far as anyone in Denver knows, you're bringing in the convicted killer, the man who refused to be named at his murder trial."

Ochs stared at him, for the moment speechless along with Riley and everyone else.

As if descending into the depths of a waking nightmare, a dark landscape where the bizarre is commonplace, Riley found himself in the weird position of taking both sides of the same argument. No greater injustice could be imagined than Matt's taking the fall for him. But Riley refused to place himself in the custody of Sheriff Hiram Ochs. He had come too close to death by hanging to run that risk again. As Hoyt used to say: *A brave man challenges the gods, only a fool tempts them.*

Riley had been serious when he had defied Ochs. He'd had no intention of backing down. But now the horns of his dilemma were sharpened by Matt's last words to him: "This is your chance to set things right. Take it . . . or run before dawn."

More protests only rode the prairie breezes. Ochs pulled

the shotgun away from Riley. His expression revealed nothing but square-jawed determination. No matter what his thoughts, Matt concluded, by his silence he acquiesced.

While Ochs brought his horse around the sod house, Matt held a tearful Anne Marie in their last embrace. Then he pulled away and strode to the corral. He ducked under a rail and caught his mare. Saddling and bridling her, he led her out and swung up. With one look back, he rode out stirrup to stirrup with Sheriff Ochs.

Micah and Samuel emerged from the doorway of the sod house. Both boys were silent and dour until Samuel spoke. "He'll come back."

Micah turned to his brother, a questioning look on his face.

As though privy to private information, Samuel went on: "Matt told me he won't leave us. He'll come back. That's what he said."

Gazing after the two horsebackers riding across the prairie, Old John slowly shook his head. "Never seen nothing like this. Never in all my days. No, sir."

The prisoner could not sleep. He lay on the hard bunk, still, eyes open. Raucous noises carried from Denver's saloon district, the jarring notes from an upright piano tangling with boot-stomping fiddle music. Against this background he heard rhythmic snoring from a drunk in another cell, and then, outside, a line of ox-drawn freight outfits rumbled past the jailhouse, the plodding hoofs adding to the symphony. At last his eyes closed, and the sounds faded.

Time passed, and the prisoner awakened. He blinked against the glare of the morning sun. Sounds outside the jail-house window reached him. He sorted them out, realizing he had been disturbed by the push-pull rasp of a cross-cut saw and hammers driving nails into wood.

He stood. Stepping onto the bunk, he peered out through the barred window. Carpenters were at work outside, half a dozen men replacing the charred timbers with newly sawn six-by-sixes and burned planks with two-by-twelves. Matt watched in a silent and strange fascination. He was unwilling to believe he would hang, yet the imposing sight of gallows made him consider the possibility of his own execution as never before.

On the way to Denver, Matt had discussed this with Ochs. The lawman had been terse. He reminded Matt that passions still ran high in town, that demands for justice were loud and persistent, that the will of the people could be slowed but not halted. The sentence would be carried out, Ochs warned him, some day, some way.

Matt did not dismiss this fair warning. But he counted on the fact that Ochs would not stomach the hanging of an innocent man. The sheriff had readily agreed to arrest Jimmy, and said he would consider assigning deputies to observe the comings and goings of Tug Larkin. Matt felt heartened. Taken together, these concessions hinted that Ochs was inclined to believe Riley's version of events, after all. Now the overriding question was what would Riley do? Would he dig up the money and flee with as much gold as he could carry? Would he put this hayseed territory behind him as he had so often threatened?

Not long ago, Matt would have bet on it: Riley would leave. Whether the conscience of a man is learned or earned was a question beyond Matt's ken, but he believed Riley would be guided by his notion of right and wrong now, that his twin would not run before dawn. Matt was no gambler, but he had wagered on that one. In fact, he had bet his life on it.

He dozed after a late breakfast, roused by a skeleton key rattling in a door lock. The hard, metallic sound was followed by the shrill squeal of hinges. He sat up just as the steel-reinforced door between the sheriff's office and the cell-block swung open.

Matt left the cot. He saw two burly deputies struggling with their prisoner, a slender man who was tossing his head and kicking like a calf touched by a red-hot branding iron. One deputy punched him below the belt, hard. The prisoner buckled. Matt watched as the two deputies dragged him into the cell-block. They manhandled him toward the next cell. One took off the wrist irons, and then the other gave him a last shove into the cell. They slammed the barred door shut with a *clang,* and locked it.

The new prisoner slumped down on the cot, head bowed, breathing raggedly. Hatless, his red hair was mussed, his pink-skinned face glistening with sweat. Matt waited until the deputies had departed and closed the heavy door after them.

"Jimmy."

Jimmy raised his head in surprise. He blinked slowly and turned toward the sound of Matt's voice. Recognition crept into his eyes.

"Damn . . . it's you." Jimmy sat up. After a moment he stood and moved closer to the bars separating their cells. "Looks like the law caught up with you, Riley."

Matt did not correct him. He had not expected Jimmy to mistake him for Riley, but quickly realized he should have. By now Jimmy had learned from Tug Larkin that Riley had been found guilty of murder in Denver. For Riley to be in jail was a logical outcome of his trial.

"Reckon so," Matt replied, wondering if he sounded anything like Riley. In the following moments, he realized the sound of his voice did not matter. Jimmy had reached a conclusion about his identity, and did not think beyond it.

"How I see this," Jimmy said slowly, "you'll hang. Those gallows out there, they're for you. I'm right about that, aren't I?"

"You're second in line," Matt said, "if Maude Riley has anything to say about it."

"That sour old bitty treated me like dirt . . . ," he began.

Matt interrupted him: "You sold that salted mine to her for the eight hundred dollars she stole from Sarah Painter. She wants her money back. Or is it Collier's money?"

"I don't know anything about that."

"Tell the truth, Jimmy."

He glared at him. "Who do you think you are?"

Matt cast a glance toward the steel-reinforced door. "If you don't tell the truth now, the rest of your story will fall to pieces after Ochs learns what happened in Valmont City."

"I don't know what the hell you're talking about."

"I'm talking about the money you and Larkin stole," Matt replied, "after you gunned down Eldon Collier."

"That's a damned lie," Jimmy said.

"If it's a lie," Matt said, "then you aren't worried about Larkin, are you?"

"Worried? What about?"

"About him taking that money for himself," Matt explained, "while you sit here like a bird in a cage."

Face flushed, Jimmy said: "Go to hell."

"Larkin killed Miss Augusta Benning," Matt said, "and he robbed her of eleven hundred dollars. In Valmont City he shotgunned Eldon Collier. You two cleaned out that big floor safe and loaded the money into six monogrammed panniers. Then you stole Collier's coach and horses."

Jimmy stared. "How did you . . . ?"

Matt went on: "Now that I think about it, Larkin's the one

who ought to hang, not you. He's the killer. You're just a thief. You planned to rob Collier from the day he hired you. That's the truth, isn't it?"

When Jimmy did not answer, Matt added: "You'd better give it some thought."

"Give what some thought?"

"Testifying against Tug Larkin before he leaves the territory," Matt said.

Jimmy answered with stubborn silence.

"Put yourself in his boots," Matt continued. "While we stand here jawing, he's thinking he's a rich man. He's thinking he'd better clear out of Colorado Territory. If he stays, he'll face two murder charges."

Eyes widening, Jimmy looked startled. "I just figured something out."

"You're slow at figuring things out," Matt said, "if you believe you'll ever see Tug Larkin again. Or that money." He gazed at Jimmy. "But what the hell. It didn't belong to you in the first place. Easy come, easy go."

"You've got a bad mouth on you," Jimmy said. "I just figured out you're not Riley. You're the ugly brother. Damned if you aren't. Matt something-or-other. What the hell's your name?"

"Lately I've wondered about that myself," Matt replied.

"I'll sic that lawman on you," he said. "I'll tell him that you aren't Riley."

"What will Ochs do then?" Matt asked. "Hang me twice?"

Jimmy cursed him, uttering murderous threats as he turned his back on Matt Something-or-Other and moved to the cot in his cell.

Chapter Sixteen

Hand over hand, Riley pulled a sloshing bucket of water out of the well. He watered Old John's horse while the rancher tugged at the saddle cinch and then pulled the stirrup down. Riley saw a gnarled hand grasp the horn. Old John mounted, grimacing and grunting as he swung his leg over and settled into the saddle. He had said his good byes. Now he was headed for the Two-Bar, aiming to be home before dark.

Riley moved to the horse's shoulder. He gazed up at the aging stockman, seeing a lined, leathery face against the cloudless blue sky. He offered a word of apology again.

"Like I told you," Old John said, "no hard feelings, not on my part. You figured I brung that lawman to hang you, didn't you? A man has call to get testy over a thing like that." Old John looked off toward the horizon. "Reckon I'm the one who oughta do the apologizing. Wisht I had knowed Ochs was bent on taking in a prisoner. If I hadda knowed, I wouldn't have brung him out here. No, sir."

"Matt won't be a prisoner for long," Riley said.

Old John studied him. "He busted you outta jail. You aim to return the favor?"

Riley nodded.

"How?"

"Don't know yet."

"Ochs is no man's fool. He'll be watching for you."

"I know," Riley said.

Saddle leather creaked when Old John leaned down and extended his hand. "Good luck to ye." After Riley shook his claw-like hand, Old John added: "You need anything, anything a-tall, my house is your house."

"Obliged."

Riley stepped back as Old John neck-reined the brown and white horse around. He watched the pioneer rancher head for home until he heard his name called from the house. He looked back. Sarah and Anne Marie stood in the shadowed doorway. They beckoned to him.

Riley found the interior of the soddy to be cool even in this midsummer's blast of furnace-like heat. The sisters, rather formally, invited him to sit in the wide-armed wicker chair once occupied by Paul Painter. Sarah brought a footrest. The boys watched from the other side of the room, clearly under orders to be seen and not heard.

His booted feet up, Riley held back a smile as the sisters launched into an account of Matt's heroism when he had rescued them from the gunmen shooting up the Painter homestead. Finally he had heard enough trumpeting.

"You think I'll run, don't you?" Riley broke in.

The sisters exchanged a quick glance. Sarah spoke up: "We know of your wish to leave the territory."

"You want to get out, too," Riley said to her. "But that doesn't mean you'll leave your sister to the wolves . . . not after what she did for you in Valmont City."

Sarah shook her head. "No, of course not. But Annie and I, well, we've been close all of our lives. . . ."

"Matt and I didn't grow up together," he allowed, "but in our own way we've learned to tolerate each other." He reached inside his jacket. Palming his two-shot Derringer, he drew looks of surprise from the sisters and the two brothers when the little gun appeared in his hand. "Just so you'll know," Riley went on, "if I had planned to run, I would have gotten the drop on the sheriff, grabbed as many gold eagles as I could carry out of that stink hole, and galloped for hell-and-gone on a stolen black horse."

"You were planning to help Matt all along?" Anne Marie asked.

Riley nodded. "He went to jail for me. Now it's my turn to give him a hand."

"But how?" the sisters asked in unison.

Riley grinned. "Sometimes you two echo each other like twins."

"What about us?" Micah asked, unable to remain quiet any longer. "Me and Sam, do we ever act like twins? Do we?"

"You'd better hope not," Riley replied wryly.

"Why?" Micah asked.

"Trouble," Riley said.

"Trouble?" Micah asked.

"A twin is trouble times two," Riley replied. "Double trouble." He thought about that. "The only thing worse is triplets."

"Triplets?" Micah repeated.

"Three of a kind," Riley explained. "Triple trouble."

They laughed until Sarah repeated her question. "How will you help Matt?"

"Don't know yet," Riley replied.

"You must have some idea," Sarah said.

He shrugged. "Larkin pinned a murder on me. I'll start with him."

Sarah cast a glance at her sister, and then turned to Riley. "I'm going with you."

Riley shook his head. "No, you're not."

"Yes, I am."

In his years of riding as a civilian scout for the cavalry in the Western territories, Matt had heard tales detailing the agonies of imprisoned men. Consumed by madness when

locked in a cell and deprived of food and water as further punishment, some wiped the walls with their feces. Others drank
their own urine. Still others bit at their arms in vain attempts
to puncture arteries. A prisoner Matt had brought in to Fort
Lincoln beat his head against the bars after long confinement.
Blinded by blood, he banged his forehead against the steel
until his skull cracked like the shell of a hard-boiled egg.

For Matt, one long day stretched into two. Jimmy lay on
his cot. He stirred and sat up. A cork squeaked. He brought a
flask to his mouth, gulping rum that smelled like rancid mo-
lasses. The liquor was supplied by a deputy for the price of a
half eagle from Jimmy's money belt.

Matt watched Jimmy cork the flask and look around as
though awakening from a bad dream. His gaze moved to the
bars separating their cells. Then he cursed Matt again and
laid back, eyes closing.

Matt tried but could not surrender to sleep. Long hours
dragged him into a dark mood, a hot mist that clouded his
brain. He had not gone mad in this short time, but as the
hours wore on, an act of lunacy seemed not only reasonable
but necessary. He fantasized about throttling the deputy who
brought his meals, the same one who profited by smuggling
liquor to Jimmy. The man was rotund, frog-faced, offering to
fetch food and drink for a price. Matt visualized himself
reaching through the bars to strangle him, squeezing his
throat until the froggy eyes bugged out even farther, and
then, somehow, escaping this cell. Matt would be free, once
again a man of the open spaces. He would cross the prairie on
the back of a white horse, a mighty stallion galloping through
the powdery snow of a cold winter day. . . .

Winter? At once he knew those images were fantasies,
nothing more than waking dreams chased away by rational
thoughts and summer heat. Matt sensed the longer he was

confined here, though, the less control he could exert over his rage. For he knew anger was the wellspring of madness. Taking his twin's place within spitting distance of the gallows seemed foolhardy and reckless now. The fact that he had de-fused a crisis and saved Riley's life—for the second time—was compensation that was quickly diminishing.

If anyone deserved to be throttled, it was Jimmy. His slurred taunts fueled Matt's frustration, and the shouted curses even drew Sheriff Ochs into the cell-block. Door hinges squealed when the lawman entered. Jimmy quickly re-ported Matt was not who he claimed to be, that the twins had been switched. When Ochs showed no particular interest in this news, Jimmy demanded to be set free.

"Not until I get word from the law in Valmont City," Ochs said. "Last I heard, Maude Riley's pressing charges against you."

"You believe that lying whore?" Jimmy demanded.

"That's a question for the federal judge to answer," Ochs said.

"There's a whole lot more I could tell you about that salted mine," Jimmy said with a knowing glance at Matt. "A whole lot more."

Ochs eyed him. "Why should anyone believe you?"

Jimmy wished him a quick trip to hell.

Drunk or sober, Jimmy knew more than he was telling. Matt felt certain of that. But even with a few well-placed in-sults, he could not pry the words out of the flame-haired man-servant, no hint of a confession to his rôle in the murder of Eldon Collier—not even after gulping the contents of another flask. With a squeak of the cork when he capped the vessel, he lay back and closed his eyes.

With Sarah riding behind his saddle, Riley felt her hands

grasping his waist. She wore a sunbonnet to shield her face from a hot sun. This trek that had begun after sunrise was long and arduous for her. Riley frequently drew rein, dismounted, and handed her down. She protested each stop, calling them unnecessary delays on their way to Denver. But Riley insisted. They stretched their legs during the rest stops, walking short distances through sage and tufts of buffalo grass. They watched jack rabbits bound away, long ears up. Their conversations moved from complaints of the blistering hot summer day, the foul canteen water, and the stinging horseflies to a question from Sarah and a reply from Riley that surprised even him.

"What is your greatest fear?" she asked, slipping her arm through his as they stepped around clumps of gray sage. Their footfalls stirred and scattered small lizards camouflaged by gray, wrinkled skin. Sarah pushed: "The one you've never told anyone, ever."

He looked at her. Her gaze was steady as she looked up at him, her question sincere. He remembered their conversations over campfires, his first with a woman since Nell. Now Sarah's question, her tone of voice, her gaze—all indicated an interest in him. He was flattered, but did not open up to her. He had never told her about his upbringing, and now he found himself thinking of Hoyt Wilcox while he pondered her question.

"Being alone when I die," he replied.

She nodded, emphasizing her agreement with him. "Alone and unloved. Deep down, we all fear that fate, don't we? That's why I'm envious of the love shared by Matt and Anne Marie. Have you seen the way they look at one another? They'll be lovers forever."

"I wish I could believe that."

She halted and gazed at him. "Why can't you?"

"Forever ends," he replied, avoiding her gaze, "when one of them dies."

On horseback again, Sarah spoke after a long silence, her voice soft and close to his ear. "I see sadness in your eyes. Someday I want you to tell me her name."

In long, hot miles across the prairie, the quietude was broken only by the *clip-clop* of shod hoofs. Riley's mind filled with memories of Nell Bloom. She had declared her love for him, only to leave a cryptic note before she died by her own hand:

We eat and drink and blaspheme,
we who live and breathe in sin.
For us the cemetery is the place
where we shall all gather again.

Her betrayal was beyond his understanding. The finality of it left him stunned, as though pole-axed. The pain came later. In the aftermath he never spoke of her death, believing the searing pain would only be sharpened and driven deeper if he gave voice to it. Telling Matt about Nell Bloom had had that effect on him, a painful recounting that stirred old feelings. Besides, Hoyt had long advised him to trust no one. . . .

Trust.

Trust the hair on the back of your neck, pistol. When those fine little hairs stand up like barbed quills on a porcupine's back, get the hell out of wherever you are. With the pall of smoke hanging over the outskirts of Denver drawing into view ahead, Riley recalled Hoyt's words. It was the gambler's colorful way of advising him to rely on instinct, a code of survival for one who lives outside the bounds of society. *If you feel trouble coming,* Hoyt had often said, *cut your losses. Run out the nearest door. Steal a horse and ride over the next hill. The faster the horse, the better. Hear me, pistol?*

Arriving in Denver, Riley again recalled the advice. He remembered the urgency in Hoyt's voice, too. Hoyt had a way of justifying his actions by declaring all others to be lying hypocrites while he pursued his time-honored profession with honesty and integrity.

Now Riley stood beside Sarah on the plank walk across Sixteenth from the Inter-Ocean Hotel. The thought of entering the lobby raised the hair on the back of his neck. He had figured Larkin would come out sooner or later, but the wait dragged on while the long shadows of afternoon faded under the red skies of sunset.

Sarah gave voice to the question that had been rolling around in his mind: "How much longer will we wait?"

Riley pulled the brim of his hat down. He felt conspicuous, aware of passers-by taking note of them as they stood in a widening margin of shade cast by the false front of the shoe and boot repair shop. If Larkin did not come out on the portico, Riley knew he would have to go after him. He said so to Sarah.

"But if you go in there," she said, "someone may recognize you."

Riley acknowledged the possibility with a nod. Without another word she left the boardwalk. He stared helplessly after her as she crossed the street to the portico and pushed through the front doors of the Inter-Ocean. Only moments later she came out. After waiting for a pair of mule-drawn covered wagons to pass, she hurriedly crossed the street and rejoined him.

"Tug Larkin's gone," she said.

"Gone," Riley repeated.

"The desk clerk told me he checked out at noon."

They started back toward the livery barn. Riley heard prancing horses. He halted, grasping Sarah's arm as he pulled her back. The lamps from the hotel cast dim light on a stocky figure mounted on a spirited black horse. Tug Larkin was coming toward them from the livery, leading a saddle mount, also black.

Riley and Sarah eased into the deep shadows between the Rocky Mountain House and the shop next door. In the failing light, Larkin passed by without looking left or right. They moved out of the aperture between the buildings and followed him from a safe distance. Four blocks away they made their way along plank walks crowded with men in the saloon district. Barkers shouted their come-ons from gaming hall doorways. Clearly intent on his destination, Tug Larkin was not headed for an evening of gambling and drinking. Not tonight. He turned, rounding a corner a block away from the jailhouse.

Riley spotted someone else then, no more than a shadow in the night, moving swiftly ahead of them, someone following Larkin as he rounded that corner.

At last Matt succumbed to sleep. A squeal of hinges and the clink of skeleton keys seemed to come from a distant place. Urgent voices brought him out of an impossibly tangled dream. Bizarre images of a white stallion tumbling into an open grave slipped away when he awakened fully.

Matt's eyes opened. He raised up. Tug Larkin had let himself into the cell-block. In all this time Matt had never taken a good long look at the man. Even in Valmont City events had moved too fast for that. Larkin had always been on the fringe, a silent, menacing figure, a murderer who roamed freely. Now, by lamplight, Matt saw the small, dark eyes, a broad nose, and thick lips cracked and scabbed over in this bone-dry climate.

Matt heard Jimmy's voice. Slurring his words, the manservant cursed and swayed drunkenly in an effort to stand while Larkin unlocked the barred door to his cell. Matt overheard their words: "The money is gone." Tug Larkin had ridden out to the wash and made the discovery. "Gone! The money's gone! All of it!"

As Jimmy's head cleared, he recalled an earlier exchange with Matt. A new anger surfaced as he left his cell and halted outside Matt's. "You!" he shouted. "You stole it, didn't you? No other way you coulda known the money was packed in Collier's panniers."

Matt silently studied Jimmy through the bars of his cell. To his right, the steel-reinforced door to the sheriff's office stood open. Tug Larkin was there. He had either bribed the night deputy, Matt figured, or clubbed him. Matt saw something else—a cut-down shotgun in Larkin's hand.

Matt sat up. "Collier hired you to protect him after he was cheated by Hoyt Wilcox, but you planned to rob him all along. That's the bald truth, isn't it?"

Jimmy ignored the accusation. "Where is it? Where's the money?" He drew a gasping breath. "We oughta gun you down just for the pleasure of it . . . or maybe we'll start with those Painter sisters you favor."

"You had your chance," Matt said, "when you sent those three gunmen to their homestead."

"What the hell happened to those men?" Jimmy demanded.

Matt shrugged.

"You ran them off?" Jimmy asked.

"You might say that," Matt replied.

"I might say what?"

"Your men ran into some trouble," Matt replied. He was aware of the vagueness of his answers; it was as though he had taken on Riley's personality while impersonating him.

"You killed them, didn't you?" Jimmy demanded. "Didn't you?"

Matt did not answer. "I know you killed Eldon Collier. Then you robbed him. . . ."

"If we hadn't taken that money off Collier," Jimmy insisted, "someone else would have."

"The truth is," Matt went on, "you had to stop him before he went to Denver and deposited his fortune in a bank. And if you let him travel that freight road alone, Dad Anders or some other hardcase might have robbed him. You had to take him in his own house, in the night, when he least expected trouble."

"Collier was a dying old man," Jimmy said, as though that excused everything.

"So you put him out of his misery?" Matt asked. "What's your excuse for putting Miss Augusta Benning out of hers?"

"Folks around here didn't know that bitty," Jimmy said angrily. "Not like Collier did. She claimed to be sight-seeing when she left on her holiday trips. Truth is Miss Augusta Benning left town to gamble in private games. That's how Collier met her. Turns out she married him to get money for her gambling. She lived for the games." He exhaled, reeking of rum. "Collier told me all about her. He gave her a satchel full of money, and ordered me to take her to Denver in the Concord, one way. Don't bring the bitch back, he told me. Then she got uppity with me when I carried her trunks into the Inter-Ocean and took her to her room. Treated me like dirt." A crafty look crossed his face. "The bitty had told me about her debt to some crooked gambler. She wanted him killed. I told Larkin about it. We partnered up."

"And you brave men went after her," Matt said.

Jimmy grabbed the barred door to steady himself, his words slurring again. "Listen to me, you ugly son-of-a-buck.

You'll hang. Hang! Me and Tug, we're walking outta here, free. But you're gonna hang."

"If I do, you'll never see any of that money."

"Where is it?" Jimmy demanded.

"You'll never guess."

Swearing in frustration, Jimmy said: "How I see this, we got no choice. Divide the money two ways, and we all walk away."

Matt stood and moved closer to the cell door. "No deal."

"No deal!" Jimmy exclaimed in frustration. "No deal! I'm standing between you and the gallows out there, and that's all you gotta say . . . no deal?"

"We both know what's going on here," Matt said with a glance at Larkin. "I take you to the money, and your man kills me. That's your deal, isn't it?"

Jimmy studied him. "How I see this, we've got a deadlock. Take your chances with us . . . or stay here and hang. What's it gonna be?"

"Neither one," Sheriff Ochs said. The lawman stepped into the doorway, leveling his shotgun at them.

Startled, Jimmy jumped as though stung. Larkin spun around, bringing his weapon up.

"Shoot him!" Jimmy shouted. "Shoot him!"

Ochs jabbed the barrel of his goose gun at Larkin's chest. "Drop the Greener, Tug. Drop it!"

Larkin made no move. The two men stared at one another, unblinking.

"We go back a few years, Tug," Ochs said. "You were a good deputy until you met James Quinn. I don't want to kill you, but you know I will if I have to. Drop the gun. Now."

"Shoot him!" Jimmy repeated.

A long moment passed before Larkin decided this was not his day to die. He set the gun down, straightened slowly, and raised his hands. Jimmy swore again.

"You're a coward, Tug," he said. "Nothing but a coward."

Larkin turned away from him.

"You don't get it, do you?" Jimmy said to him. "Somebody's gotta hang for those killings. Who do you think it's gonna be? Huh?"

As surprised as Matt had been by the sudden appearance of Sheriff Ochs, he was even more surprised when his twin stepped into the cell-block behind the lawman, followed a moment later by Sarah Painter.

Within minutes Ochs locked Tug Larkin and Jimmy Quinn in separate cells. Larkin was characteristically stoic. Jimmy cursed the world at large as he staggered into his cell and the door clanged shut behind him.

The sheriff turned to Matt. "I followed your idea."

"What idea?" Matt asked.

"Keeping an eye on Larkin," he replied. "I figured if Tug was guilty like you said, he might try something. I made it easy for him, and sent the night deputy home."

"Well, the right outlaws are locked up now," Matt said.

Riley stepped forward. "Looks like folks in this hayseed town will get their wish."

"Which one?" Ochs asked.

"They've been hollering for the gallows to be put to use, haven't they?"

Ochs nodded.

They left the cell-block, leaving Jimmy's muttered curses behind as they entered the outer office. Ochs closed the heavy door. He opened a floor safe and took out a money belt and a Barlow knife. He handed them to Riley who uttered a sheepish word of thanks. "Now I want to know about Collier's fortune," he said to the twins.

"What do you want to know?" Matt asked.

"Where the hell is it?"

Matt grinned. "You'll never guess, Sheriff."

"Looks like you won't have to," Riley said with a scowl.

Chapter Seventeen

Riley threw his hat to the ground and kicked it. He had given up trying to talk sense to his twin. He charged Matt, fist cocked. Matt spun away, but the moment he turned to face Riley, he caught a hard punch to the jaw. Already off balance, he went down.

"I'll be damned," Riley said, standing over him. "You were right. I didn't drop my shoulder that time."

The money was gone, the panniers dug up and hauled away in a buckboard by Sheriff Hiram Ochs and two deputies. Matt was not surprised by the fact that Collier's fortune had been seized by the federal government. Ochs said the money would be disbursed among his heirs, if any were ever found. No finder's fee was offered, either. Earlier Riley had argued in favor of keeping some of the money for themselves—"No one would ever know," he had said.—but Matt would have none of it. Not one silver dollar.

Now Matt struggled to his feet.

"That felt good," Riley said.

"I want a re-match," Matt said.

Riley raised his fists.

Matt winced as he rubbed his jaw, and thought better of it. "Some other day."

"You name the day, brother," Riley said, grinning.

The next day Matt and Anne Marie came out of the sod house to greet a visitor, Old John. The rancher proposed an offer he had been mulling for a spell. Matt would continue to work as the outrider for the Two-Bar. In exchange, Old John would advance enough money for him to make a payment on this ranch property.

"Reckon that'll make us neighbors," he said, "if yer agreeable to the notion."

Anne Marie clenched Matt's arm as he accepted.

The stockman waved off expressions of gratitude, claiming the offer was based on his own self-interest. He would keep a good, dependable man on the payroll, he said, an outrider to protect the sprawling Two-Bar Ranch from thieves and gold-diggers.

"Onliest thing I ask out of you two," Old John said, "is to invite me to the wedding."

"Oh, you will be invited," Anne Marie assured him. "We have an announcement of our own."

"What would that be?" he asked.

She called to Riley and Sarah. They came out of the sod house, followed by the boys. When they joined them, Anne Marie turned to the stockman.

"Mister Souter," she said, "you are invited to a double wedding."

"Double?" Old John said.

"Twins marrying sisters," Anne Marie explained, smiling.

Matt and Riley looked at one another and said in unison: "Trouble . . . double."

"I'll ride as far as it takes to see it," Old John said. "Just tell me the when and the where. Yes, sir."

Matt had not needed Anne Marie's perceptive eye or elbow jab to know what had happened to Riley. For the first time he saw genuine happiness in his brother's expression, a lightness in his stride. Nor did he miss Sarah's glow when her gaze met Riley's.

Matt was surprised by the turn of events, since he had expected Riley to haunt Denver's gaming halls until his winnings paid Sarah's way to Ohio. When Riley headed him out of the sod house to the corral, though, he realized he could never have guessed what was on his mind.

"We'll rebuild the homestead," Riley said.

"The homestead," Matt repeated.

Riley nodded.

The twins leaned against the top rail of the corral. A phantom white stallion had once been penned here. So it was said. Matt had been inclined to believe that tale. But now he stared in disbelief at his brother.

"Sarah and I talked it over," Riley went on. "Even with the boys to help you out here, you and Anne Marie have your hands full. So we've been thinking. We need money. All we have to do is put two more years into that property. Then we can sell it. The sisters will divide the profits. It isn't exactly what either one of us wants, but it would be a shame to lose good land to a squatter. Besides, Ochs put the word out on me."

"What word?"

"I'm officially banned from gambling in Denver," he said with a shrug. "If I'm caught, I'll be jailed."

Matt eyed him. "You don't sound too unhappy about it."

"Sarah tells me things usually work out for the best," he said. "Maybe she's right. Maybe this is the right time for me to turn my life upside down and get a new handle on it." Matt watched as Riley paused in thought, eyes downcast. At last he spoke, his voice soft and somehow distant, yet intense. "I don't think about Hoyt very often any more. Mostly I think about Sarah and the journey we're starting on. I don't know where we'll end up."

"Run before dawn?" Matt said.

"No more of that," he said with a quick smile. He drew a

deep breath and let it out. "Hoyt hated people. He hated everyone. Maybe he hated himself, too. I don't know. But I know I can't live out my days that way. The lies and the cheating and the running, that's all behind me." Riley fell silent, looking off toward the horizon. "I told Sarah about Nell Bloom," he finally said. "She asked me, so I told her. I told her everything. Funny thing is, afterwards, I felt like a weight had been lifted off my shoulders. A big one. How that happened, I don't know."

Matt grinned. "I think I do."

Gazing at his twin now, he thought back to the first time he had laid eyes on Riley Wilcox. That encounter in the cellblock was vivid in his mind even today. From that moment to this one, he had yearned to discover the circumstances of their births. He had failed. And he was coming to accept the fact that he would never know the truth, as Riley believed, and that the couple who had raised him had had good reason never to tell him. He could let it go.

Almost. He knew he would always wonder about his birth. Maybe someone, somewhere knew the answer. . . .

The inner turmoil had left him when he had declared his love for Anne Marie. That was how he understood what had happened to Riley. The workings of some mysterious alchemy of his mind, the prospect of spending the rest of his life with the woman he loved had purged him of his torment. He was interested in the future now, in developing this ranch, in starting a family.

Riley met Matt's gaze. Neither of them spoke as their eyes held. Words were not needed. The past was behind them. The twins were ready, as Hoyt used to say, for the curtain of life's stage to open, for the future waiting in the wings.

About the Author

Stephen Overholser was born in Bend, Oregon, the middle son of Western author, Wayne D. Overholser. Convinced, in his words, that "there was more to learn outside of school than inside," he left Colorado State College in his senior year. He was drafted and served in the U.S. Army in Vietnam. Following his discharge, he launched his career as a writer, publishing three short stories in *Zane Grey Western Magazine*. On a research visit to the University of Wyoming at Laramie, he came across an account of a shocking incident that preceded the Johnson County War in Wyoming in 1892. It was this incident that became the inspiration for his first novel, A HANGING IN SWEETWATER (1974), that received the Spur Award from the Western Writers of America. MOLLY AND THE CONFIDENCE MAN (1975) followed, the first in a series of books about Molly Owens, a clever, resourceful, and tough undercover operative working for a fictional detective agency in the Old West. Among the most notable of Stephen Overholser's later titles are SEARCH FOR THE FOX (1976), TRACK OF THE KILLER (1982), and DARK EMBERS AT DAWN (1998). The author is currently at work on his next **Five Star Western,** SHADOW VALLEY RISING.